THE BREAK OUT

DENVER DRAGONS SERIES

MADI DANIELLE

Cover Design: KBGDesigns

Editing: Kay with KMorton Editing Services.

❀ Created with Vellum

PLAYLIST

Home with You – Madison Beer
Middle Fingers – ASTON
Don't Need Nobody – Ellie Gouling
Broadway Girls (Feat. Morgan Wallen) – Lil Durk
DBE – Sarah Saint James
To My Younger Self – Britton
Bad Together – Dua Lipa
I Can Do It With a Broken Heart – Taylor Swift
Dirtier Thoughts – Nation Haven
Stay – Colorblind
Not my problem – TAELA
Like You Mean It – Steven Rodriguez
I Like You Best – Ella Red
Maybe – Kelly Clarkson
Damaged – Britton
Lip Service – Xana
Sabotage – Bebe Rexha
He loves me, he loves me not – Jessica Baio
That's all folks (finale) – emlyn

CONTENT WARNING

As always, my stories are sexy and fun, but this one has some triggers to be aware of including: mention of child neglect, death of siblings, child illness, discussion of addiction and toxic relationships.

For those of you that pretend you're fine when you really aren't. Colton will take care of you.

Working as my best friend, Spencer's, publicist has its pros and cons.

Pro, we get to spend a ton of time together. She's an extremely well-known singer and the most talented person I've ever met. It's amazing to get to travel with her and watch her perform all the time. I get to hype her up constantly. Honestly, it's a dream come true for both of us.

Con, she goes rogue and announces her new relationship while her ex is still pissy. I then have to deal with the massive fallout for her because I don't need her stressed about it. Plus, that's what I'm there to do for her.

And as her best friend, I want to be on her side about the picture she posted as a "fuck you" to her shitty ass ex. As her publicist, I kind of want to kill her for doing so without talking to me first.

Right now, I'm on the phone with Spencer's ex, Kenneth's, publicist.

"I just think we should have had a heads up so we could have approached this together," she says.

"I know, I get that, but Spencer did approach Kenneth about a joint statement, and he basically told her to kick rocks. Which is why she posted her *solo* statement."

"This is why *you and I* handle these things."

I sigh, "I know. She was mad and vindictive, so she posted the picture. Can we just move past this. Spencer would like to cut all ties with Kenneth."

"Fine. I'll figure something out."

"Thank you."

We hang up and I toss my phone across the hotel bed in annoyance. There's several texts, emails, and phone calls that need to be returned and I don't feel like dealing with any of it.

Spencer is currently on tour, and we are in Denver because she had some days off, but we fly out in the morning to her next stop. *Which is Kansas City, I think. Or maybe it's Detroit.* Honestly, I can't keep up without my planner on my tablet. We're here because her new boyfriend, Jared, is a goalie for the Denver Dragons hockey team. The same team that my brother, Brent, is the captain of.

We went to a game tonight against the Spartans, which is the team her ex played for. Then, she decided to post a picture holding hands with Jared and shut off her phone. She'll be hearing about all of this from me on our plane ride.

For now, I'm here in my hotel room about to drink myself to sleep. I like being in Denver and being able to see my brother and his unconventional family. His girlfriend, Chandler, is also dating two of his other teammates. It's a little weird, but not my business and I like her a lot.

Could never be me. I don't want to deal with one hockey player, let alone three. My brother and I have a good relationship, though. He basically raised me because our parents suck and he's the oldest. We have three other siblings with me being the youngest.

Well, I guess we *had* three other siblings.

Two years ago, my second oldest brother, Brandon, died of an overdose.

I shake away the memories because I don't have the mental capacity to deal with the spiral that will send me down right now. Though, the single reminder is sobering enough to remind me not to grab a bottle to deal with my problems.

Instead, I take a nice, hot therapeutic shower before climbing into the cool sheets and do my best to fall asleep. If only it were that simple, because as soon as I do my mind is consumed with all my thoughts I suppressed during the day. All the guilt and resentment that comes from being a Collee comes rushing back and sleep is a lot more elusive than I would like it to be.

———

SPENCER IS ALREADY SEATED on the private jet when I arrive because I'm late, which is unlike me. She's texting and looks up when she hears me enter.

"Hey, I was starting to worry about you," she says right as her phone goes off signaling another text and she looks down smiling. I assume it's Jared.

"Yeah, sorry, I couldn't sleep," I plop down in the seat across from her.

"Someone keeping you awake, too?" She wiggles her eyebrows at me, suggestively.

I bark out a short humorless laugh, "Not in the way you're suggesting. Mine was all work related."

She sets her phone down on the seat next to her. "Yeah, I'm sorry about posting that picture."

I wave her off, "Don't worry about it. That's why you pay me."

"I was just so mad and annoyed at Kenneth and wanted to make it known that I'm happier without him," she explains.

"It's really okay. I get why you did it, I'll get it handled."

"You're the best. Did you happen to see the rumors about Colton Wheeler possibly getting traded?" She asks.

"Nope, I only have eyes for you and your news," I joke, batting my eyelashes at her.

"Aw, how sweet. And hilarious. Now tell me what that guy's deal is."

I groan, shaking my head. "He just likes annoying me because I turned him down before."

"Wait, I don't think I know about that."

I shrug. "It wasn't a big deal. You know how I feel about dating a hockey player. One of the times we went to Kenneth's game he came up to me, flirted with me, and asked me out. I said no and to never try again. He's taken that as a challenge and made it his personal mission to bug me every time he sees me."

"Where was I when that happened?" She looks confused.

"I don't know, talking to someone, I'm sure. Seriously, Spence, it's not a big deal. I can handle it."

Spencer's phone goes off again and I see she wants to grab it, but then looks back at me. I chuckle, grabbing my own from my purse. "Talk to your boyfriend, we have the whole flight to talk to each other."

She picks up the call from Jared while I go through my emails and flag the important ones I'm going to need to get back to once we land.

The flight takes off and Spencer passes out almost immediately. I try to do the same but am widely unsuccessful and end up looking out the window in the distance as we pass through the clouds. Flying never ceases to amaze me, how we can be so high up in this flying tube of metal.

It also makes me think about the way my life has turned out. No one back home would have believed that Brynn Collee would end up on a private jet regularly.

Honestly, no one would believe any of the Collee kids turned out to be anything. I love proving them wrong. Brent shielded me from a lot of the horrors in our house, but once he moved out there was only so much he could do. Brandon was rarely around after that. Bryson did what he could for Bailey and me, but eventually he left too.

Once again, I shake off the negative thoughts in regard to my childhood and focus on the here and now. And the here and now has me doing a lot of work with no need for distractions.

I start my morning on social media, seeing what the latest news is on trades in the league since the trade deadline is approaching. There are some rumors of me getting traded to Denver but I'm hoping that's all they are. I like L.A. I don't want to leave. There are models, actresses, hot chicks of any kind I could ever want. Whenever I need a woman in my bed. I have one. Sure, I can get that anywhere, there's just *more* here. Plus, Denver hates us, and I know it would cause issues being there. And it's fucking cold. I'll stick with California.

There aren't any missed calls from my agent or anyone on the team, so I feel like I'm safe for another day. There are plenty of accounts online talking about the possibility and benefits to trading me along with a handful of other players from various teams.

Tossing my phone aside, I get up to brush my teeth and grab my gym bag before heading to morning skate at the practice arena.

We run some drills on the ice and of course Kenneth

Richardson starts bitching about something to one of the assistant coaches. We all have our reputations, and mine is far from great, but he's the worst.

"Entitled prick," I mumble, skating past him to continue what I was doing.

"You got something you want to say to me, Wheeler?" he calls out, turning his rage from our assistant coach onto me.

"Get back to practice," I call back right before shooting the puck past our goalie right into the net.

"Wheeler!" Coach calls from the bench.

I skate over. "What's up?"

"We just got the news, pack up your stuff you've been traded."

I drop my stick. "Fuck. Where?"

I can see he tries to stop the cringe from taking over his face but fails miserably. "Denver."

———

FUCKING TRADES. It all happens behind closed doors like we are some sort of pawn to do with what they will. Here I am, having to uproot my entire life, get on a plane to an entirely new place and get ready to play with a whole new team in the morning.

This is the second time I've been traded since entering the NHL. The first time, I was happy to get to L.A. and planned to spend the rest of my career with this team.

Which clearly isn't in the cards for me now.

Back home, I pack up my really important shit and plan for a moving company to come get the rest. I'll end up staying in a hotel until I can find somewhere to live. A hotel the league pays for which means it's nice as fuck. Too bad that still doesn't take away the sting that I'm headed to Denver.

Fucking Denver. It's pretty I guess, but it's cold and all those damn Dragons players are dicks. Yet, they're my new team and now I'm considered a Dragon as well.

The second I step off the plane I'm pissed off. The strong wind is whipping me in the face and chilling me even through my jacket, which is clearly not thick enough for my new environment. I continue to be pissed off as I get my rental car while I wait for mine to be delivered.

Once I'm at my hotel room I toss my bag onto the bed and scowl at it. Tomorrow is going to fucking suck.

WOULD YA LOOK AT THAT? It already sucks.

I showed up to the practice arena to scowls and quiet mumbles of shit that just pissed me off more. I try not to pay attention to any of my new teammates while I gear up. Right before I head out to the ice, I'm approached by the team captain, Brent Collee.

"Wheeler," he greets, completely straight faced.

I'm pretty sure I fought him last season, and just grunt in response.

"Look, I know our teams haven't always gotten along. But you're not with them anymore. You're with us. So, let's all put the shit behind us and focus on being a team," Collee says.

I narrow my eyes at him. "I may have to wear your jersey, but I'll never accept being a part of this team."

Without giving him a chance to respond, I push past him and head out onto the ice.

I'm not here to make friends. I'm here to do my job, play hockey, and get paid. I'll play my best, because no matter what I still want to win. But I'm not going to make up for anyone else's shitty playing and I'm not going to hold anyone's hand out there.

The coaches tell me what drills to run, and I do it without a word. The looks continue, but no one says anything to me. Just the way I want it to be. We have a game tonight and I expect to get benched for it since I just got here, but that's not what happens.

As I'm leaving the ice, Coach stops me.

"Third line with Merrick," he says, naming another defenseman.

I grunt in response before heading back to the locker room to shower and get the fuck out of here.

Some of the guys are talking to each other, but I do my best to ignore them. Until I hear Dumont talking to Collee and I hear a familiar name come out of his mouth.

"When do you think you'll see Brynn again?"

Brynn.

The baby Collee.

I smile to myself thinking of the leggy blonde. She's hot as fuck and wants nothing to do with me. I forgot she's my new captain's little sister. She was around a lot when Spencer was dating my teammate, Kenneth. I've always tried to get into Brynn's bed, but she's never budged. It kind of became a mission for me to make it happen.

"She's talking about moving here with Spencer once the tour is over," Collee responds.

"Chandler will love that, especially with the baby on the way."

I grimace thinking of having a kid. Sounds like being tied down which is *not* something that's in my future. I also know the rumors about some of the guys on this team sharing a girl. Fucking weird.

"Yeah, she's going to want to be around and since this is where Spencer will be, it kind of works out."

Smirking as I head to the showers, I think about how it may kind of work out for me as well. Maybe Denver won't be so bad at all. Especially if I can manage to fuck my captain's sister. Things may get a little fun around here.

"Did you see who the Dragons just added to their team?" Spencer asks while we are on the way to her second show in Detroit after we arrived yesterday.

"No, who?" I ask because I've been too busy monitoring her social media to make sure Kenneth doesn't pull anything shady while we aren't paying attention.

"Colton," she grimaces.

My eyes snap up to hers. "You're kidding."

She shakes her head, "Nope. Told you there were rumors about that happening, but I didn't think he would actually end up with the Dragons. How do you think your brother is handling that?"

"I'm sure he's handling it a lot better than I would," I tell her and it's true. Brent is able to keep his cool a lot easier than most people.

"And anything new from my asshole ex?"

"Nope, he's being suspiciously quiet."

"Hm," she hums, "maybe he's accepting that I'm happy and will move on with his life."

We are both silent for a second before bursting out laughing so loud the driver looks back at us with raised eyebrows.

"Don't worry, Spence, I told you I have this."

"I know you do. I just worry that sometimes I put too much on you."

"Stop it, focus on you being your beautiful talented self on that stage tonight."

————

"YOU'RE AMAZING," I tell Spencer as she gets off the stage. She's handed a towel to wipe her sweat while myself and Laura, Spencer's manager, greet her.

"What did you think of that new song?" she asks, referring to a song she just wrote that she performed for the first time tonight.

"Amazing, as always," I gush. Which is true, I never lie to her. If she plays me a song and it's not the best, I'll tell her. She appreciates my honesty.

"Agreed, and you're not going to be happy, but you have a quick interview. It's just over the phone," Laura tells her.

Spencer instantly groans, "Please tell me you're just making an excuse and Jared is here to surprise me again."

Laura winces slightly. "Sorry, not this time."

Spencer groans even louder. She hates doing interviews after shows, but Laura knows it's sometimes the best time to get her nailed down with her busy schedule. The schedule that will be much freer after the tour is over and she's taking some much needed down time to regroup, write, and record a new album.

"It'll be quick," Laura reassures.

"Fine, let's get it done."

———

ONCE I'M BACK at the hotel, even though it's late, I text my sister, Bailey. She doesn't talk to any of us that often, but I still try to reach out. After we lost Brandon, I want all my siblings to know I'm there for them.

Brent may have been the one taking care of us, but I'm determined to be the glue that keeps us together.

> Brynn: Hey, how are you doing?

Bailey left our hometown as soon as she could and hasn't looked back. She moved around a bit; it was hard to keep track where she was for a while. Recently, she settled in a little town in Washington called Amity. I did ask if it was the same place as *Amityville Horror*, but she said it had nothing to do with it. I've seen pictures of the picturesque mountains; it reminds me of Colorado, just with more trees. I tried to ask about her moving to Denver, but she says no. She has said she refuses to be land-locked again and will only live in places with the ocean nearby but won't go into more detail than that.

> Bailey: Hi. I'm fine. You?

While I'm glad she replied, this is pretty typical with what I get from her. Short responses without much substance.

> Brynn: Good. When Spencer has a show in Seattle, I was wondering if I could see you?

> Bailey: Seattle isn't close to where I live.

> Brynn: I'll come to you. Please.

I watch the gray dots appear and disappear. I haven't seen Bailey in a couple years, and I don't like the distance she's putting between herself and all of us, but I'm not going to push it. With a sigh, I toss my phone aside and get ready for bed. By the time I'm settling into the cool sheets, I check my phone one more time slightly shocked by the one-word reply.

> Bailey: Fine.

BRYNN

S pencer's tour seemed to fly by. Once the hockey season was over and the Dragons were eliminated in the first playoff round, Jared joined her for the rest of the summer, and she has been over the moon. I've been excited for her and looking forward to when things are going to settle down and we all return to Denver.

Drama has been suspiciously absent, which has made me be a bit more on edge waiting for the other shoe to drop, but it hasn't. The most dramatic thing that has happened has been the fact that my sister ghosted me when we had our stop in Washington.

I tried, I really did, but I wasn't going to chase her down. But I am determined to meet up with her during the break. I told Brent about what happened, and he just said she would come around. He can be so calm even in the worst situations and I wish I could be that way, but that's not the way I'm wired.

Here we are, the last show of the tour, and I'm standing on the side stage with Jared while he is fixated on the redhead on stage like always. I've snuck some pictures of him to show Spencer so she can see the complete awestruck, loving look he has for her at all times.

Sometimes I want what they have.

Other times I'm convinced that it won't ever happen for me.

Connections like that are rare. I've had a front row seat to a few romances that have that special, undeniable connection and I feel like the odds are not in my favor.

Spencer has it.

My brother has it.

I'm not likely to find it.

And that's okay, even just seeing it gives me butterflies. That will just have to be enough.

My phone goes off in my hand, pulling me from my thoughts and I look down to see an alert for news on Spencer that I have set up. When I click on it, I almost drop it from shock. The picture staring at me is of Spencer and her ex, Kenneth, from a happier time, earlier on in their relationship. He's kissing her cheek while she's smiling so wide her eyes are squinting. The caption says, "Loving life recently."

I want to launch myself through the screen and strangle the man. He knows what he's doing and while I know it's an old picture, the general public won't. He wants people to think he's been with Spencer when she has made her relationship with Jared *very* public.

Luckily, Jared isn't paying attention to me or his phone, so I sneak away to call Kenneth's publicist. She answers after two rings.

"Hello?"

"Delete the picture your client just posted," I snap. I don't have any particular issue with her, but I'm fuming, and Spencer doesn't need this right now.

"What picture?"

"I'm glad you don't know about it, but it needs to go away before more damage is done."

I hear shuffling then a deep sigh of annoyance. "It's gone."

Refreshing the social media, I double check that it's deleted and it is. Though, I'm sure tabloids have already picked it up and I'm about to spend all night fixing this.

"Take away his access to social media, or something," I huff.

She gives a humorless laugh, "If that was an option I would."

"Thanks for deleting it."

"You're welcome. I'll talk to him."

Using my connections at every news outlet, I'm furiously sending emails *lightly threatening* them not to use the photo or write a story if they want any further interviews or exclusive news from Spencer.

Before I know it, I hear Spencer announce the end of the show and thanking everyone that was a part of the tour. Sending off my last email, I take my spot back on the side stage to be there and not let her know that anything is wrong.

She can know, but not until tomorrow. She gets to enjoy tonight.

Of course, as soon as the lights turn off she's running our way, but only has eyes for Jared. She bounds toward him, throwing herself into his arms and he instantly picks her up in a tight embrace like they are the only two people in the world. I can't help my smile.

I can't hear what he's saying to her, but I'm sure it's a bunch of sweet and loving words while all I can do is watch in awe. When he finally puts her down, I speak.

"I'm so proud of you, Spence, your biggest tour so far is done. How do you feel?" I don't have to feign my excitement, despite the drama happening behind the scenes I am genuinely excited for her.

"Everything," she breathes, "overwhelmed and in a way glad it's over. I'm ready to relax for a bit." She leans back into Jared's hold.

"And I'm excited to have you around for the entire season." Jared nuzzles into Spencer's neck and part of me feels like I'm intruding during an intimate moment with them.

"Me too," Spencer nods. "You excited to spend some time in Denver?" she asks me.

I nod. I can only hope that the drama will be minimal in our lives so I can enjoy my relaxation time as much as Spencer is going to.

———

I'VE OFFICIALLY BEEN a resident of Denver for one whole week. Moving is always its own special brand of chaos, but lucky for me I have a brother who I love to put to work, and his girlfriend has two other boyfriends who got roped into helping me by default.

Of course, there was a lot of yelling. A little bit of crying. Okay, all the yelling was between Brent and me because that's our love language to each other. And the crying was Chandler because she's pregnant and cries over everything.

The reason this time? She's so glad I'm going to be living close to them when their baby is born.

Once everything was moved into my new studio apartment, I take it all in. My newest chapter.

"You'd think Spencer Sparks would pay you enough to get something bigger than this," Brent teases.

"You'd think as team captain you'd learn not to be such an uptight douchenozzle, but here you are."

He swings his arm around my neck, yanking me into his side roughly. My face is forced into his chest, and I start pushing against him as hard as I can to let me go.

"Get off me, you tree."

"Come on, shorty, you can do better than that."

I jam my knee against the back of his, causing his leg to buckle and he lets go just as Chandler comes back inside and chuckles, catching the tail end of our scuffle.

"You two are going to be so happy to live so close, aren't you?" She beams with a teasing tone.

"Not a chance. Chan, I will hang out with you whenever you want. Brent, get fucked." I jam my elbow into his side causing him to grunt.

She just shakes her head at us. "I'm going to make sure Vince and Matt haven't killed each other returning the moving van."

"For the record," I say to my brother, "I could afford something bigger, but I don't need to prove I have a big dick by living in some mansion."

Brent scoffs, "Me either, which is why I don't have a mansion."

I roll my eyes. "Whatever you say. Thanks for helping I guess."

"You're welcome. Are you coming to the game tomorrow?"

I nod, "You think your girlfriend and my boss would let me get out of that?"

"See you there, shorty."

With everyone gone, the silence of my new apartment threatens to consume me. I don't like the quiet, it makes me think. When I think then the negative memories come roaring back. I prefer the side of me everyone sees. The happy-go-lucky Brynn.

Instead of stewing in silence, I turn on music and dance around while I unpack, refusing to acknowledge any of the fear for this new chapter of my life.

WHEELER

24

I 'm even more pissed off that I'm here than I was the day I got traded to this fucking team.

When my contract was up last season and I was a free agent I was hoping to get picked up somewhere else. Ideally back in L.A., though I knew the chances of that happening were close to zero.

The only thing I didn't want was for Denver to offer me a contract. I told my agent, but when it came through I couldn't say no.

Literally I couldn't, unless I wanted to be out of a job because they were the only ones to offer me one. I'm a good fucking player, I know this, and so do the big wigs in the league. Unfortunately, they also know my attitude on *and off* the ice. I think it's fucking dramatic, but it makes teams not want to deal with me.

But Denver did. And now I'm stuck. At least for the next

four years of my contract. Though, I made it clear I'm open to *any* trade. But for now I'm going to be a miserable fuck constantly which includes at all our practices so far and at our game tonight. It's the first of the season and I'm arriving with my headphones in, ignoring everyone around me.

The social media people taking pictures, the reporters asking all the guys if they would be okay with a pre game interview. I ignore them all with a blank look on my face. I don't even take off my headphones in the locker room as I begin changing.

I hear some of the guys—I refuse to call teammates because I don't feel like a team with them—talking about some shit. Doesn't matter that we've had daily practice for weeks, they are all talking like little bitches catching up after not seeing each other all summer. Even though we've had practices.

Makes me even more pissed off.

I'm turning up the volume on my headphones as I tug on my gear but before I get my jersey on, one of my headphones is ripped out of my ear. I turn to whoever decided they want to be fucked up and come face to face with the captain.

"The fuck?" I snap, stepping closer to him because I don't give two shits who he is.

"Coach is talking. Which means everyone needs to listen," Collee states, straight faced. Which only pisses me off more.

"You don't tell me what the fuck to do."

"You're a part of this team, whether you like it or not and we are not going to suck this season because of you." He keeps his cool through his little speech and I want to punch him in the face just for a reaction.

I scoff, still not backing away from him. "*I'm* not going to be the reason your fucking team sucks, but I don't give a shit about any of you. Never have before and I'm not going to start. Leave me the fuck alone and let me do my fucking job."

I grab my headphone from his hand and shove it into my ear, tuning out the entire locker room once again.

———

AFTER WARMUPS, we're all back in the locker room and I'm forced to listen as starting lines are announced, which isn't me even though it should be. Then, we're heading out into the arena for the game to start.

I feed off the energy of the crowd and that's where my focus remains. The only thing that matters is when I go out for my shift and being the best fucking player out there. Tolerating the other Denver guys enough while we are out there to try and get a goal.

It's almost the end of the first period, I gain control of the puck and skate toward the other zone. I can feel their player on my ass, but I speed up to get away from him. I get over the blue line to avoid being offside, just barely, then slap the puck toward their goal. The goalie stops it and I let out a loud curse, skating back to the bench.

Before I climb over the boards, I'm checked by Matt McQuaid. "I was open and had a clear shot you asshole."

"So did I," I grit out, itching for a fight.

"We hate you just as much as you hate us, you know? But out here we have to work together."

"Fuck off, McQuaid, you're not one to talk. You wouldn't have passed either."

"Guys, bitch at each other later, we are in the middle of a game," Charlie Mann snaps as both McQuaid and I sit.

The first period ends with Vince Dumont blocking a shot before it gets to the goalie, Colver.

In the locker room I get bitched at by Coach, but it goes in one ear and out the other. Everyone on this fucking team can eat shit, none of them would have gotten that goal either. It was a solid shot on my part, their goalie just stopped it.

I have too much shit pent up by the time we go back out for the next period I'm practically vibrating with rage. The combination of everything this last year from the original trade, to being stuck, moving bullshit, and dealing with everyone on this dumb ass fucking team. When I go out for my first shift of the period I cross check the guy who has possession of the puck into the boards hard enough I know I should get a penalty.

He reacts exactly how I hoped he would by shoving me back and then we are both throwing our gloves off as I grab his jersey and start raining punches down on him. He gets a couple good hits in and I love the pain it causes from my split lip. I taste the copper on my tongue and feel the blood from my busted knuckles, but I keep going until we end up on the ice and pulled apart by the refs.

I'm guided to the penalty box and can't help but smile for the first time in weeks. Sometimes all you need is a little fight to make you feel better.

And a good fuck.

Which I'm going to make happen after the game. This isn't L.A., but there isn't a shortage of puck bunnies. Especially after I get in a fight, for some reason that gets me even more attention than normal. Which is fine by me.

———

WE LOSE by one and of course everyone is pissed off as we change. The locker room is tense, but at least no one tries to talk to me again. I rush through my shower and throw my suit on so I can get out quickly.

As I enter the hallway I see a couple different groups of WAGs waiting for their guy. I grimace, I'd rather shoot my dick off than think about settling for just one woman. I'm a twenty-eight year old, good looking professional athlete. I can have whoever I want and I plan on that being my life for as long as I can.

One particular group catches my eye as I approach, I recognize Chandler who's dating three of the guys on the Dragons. *Fucking weird*. She's standing with three other women, one is Spencer Sparks, another is wearing glasses with short black hair. It's the blonde with legs for days that are covered in a pair of tight jeans that draws my eyes to her ass that I know belong to Brynn Collee. My captain's sister.

Suddenly I'm not in as much of a rush to leave. I may have just found the perfect fuck right here. That was easy.

Approaching the women, I paste a smile on my face and drape my arm across Brynn's shoulders.

"Good evening, ladies," I turn to the woman I have my arm around, "Baby Collee."

She makes a noise in the back of her throat before pushing at my side to get my body away from hers.

"Don't call me that," she snaps. I can't help how her bitchy little voice makes my dick jump. I don't mind a little bit of a fight, she's feisty, always is with me and I like it.

"How many times does she have to tell you she's not interested, Wheeler?" Spencer folds her arms across her chest. I know she's some famous singer, but she used to date my old teammate, Richardson. Now, she's dating the goalie on the Dragons somehow.

"Spencer, good to see you again. Do you know what team you think you're going to try to date next? Or actually," I turn toward Chandler, "Maybe I should be asking you that. Seems like that's more your speed."

"Charming as always, Colton." Spencer just rolls her eyes.

It's the one with glasses that starts storming toward me, which makes me chuckle softly. She's the only one I haven't even talked to.

"Who the fuck do you think you are? You better walk away before I cut off your dick. Assuming you haven't lost it to some sort of venereal disease already." She is fuming.

"My dick is just fine, I'm so glad it concerns you...." I don't know her name.

"What the fuck are you doing?" Mann approaches, and wraps his arm around the feisty one with glasses, so I guess she's with him. "You okay, Audrey?"

"Your girlfriend was just showing some concern for my dick, Mann, not a big deal."

"You asshole!" She starts to come toward me again, but Mann holds her back.

"My bad. Baby Collee and I will just head out and get out of your hair." I drape my arm around her again, but she shoves me off instantly.

"Get fucked, Wheeler," she seethes.

"That's what I'm trying to do," I smirk.

"What is happening?" a deep voice booms behind me. I groan, turning to face the captain himself.

"Just talking," I smile.

"Brynn, is he bugging you?" Collee asks, his narrowed eyes on me and I think this is the closest I've seen him to pissed off aside from during a game.

"The same way a fly does. Shoo, Wheeler, go fly around some shit, I know that's your favorite past time."

I lean forward to speak into her ear so no one around us can hear, "Keep talking dirty to me, Princess, it only makes me want you more."

I don't wait for her to reply and just keep walking because more of the guys have started to join and I don't want to deal with them anymore. Brynn wouldn't leave with me in front of her brother. Eventually I'll get her in my bed. It's only a matter of time.

"What was that about?" Brent asks, his eyes locked on Colton's back as he walks away.

I shrug. "Same shit different day. I can handle myself though, big bro, no need to get all weird."

"I don't like him talking to you." He's still staring in the direction Colton walked even though he's out of sight now.

"Yeah, yeah, you've never liked any of your teammates talking to me." I roll my eyes. Brent is the typical protective older brother, especially of me. I'm sure he was and is protective of Bailey too, but she's always been a bit more distant.

"Whatever, you need a ride home?"

"No, I drove because I knew I couldn't rely on any of these people to take me home," I refer to Chandler, Audrey, and Spencer because I knew they would want to go home with their men without having the pit stop of dropping me off. And I know Brent would rather go right home too.

"Alright, see ya later, shorty."

I groan, "I'm not even short."

He just laughs and I ignore it while I say goodbye to Chandler who was distracted by Vince and Matt arguing about something. I also say goodbye to Audrey and Spencer before heading out to the parking garage.

I approach my black crossover when a little blue sports car races through the garage, I have to jump out of the way. It stops suddenly, behind my car, rolling down the window to reveal the driver and I'm not at all surprised.

"You could kill someone, you know." I narrow my eyes at him.

"I'm careful, unless you don't want me to be," Colton teases.

"You're disgusting."

"Last chance to change your mind and come home with me. Maybe you need a good fuck to loosen up and I'm nice enough to offer."

"I will *never* want to go home with you, so give it up."

"Aw, Princess, never say never. I can be very convincing."

I paste a fake wide smile on my face and approach his open window, leaning in with my elbows propped on it.

"You know, maybe I can be convinced." I make sure my

cleavage is accentuated, and when I see his eyes shift down to it, I know I've succeeded.

"Yeah?" He runs his tongue along his bottom lip, his eyes fixed on my chest.

"Yeah, you know, if you take this pretty little car and drive off the nearest cliff, then *maybe* I'd consider it." I stand up and start to back away.

"I meant what I said, Baby Collee, keep talking dirty to me. It only makes me want you more. I like a challenge and I know you want me."

"If I wanted you, then you'd have me already." I turn, giving him my back as I go to get in my car.

I expect that to piss him off, but he just laughs.

"We'll see about that, Princess, you'll be begging for my dick in no time."

I make a dramatic gagging noise as I start to get in my car. "Go home and go to sleep, because the only time that will happen is in your dreams."

Shutting my door, I cut off anything else he could be saying, and I watch in my rearview mirror as he drives away. The last glimpse I get of him, I expect to see him scowling or looking pissed off, but he isn't. He has a smug smile on his face like he really believes he's going to get what he wants.

But that will *never* happen.

By the time I get home my exhaustion hits me like a train.

The adrenaline from watching the game, and then the verbal sparring with Colton has me ready to curl up and pass out for the next twelve hours.

I force myself to wash my face, brush my teeth and change into some pajamas as opposed to flopping face down onto my bed, makeup, jeans, and all. Once I'm finally ready, I slide in between my cool sheets snuggling up and embracing my soft blankets.

The moment my eyes close my phone dings with a notification. I fully expect it to be Brent checking to make sure I got home okay because he loves to pull that stuff with me. I know he will end up blowing me up if I don't respond, so I grab the phone to check, but see it's not a text from my brother. It's a social media notification and I roll my eyes.

Colton Wheeler has followed you.

I could block him, but I tell myself I'll do it in the morning, because I'm too tired to deal with it right now which is why I toss my phone back onto my nightstand and fall asleep almost instantly.

———

WHEN SPENCER and I talked about her taking time off and both of us moving away from L.A. I pictured my life in Denver a little different than this. Because, for me, it hasn't changed. I'm fielding requests for Spencer with the same answer over and over about her taking time off right now and not doing any interviews.

I'm glad there hasn't been any more backlash from the Kenneth situation at this point. When I told Spencer and Jared together what happened after her last show Jared didn't react well, but Spencer has a skill of calming him down.

However, I anticipate drama to ensue at the game tomorrow. It's a home game for the Dragons and we're all going.

I'm in the middle of answering emails when I get a text from Chandler.

> Chandler: Hey! You busy?

> Brynn: Only with things I don't want to do. What's up?

> Chandler: Want to go shopping?

> Brynn: Only if you let me buy things for my niece!

Chandler is pregnant and due in a little over a month and has been weird about getting presents from anyone because she said the guys have already bought too much. Mostly Vince, but Matt and my brother have overdone it as well and she insists she doesn't need anything else.

> Chandler: One thing!

> Brynn: I'll pick you up in an hour. *smile emoji*

When I get to Chandler's house, my brother answers the door and fake scowls at me.

"What do you want?" he asks.

"To steal your organs and sell them on the black market. Let me in, I'm not here for you."

"What's the password?" He folds his arms and leans against the doorframe.

I groan and push forward using all my strength to move him away from the entrance. Even though I'm five-foot-nine, I'm the shortest of my siblings with the rest of them being over six feet, including Bailey. Brent is the tallest at six-foot-six, and since he's a hockey player he's essentially a wall and I haven't lifted anything heavier than a laptop in years.

But I'm stubborn and determined so I still attempt to bull-doze my brother out of the way.

"What's going on?" a male voice asks from inside the house.

I peek around Brent to see Vince standing a few feet away looking extremely confused.

"Vince! My favorite out of Chandler's boyfriends. I'm here for your girlfriend and this asshole is acting like a child."

Brent scoffs, but still doesn't move.

Vince looks between me and Brent before shaking his head. "You two make me appreciate the relationship I have with my sister. I'll go get Chan."

"Thank you!" I call after him before narrowing my eyes up at Brent. "You're a child. And you're about to have one so you may want to grow up."

"I'm just standing here. You're the one trying to push me out of the way like a tiny little child."

I snarl, "Count your days big bro. Count. Your. Days."

"Brynn," Chandler calls from inside and that is what finally makes the big doofus move because he turns to look at her and gives a small smile. I love that he's so happy, but also...gross.

"Chandler, let's get out of here before this one drives me to drink," I hook my thumb in Brent's direction. "And I know I'll be in trouble if I drag you into a bar at eight months pregnant."

Chandler chuckles and presses her hand on Brent's chest which gets him to move instantly. I scowl at him while slicing my thumb across my neck in his direction while he kisses the top of her head.

"Love you, beautiful, have fun," he tells Chandler.

She leaves his embrace, and he starts to go back inside. "Love you, big brother!" I shout. Loudly.

He just shakes his head before shutting the door and I laugh as we walk back to my car.

"He does love you, you know," Chandler clarifies.

"I know. He'd be totally lost without me."

C handler's best friend, Audrey, meets us at the outdoor shopping center. I invited Spencer, but she said she was extremely inspired and needed to focus. Audrey insists we start at the store that sells lingerie because she needs some new options for her shows as a cam girl.

I feel bad for the amount of walking we're doing because Chandler seems to struggle to keep up a bit with her extremely pregnant belly. She says she's okay, but I'm finding it hard to believe when she presses her hand to her lower back as she walks.

While Audrey is in the changing room with a whole armful of lace and string that I couldn't even imagine trying to get onto my body, Chandler turns toward me on the plush couch outside the changing rooms.

"So, we haven't gotten the chance to talk about that Colton situation," she starts with a raised eyebrow.

Audrey must hear because she calls from behind the curtain, "Yeah what the fuck was up with that asshole?"

They've known about my aversion to a certain annoying hockey player since last season, but that was the first time anyone except Spencer has seen his handiwork firsthand. And it's definitely the first time he's tried any of his tactics around my brother.

"I think he either has a death wish or has some weird goal to try and fuck me." I shrug, those are the two possibilities I've thought of when it comes to Colton Wheeler's attention.

"If he keeps trying to pull that in front of Brent, he *definitely* has a death wish," Chandler nods.

Audrey comes out wearing a tight purple corset top that pushes her boobs up and some lace underwear that match. I respect her confidence to wear things like that because I'm comfortable with my body, but I wouldn't dare.

"I think he really wants to fuck you." Audrey shrugs.

"Hot. That's a yes," Chandler says pointing to the outfit.

"Done." Audrey nods.

"I think he wants to fuck anyone who looks at him," I grumble.

"Charlie has said he's a total prick and acts like he's still a part of another team," Audrey adds while walking back behind the curtain.

Chandler nods, "Yeah, even last season after he got traded

Matt would come home and talk about how badly he wants to beat him into the ice."

"You know, I would love to see that, actually," I smirk.

"Same!" Audrey exclaims while changing.

I chuckle, "Anyway, it doesn't matter. I don't care what he does or who decides to fight him, he can keep trying to get with me, but it'll never happen."

Chandler raises her eyebrow at me. "Those are famous last words."

Audrey peeks her head out of the curtain. "Yeah, they are. I would know, I said it'd never happen with Charlie and...well... here we are."

"I mean it though; I've gone the last twenty-five years knowing I will never date a hockey player because of my brother. That won't change, especially for a guy like Colton."

Audrey gives me a skeptical look before disappearing back behind the curtain. Chandler also looks at me suspiciously.

"You guys suck, I mean it. I have *zero* interest," I insist.

"All I'm saying is that I will get to say, 'I told you so.'" Chandler shrugs.

"I give it a month," Audrey adds.

I just roll my eyes at the two of them. Clearly, they underestimate how stubborn I am. Because when I set my mind to something I mean it. And I've had my mind set on this my entire life. It's not changing.

———

WE ARE all in the WAGs suite at the game against L.A. Audrey and Chandler spend the warmups down at the glass because they insist they need a prime view. Spencer was tempted to go with them but knew that might create some chaos and she's trying to keep a low profile these days.

I have no desire to watch that up close. Or really at all, which is why I spend the time getting myself a drink. I'm only allowed one at the beginning of the game since I'll have to drive myself home.

I return to Spencer's side with my cider in hand and as soon as I sit down, I overhear a particular group of women gossiping about my friends and I just roll my eyes.

"Give it a rest," I sigh.

"Why are you friends with the outcasts, Brynn? Your brother is the *captain*," Rosie says.

"And he's one *hot ass captain*," another woman, Helen, adds.

I grimace, "Gross and he's *very* taken."

"She gets to have more than one guy, why can't they do the same?" Rosie scoffs.

I roll my eyes, "Stay out of their lives. It doesn't concern you. It's been years and if you don't knock it off, I'll let Audrey loose on you."

Last season I heard about Audrey putting them in their place, but apparently it hasn't stuck like it should. It shuts them up for now, though, and they don't say anything when my friends return right before the first period starts.

"How were warmups?" I ask them as they take their seats.

"Amazing as always. Spencer, I'm always impressed that Jared can do the actual splits." Audrey fans herself with her hand.

Spencer chokes out a laugh, "Thanks, I'll make sure to pass that compliment along to him."

I chuckle, taking a sip from my drink.

"Colton looked good out there, stretching his hips," Chandler says, side eyeing me.

I cough. "Don't even try. I love you, Chan, but I will tell my brother what you just said."

She giggles. "Good. I'd love to see him lose his shit for once."

I cringe. "Never mind."

The game starts and it's clear the team is putting in serious effort to win this one after their less than stellar start to the season. I've always been forced to watch hockey because Brent would drag me along to his practices and games because he didn't trust to leave me at home with our pieces of shit parents. Sometimes it was fun, but I got bored of it eventually. I'm not like my friends who are glued to everything going on down on the ice and drooling over their men.

They're happy and good for them, that's all that matters.

The crowd gets louder, and I focus on what's happening when I see a Dragons player racing toward the goal in the opponent's zone, and when he shoots it, the horn that signals a goal goes off and the arena erupts in cheers. I jump up along with everyone celebrating the goal.

The jumbotron highlights the player that just scored, and my cheering instantly stops. Because the smug handsome face that is filling the screen is the one man in this entire arena, I wish I never had to see again.

Tensions begin to creep up on the ice between the teams during the next play, now that the Dragons scored. My eyes catch on a small altercation between Spencer's ex, Kenneth, and Colton. They shove at each other, but it doesn't progress. I'm sure it was just playful and them being all buddy-buddy.

Dickheads have to stick together. I'm sure it's a code somewhere.

The teams continue trying to get control of the puck, and a couple line changes later things start to heat up a bit. Matt shoves some player into the boards at an awkward angle and they end up sprawled out on the ice. Instantly, players are descending on Matt, punches are being thrown and the crowd screams louder than when Colton scored his goal.

More players jump in on both teams and it's an all-out line brawl with the Dragons against the Spartans. Matt swings the guy he's fighting around by the jersey and throws him onto the ground before he's on him. The refs and linesmen are struggling to break up all the fights happening.

Brent's on the ice, mostly just holding back an L.A. player instead of full on fighting him. My brother, the controlled peace-keeper. Except when he's antagonizing me.

The cameras on the jumbotron change their view to the benches and all the Dragons players are hitting their sticks against the boards in solidarity, except Colton. He's resting his chin on his hands that are balancing the stick underneath him where he stands as he watches what's happening on the ice. The camera cuts away, but not before I see the smirk on his face.

The fights are finally broken up, and the first period ends with one goal for the Dragons.

"Matt is going to be riding that high for the rest of the night." Chandler shakes her head.

"Which means you'll be riding *him*." Audrey winks at her best friend and I chuckle.

Chandler scoffs, "He doesn't get that privilege alone, it's more fun to mess with him by messing with Vince or Brent."

I gag, making sure to exaggerate my retching noise.

Chandler cringes. "Sorry, sometimes I forget you're not just one of my best friends."

I wave her off. "It's fine, it's just my initial reaction to anything having to do with my brother regardless of the subject matter. But also, gross."

"Well, you're not related to Charlie so I can tell you all about what his reward is if they win tonight," Audrey beams.

"Thanks, but no thanks on that one too," I say, laughing.

During the next period there's a small altercation between Kenneth and Audrey's boyfriend Charlie. It gets broken up before anything really happens and I just shake my head at all the drama between these guys. I know it's the nature of hockey, but these teams have a hatred that runs deeper than just the game.

The crowd loudly opposes when the Spartans get a goal, and it fires up the Dragons even more. Every time Colton is on the ice I notice that he's not as aggressive toward his old team as he usually is during a game.

I hate that I notice that but considering he's usually one of the players causing massive fights, with some dirty hits. Not this game. If anything, sometimes it almost looks like he's playing against his teammates rather than with them. Even though I can't see my brother, I know he's probably pissed, but hiding it like he always does.

The teams are tied going into the third period and they are both playing like its game seven of the playoffs, not just one of the first games of the season. Everyone's eyes are glued to the ice, I'm hoping the Dragons win purely because I don't want to deal with any moping.

That dream fades when the Spartans score once again putting them ahead by one with only five minutes left in the game. Hockey can change in a second and I know this doesn't mean it's over at all.

And yet, after five minutes it is over. The Spartans won.

"Well, that fucking sucked," Audrey huffs as we all start to make our way down to the tunnel to meet the guys.

It doesn't take long before some of the players start to exit the locker room, clearly wanting to get out of here as soon as possible after the loss. Vince greets us with a smile on his face the second he sees Chandler, like the shitty game doesn't even phase him now.

"Hey baby," he greets her with a kiss on her cheek. She blushes, leaning into him.

"Are we going out to commiserate?" Audrey asks.

Chandler groans, rubbing her hand on her stomach. "Not me. You all can enjoy, but I'm going to sleep for the foreseeable future."

"I'm going wherever you go." Vince wraps his arms around Chandler, placing his hands on her very pregnant belly.

Charlie joins us, his girlfriend turns to him and asks, "Are we going out?"

"Uh, I didn't really have any plans to. Are you wanting to?" Charlie looks around at the rest of us, clearly caught off guard by her question.

"I'm down," I announce, even though I'm exhausted too, and want nothing more than to crawl into bed like Chandler.

"Down for what, Baby Collee? Me? It's about damn time," Colton says, sneaking up on me and throwing that damn arm around my shoulders again. I immediately push him away, but he just chuckles.

"Give it up." I roll my eyes.

"I'm going out with some of my old teammates, so if you decide you want to have some *real* fun tonight, Princess, hit me up."

"Won't happen."

The words don't leave my mouth, instead, Brent beats me to it as he approaches. His eyes locked on Colton who's already walking away.

I turn toward my brother. "What did I say? I can handle myself."

"You're still my little sister," he grunts. I know he's already mad about the loss and catching Colton hitting on me yet again is not helping the situation.

"Ew don't call me that," I joke, trying to dissipate some of the tension that's surrounding us.

"Anywayyyy," Audrey exaggerates the syllable, also trying to relieve some of the weird tension that's fallen over all of us. "You're still coming out, Brynn?"

"Yup, let's leave these party poopers to their lame night in."

I meet up with some of my old teammates at a bar downtown near the hotel they're staying at. Kenneth is with them, which is not someone I want to hang out with, but I'd rather see my old team, my *real* team, than go out with the fuckers from Denver.

"How has it been slumming it, Wheeler?" McEntyre asks.

"Fuckin' brutal. And it would be one thing if these guys could play, but they are just dragging me and I'm fucking over it." I take a swig of my beer.

"Wish we could say we missed ya, but we just kicked your ass so," Thompson shrugs.

"Oh, fuck off, that wasn't my fault."

"It was your team though," McEntyre ribs.

"Those guys aren't my fucking team," I grumble.

Kenneth Richardson snorts out a laugh. "Say what you want Wheeler, but those guys *are* your team now."

Glaring at him, I can't help but say, "Which means I get a front row seat to how happy Spencer is to be free of your pining ass."

He scoffs, "I'm not pining for anyone. He can have my sloppy seconds."

He's acting like we all didn't see the weird ass picture he posted making it seem like they were still together. He may not want to be with her, but he sure as shit doesn't want anyone else to have her either. But at the end of the day, it's not my business.

"Oh shit, hey Wheeler, isn't that your captain's hot ass sister over there?" Thompson nods behind me.

Taking another deep pull from my beer, I turn over my shoulder to see if she really is here. And sure enough, standing at a high-top table with Mann and his girlfriend is a certain tall blonde, her wavy hair falling to her mid back. Her jeans hugging her long legs and perfectly round ass have me dying to go over and fuck with her more.

She throws her head back laughing at something someone said. Even though I can't hear her, for some reason that's what does me in and I find myself walking closer. The music playing in the bar is loud, but I hear my old teammates saying some shit I just ignore, focused on the one girl I know I'm not allowed to have, which is probably the only reason I want her.

At least just for a night. I don't want a relationship, but to fuck her at least once? That I do want. Her laughing stops the second her eyes meet mine as I get closer to where she's standing.

"Your protector let you out without supervision tonight?" I ask, sliding up next to her, ignoring the glare I'm receiving from Audrey and the look of confusion from Mann.

"I'm her protector and I will make you disappear where no one can find you," Audrey snaps.

"Come on, pretty girl, let's get a refill." Mann starts to lead her away from the table with a serious look in my direction. As they pass by me, he speaks low so only I can hear him, "Don't do anything too stupid."

"We will be *right back,*" Audrey yells as she's pulled away by Mann.

I lean against the table in front of Brynn, and she just glares at me. I like how she has to bend her head back just slightly to look up at me. At six-foot-five most girls have to strain to meet my eyes. Brynn is on the taller side, and it puts her at the perfect height for me. For everything my mind can conjure up. Which is a lot.

"I think it must be fate or some shit we ended up at the same place," I tease.

"What do you want, Colton?"

"You in my bed would be ideal." I step closer to her.

"I *hate* you."

"I hate you too, Princess. Now, let's hate fuck it out of each other."

She scoffs, "You're disgusting."

"Just once, we can get it out of our systems."

"Or I could smack you once, you know, just to get it out of my system."

"If that's what you're into, Princess. I like a little pain." I edge closer to her, as she tries to step back, she realizes I have her caged in with her back to the table.

She raises a hand onto my chest, her eyes locked on it. My heart rate kicks up at the contact. The heat from her palm feels like it's burning through my shirt onto my skin. I want that heat wrapped around my cock. Then I want to be wrapped in the heat of her pussy.

"You're right, Colton, just once. It would be good for us," her voice is breathy, and I'm actually shocked this seems to be working. I fully expected to have to work a little harder than this, but I'm not going to question it.

I grip the edge of the table on either side of her body. "I'm so glad you agree. Let's get out of here and back to my place."

"No, you want this. Do it right here. Right now." Her hands grip my shirt in her fists.

I'm taken aback at her boldness, looking in her green eyes that are shining up at me, she doesn't falter. She's dead serious.

"You want me to fuck you right here?" I ask cautiously.

"Right here," she smirks. "Unless you can't handle me."

"Oh, I can handle you, Princess." I press against her completely so she can feel that I'm already hard for her.

"Mm, you sure about that?" She arches into me.

I lean down, running my lips along the side of her neck while she pulls me tighter against her by my shirt. When my lips graze her jaw, she whispers my name. I can't wait to hear her scream it.

"Yeah, Princess?" My lips are barely an inch above hers, breathing the same air.

"No matter what you say, or what you do. You will never, ever get to touch me." I'm pushed back from her grip on my chest, stumbling at the force, meeting her devilish gaze.

I chuckle. "You got me good, Baby Collee, but you're wrong, because I'm still not going to give up. You want me, you just don't want to admit it."

Audrey and Mann return with drinks in their hands, both staring daggers at me.

"If I change my mind, which I won't, you'll be the last person to know." Brynn smirks.

I shake my head, walking backward toward the table with my old teammates. "Challenge accepted."

I turn around so I can't see whatever remark was on the tip of her tongue.

As I get back to the table the guys are already giving me shit.

"That went well."

"Strike out for Wheeler."

"I'm playing the long game, guys. She's the captain's sister and he fucking hates me. What better way to get back at him." I down the rest of my drink.

"You're fucked up, Wheeler. Sounds like a great plan." Thompson chuckles.

While the other guy's joke at my expense, I can't help but notice how Richardson is looking at me. He doesn't say anything, but something about his smug little face makes me think he sure as shit is thinking something. And something tells me I don't want to know what that could be.

Chapter Nine

BRYNN

I say goodnight to Audrey and Charlie not long after the run in with Colton. I'm tired and didn't want to run the risk of him trying to shoot his shot again. Turning him down is annoying and I know that's probably his goal, to just wear me down, but it won't work.

"You're my new going out buddy since Chandler had to go get knocked up," Audrey jokes as we are parting.

"As long as you don't ditch me by doing the same." I wave as my ride-share pulls up.

"Not a problem here. No babies will be had, we just enjoy practicing making them."

I choke out a laugh. She's not shy about anything in regard to sex, being a cam girl. Charlie just shakes his head, accepting his girlfriend announcing that, loudly, on the streets of downtown Denver.

I climb into the car and right before he pulls away from the curb the back door opposite to the one I got in swings open. I gasp loudly, terrified some random person is going to reach in and snatch me or something while I try to crowd myself against the other door.

The fear turns into annoyance instantly when I meet the blazing blue eyes of my nemesis.

"What are you doing?" I snap.

"Do you know him?" the driver asks.

"No."

"Yes."

We answer at the same time, and Colton climbs into the car without an invitation.

"I need a ride," he says calmly.

"That sucks. Go get your own ride, this one is going to my house."

"Perfect. That's where I was needing a ride to."

"Get out." I push at his chest.

The driver looks in the rearview mirror, clearly confused as to what is happening and what he should do.

"We got into a fight earlier, you're good to go," Colton tells him, to which the guy just shrugs and starts to drive.

I stare at him, extremely concerned for any woman who gets

into his car in the future. "You could be assisting in a murder right now, you know? Or some other horrible crime. I said I don't know him."

"Pretty sure you'd be screaming and jumping out of the car if that was true," the driver retorts.

My eyes narrow at him. "This isn't safe."

"Come on, Princess, I'm sorry for what happened back there, no need to harass the nice man." Colton pulls me back against him and I scramble away, pressing myself as tightly as I can on the opposite side of the car.

"Hope you enjoy the ride, as soon as we get there, you're ordering your own car to take you back to *your* house," I demand, facing the window, refusing to look at him.

He just chuckles like I'm the one being ridiculous right now.

Neither of us say anything the rest of the way back to my apartment and as soon as the car stops, I'm rushing out, holding my tongue because I want to yell at the guy that he's not getting a tip. My desire to get away from Colton wins as I rush toward my building. Colton is clearly taking his time because I hear the car door shut while I'm almost to the door. I debate taking the stairs, even though it's going to suck going up the five flights.

Somehow, Colton catches up to me before I make it to the door, and I know I can't lead him right to my actual apartment. Spinning around to face him, I fold my arms across my chest. "What do you think you're doing?" I snap.

"Walking you to your door like a gentleman," he replies, calmly.

"No."

"No?"

"I. Said. No."

"It's about safety, Baby Collee."

"What can I do to make you go away?"

He smirks, his eyes trail my body and I roll mine at his blatant perusal. I'm not wearing anything revealing so he can enjoy his fill of my jeans and Dragons sweatshirt with my last name on it. His *captain's* last name on it.

"Go out with me."

"No."

"You seem to like that word, don't you?"

"With you? Yes."

"Look at that, you know another word."

I groan, throwing my hands up in the air. "I'm not going out with you. Give it up."

"One date."

"No."

"What if I say please?"

"No."

"Is there anything—"

"No."

"What if—"

"No."

"Baby—"

"No."

"Brynn—"

"You do know my name. Oh my God, I assumed you thought my first name was baby."

He laughs and I scowl.

"Fine, I'll leave on one condition."

"What?" I ask, exasperated by this entire exchange.

"You let me know you made it home okay."

I roll my eyes, "I'm home now."

"Into your apartment," he smirks.

"Yeah, fine, sure, bye."

I press the button for the elevator and hope he won't try following me, completely over this entire interaction. He's exhausting and I can't stand him. Good on any woman who chooses to put up with him because he would drive me *insane*. Luckily, he stays outside the elevator as the doors close in his face.

Once I'm inside my apartment, safe and sound with the door locked, I breathe out a sigh of relief. My exhaustion hits me like a ton of bricks, and I get ready to crawl into bed. While I'm brushing my teeth my phone goes off with a notification. I see it's a message on social media and roll my eyes so hard I'm convinced they may get stuck.

Colton: You didn't tell me you got home.

Brynn: I got home.

Colton: Too late, the deal is off, guess I won't stop leaving you alone. Goodnight, Princess.

I toss my phone down before rinsing out my mouth. I don't know who I pissed off in one of my lives to deserve this annoyance, but I'm sorry. I apologize to whoever it was, just please, *please* make this man go away.

And yet when I start to doze off to sleep the last thing I think about is how his body was pressed against mine and how in that moment, I didn't entirely hate it.

———

THE NEXT DAY I go over to Spencer's place because we have to talk about some things while she's technically "off the grid" working on her next album. Jared and the team left for a week-long road trip, and I'm thankful I get a week reprieve from Colton and his bullshit.

When Spencer answers the door in her sweatpants, tank top, and auburn hair in a messy bun she still looks very much like the rock star that she is.

"How's it going?" I ask, as I walk into her huge house she shares with Jared.

"Good, I've got some songs I'm excited about and now going to have the emotions for sad ones while Jared is gone," even though she says that she chuckles.

"Sounds like you've got it all figured out," I tell her while sitting on her soft couch that threatens to suck me in. I may never leave.

"What about you? What's new in my outside life?"

"Things have been surprisingly quiet since Kenneth pulled that BS on the last day of your tour," I shrug.

She groans, dropping down onto the couch next to me. "I'm so glad Jared is understanding because I know not everyone is as lucky as I am when it comes to drama like this."

I nod. "He's amazing and you deserve it. I can't believe you put up with Kenneth for two years."

Cringing, she replies, "Don't remind me."

"The label is wanting a tentative date that you'll be finished recording just as a heads up," I tell her. I'm the only one from "work" she's communicating with right now, so it all has to go through me.

"I *gave* them a tentative date; they are just hoping it'll be sooner. You can tell them nothing has changed."

"Sounds good, and of course I'm being hounded for interview requests for you but turning them all down."

"Good, everyone can sweat it out for a bit. Or forget all about me so I can live in peace for the rest of my days."

I furrow my eyebrows at her. "You really think you might want to retire?"

We're only twenty-five, but she's had enough success to never have to worry about anything again. I just figured she would want to do this for a long time, she worked hard to get where she is and I know it's been insane these last couple of years, but I know she enjoys herself.

She waves me off. "No, not yet. The peace is nice, but I would miss performing. Don't worry, your job is safe."

I breathe out a laugh. "I wasn't even worried about me. I know you would give me a killer recommendation for working with anyone else in the industry. I'll never be unemployed again."

She points a finger at me. "You're not wrong. Now, I've heard things through the grapevine about a certain player bothering you."

I roll my eyes. "Yeah, Colton getting traded here is horrible for everyone, honestly. He's doubled his efforts to get into my pants."

"Don't do it!"

"*Ew*, never. You know how I feel about hockey players, and assholes. Since he's both, there is zero concern to be had." I'm reminded of the other night; how persistent he was. How I could feel how hard he was pressed against me. How big he felt...*nope.* Never going to happen.

"What does your brother say about it?"

I burst out laughing. "Brent only knows what I want him to know. Which is nothing."

"I'm sure he knows more than you think," she gives me a pointed look.

"He's seen Colton try to hit on me, but he's also seen that I can handle myself."

"Oh, I know you can, but I also know that you're his baby sister who he's *super* protective of."

I roll my eyes again. "Yeah, yeah. He needs to let me be free. Like a bird that's flying away and trust that I am okay. *Oh*, there's some inspiration for a song. You're welcome."

Spencer shakes her head at me. "Thank you. I will write a song called 'my protective older brother needs to leave me alone.'"

"Perfect, I sense your next smash hit."

S pencer and I hung out the rest of the day because I insisted she needed a break from all the work she's been doing. To which she told me Jared gives her *plenty* of breaks. I argued that technically that was inspiration, and she needs a true break, which led to us eating too many snacks, watching dumb movies, and having one of the best days I've had in a while.

Which is why I'm in a great mood by the time I get home, overly full from all the snacks and tired from all the talking and laughing we did. It felt nice to hang out with my friend again without the outside pressures of who she is.

We met in college, and at that time Spencer was just posting videos of herself singing on YouTube. Eventually, it became more than that and she got widely popular, and the rest is history. I was studying public relations in college so when she needed a publicist, she hired me, and it's been a balancing act of our friendship and work ever since.

So days like today are nice. It reminds me of college when everything was easier. When my family wasn't as strained with Bailey's chosen absence and Brandon's...well anyway. Shaking the depressive thoughts away, I decide to reach out to my other brother, Bryson. I'm not as close to him as I am Brent, but we keep in touch every so often.

When I pick up my phone to call him, I see a message I must have missed on my social media. I scowl at the screen when I see who it's from.

Colton: Missing me yet, Princess?

Not even slightly, I think to myself. Ignoring the message I call my brother.

Bryson answers and the background noise is loud like he's at a club or something based on all the voices and music.

"Hello?" he answers.

"Hey, where are you?" I ask.

"Uh, out with some friends. Everything okay?"

"Yeah, just calling to say hi." I pick at some lint on my pants because it's clear he's busy and will want to get off the phone quickly.

"Oh, hi. Sorry, Brynn, can I call you back tomorrow?"

"Yeah, sorry to bother you!" I fake cheeriness in my voice because if I'm honest I'm a little disappointed. I wanted to talk to him. Sometimes I just want to talk to someone in my family, but they are all too busy or too preoccupied with other things to talk to me, and it just makes me feel silly for trying.

"It's okay," his voice is sincere, but I hear his name called in the background. "I'll call tomorrow, okay?"

"Yeah, whenever you're not busy. It's okay."

"Okay, talk later, sis."

"Love—" The call cuts off and I feel the tears brimming, but I blink them away. I'm not going to cry.

And because I clearly am some sort of masochist, or the loneliness has driven me to insanity I actually reply to Colton.

> Brynn: You wish.

Colton: Go out with me when we come back.

> Brynn: No.

Colton: One drink.

> Brynn: How many times do I have to tell you no?

Colton: Until I have you under me screaming, "yes."

Ugh. I regret replying. Staring at the screen I don't know what to say. And I know I shouldn't say anything else. He just likes to fuck with me and wants what he can't have.

And yet, it reminds me how long it's been since I've been with someone. I've never dated anyone seriously, just a handful of dates that lead to more, but then it just kind of fades out. I've

never had those butterflies, fireworks, seeing stars type of feelings that I hear about. The same feelings Spencer sings about in
her love songs and yet I've never felt it.

I've also never felt the heartbreak she sings about either
because I've never felt so strongly for anyone I've been with to
be upset when it ends.

Sometimes I think I'm defective.

Other people have it, but I don't.

Since I started working with Spencer, I became so busy that
dating took a back seat and that includes sex. Rereading Colton's
text makes me think even more about that and realizing how
long it's been since I've even gotten myself off.

I refuse to admit that his words may have made me feel a
certain way. Which results in wetness between my legs. But it's
not *because* of him. No, just the thought of being under *anyone else*
screaming yes.

The faceless man of my fantasy giving me pleasure I've never
experienced with anyone else. His fingers rubbing me, his mouth
on me, before fucking me in a way that has me exploding all
around him.

I find that my hands have slid underneath my underwear and
I'm swiping my finger through my desire and bringing it up to
my clit to rub tight circles, exactly the way I need to get off. I
close my eyes and the fantasy takes over.

The man moving me exactly how he wants me, flipping me
onto my stomach as he drives into me from behind. His hand is

rubbing me between my body and the mattress while he fucks me in punishing thrusts.

His voice is in my ear, *"Such a good girl for me."*

"You're taking my cock like the perfect little slut you are."

"Your pussy was made for me."

The voice becomes more distinct the closer I get. The telltale signs of an orgasm starting to form. I bring myself closer and closer to the edge when the voice becomes familiar. And in my fantasy, I'm flipped around on my back and the faceless man isn't faceless anymore.

When my release hits me, I realize who my brain assigned this fantasy to. I almost want to stop myself from coming, but I can't. It's too late. When I bite down on my bottom lip to stifle my moan, it's in punishment to myself that the face and voice my brain decided to add to my fantasy is that of Colton *fucking* Wheeler.

————

THE NEXT DAY I refuse to think about what I did last night. I didn't reply to Colton, and I don't plan to. I'm avoiding him and pretending like I never fantasized about him while I...*nope*, see I'm not thinking about it.

Chandler needed my help with something for the baby today and I head over as soon as I see her text. She greets me looking completely disheveled and out of breath. If the guys weren't out of town, I would assume to know why she looks like that and would probably throw up in my mouth a bit because that would include my brother.

"Hey," she greets, panting.

"You okay?" My concern rising. I've never been around anyone in labor, and she could be right now for all I know.

"Yeah, the stairs are killing me," she heaves.

"Maybe you guys should've thought about that before buying such a huge place." I step inside. "Or even better, make them build you an elevator."

She shakes her head. "It's only for a couple more weeks, I can handle it."

"I don't know. That elevator seems like a good idea in general," I coax.

Chandler huffs out a small laugh. "You might be right. If I had an elevator I wouldn't need your help."

She leads me to a box leaning against a wall. It's not heavy, but it is awkwardly shaped, so I have to walk sideways up the stairs to get it up to the nursery.

I set it down in the immaculately decorated baby room, placing my hands on my hips. "Could this not have waited until the guys were back? I feel like this is all they would be good for."

Chandler smirks, "They are good for much more than that."

I exaggerate a gag. "Gross. No. I love you, but those comments are okay for Audrey, not me."

She laughs. "Sorry, but that's what you get for questioning me being an independent woman."

"I know you are. What is this anyway?" I ask, moving the box to see for myself.

"It's a nightstand. I realized we needed one when I ran out of room to put things for her."

"I assume you need my help building it too?" I ask, already starting to open the box.

"Nah, I got it. I just need you to keep me company." She takes over for me, opening the box.

Over the next couple of hours, Chandler fights off my attempts to help beyond handing her things she needs for the project. After a short interlude when Vince calls her, and another one when somehow a piece was put on the wrong way resulting in her having to undo a couple steps and try again, it's finished. We ordered dinner to have together and it's nice to spend some one-on-one time with my sister-in-law.

I head home and only realize I haven't paid my phone any attention when I see all the notifications that have piled up throughout the day. While I hope to see some from Bryson, or even maybe Bailey, that's not the case. Most of them have to do with Spencer which means I'll be spending tomorrow *gently* reminding people that she is not available at this time.

One message makes me narrow my eyes at the screen, and yet again while I debate blocking him, I still don't. At least this time I don't reply. Not after what happened last night. I refuse to let my fantasies include this asshole again.

I know that if I ignore him long enough, he'll eventually give up. Guys like Colton Wheeler only like the thrill of the chase for so long. At the end of the day, he wants convenience and that will never be me.

Colton: Can't wait for our drink when I get back, Princess.

Chapter Eleven

WHEELER

24

M y new favorite pastime is fucking with Brynn. When I'm bored, I fuck with her. When I need to cheer myself up, I fuck with her. When I'm horny, I fuck with her. I don't know if it's because of who she is, or because she can't stand me, but the woman makes me want to fight with her and then fuck her all within the span of ten seconds.

The way she fights back and argues makes me want her even more. I mean, makes me want her *under* me. Because that's all I'm looking for. And the fact that it would piss off her older brother really is the icing on the cake.

Every day that we're on our road trip I send Brynn at least one message a day. Why? Because I know it'll piss her off. I half expect her to block me, but she doesn't, which tells me everything I need to know. Baby Collee is enjoying our little back and forth as well.

The next step for me is going to be taking it further. Now

that we're back, I want to piss her off *in person* again. It's a sure-fire way to get my dick hard and then I want her to do something about it. Hand, mouth, pussy, I'm not picky, but she will at some point.

As soon as the team plane lands back in Denver, I can't get off it fast enough. I don't talk to anyone, and they don't talk to me. Which is fine and makes me want to get some release. Mostly in the form of a certain little blonde.

Once I'm in my car I send her the first message of the day.

> Colton: I'm back, Princess. Meet me at Twisted Snake tonight at eight.

She will probably ignore me. Likely not to show up, but that's okay because if she doesn't then I'll just find someone else to go home with. It's a win-win either way for me.

I smirk at the screen when I see the message has been read and she doesn't respond. It's fine, though, I have a feeling she may surprise me.

When I open my texts, I see one of the simple obligatory texts from my mom. You'd think being the only child she has left she would care more, but every message I get from her just reminds me that she feels like she *has* to check on me. Not that she wants to.

And my dad doesn't even pretend to try and care.

So, I stopped caring a long time ago. They aren't the only ones that were affected by losing Josh, but they sure as shit act like it.

> Mom: How are you?

Colton: Fine.

It's all I say before tossing my phone into my bag strapped around my shoulders before I straddle my bike and take off toward my place. I love the chance to ride whenever I can. I can't take my motorcycle on game days, but any other time it's my main ride.

I speed down the streets of Denver to get back to my rental house just outside of the city. I like the distance away from everything that reminds me where I actually am. Out here I can pretend I'm anywhere else. At least until the snow starts, then I'll remember I'm not in L.A.

As I get closer to my house, I'm tempted to keep driving up into the mountains to kill time, but I end up doing a loop around the hills near my house instead of navigating the mountain roads. I park my Ducati Supersport in the garage and go inside. It's completely silent, which isn't unusual and is how I prefer it.

No one comes into my house. When I hookup with a chick, we go to her place, or a hotel.

I head up to my bedroom, tossing my bag on the floor and immediately stripping out of my clothes before getting in the shower. My mind drifts to the feisty little baby Collee as the hot water pelts my skin. The smirk pulls at my lips as I think about the possibility of her showing up tonight.

My dick stands at attention at the thought of her tall, little body pressed against mine again. How it would feel if she wrapped those long legs around my waist while I pushed inside her. I dunk my head under the water and shake out my hair. I'm not going to fuck my fist to the thought of her. Not yet, because I want to feel the real thing first.

————

I GET to the country bar a little after eight because I know if she's going to show up, there's not a chance in hell she would show up at the time I told her to. Defiant little thing.

When I walk in, my eyes scan the area looking for the familiar head of blonde hair. When I don't see her at the bar or by the bull riding machine, I decide to grab a drink and scope other possible options for the night. Because it's been too long and I need to get laid tonight, regardless.

Some guy steps up to the mechanical bull and I see the cocky look he sends a group of girls right before he hops up onto the machine. It starts before he's ready and he attempts to hang on, but after a second he's thrown onto the soft ground.

Shaking my head, I turn back toward the bar as my beer is being slid toward me. I nod at the bartender. "Go ahead and leave it open," I tell him.

"You know, you should try that out," a feminine voice says next to me, and I can't help the pull at the side of my mouth in a smirk.

Turning toward the voice, I'm met with a conflicted looking Brynn.

"I will if you will, Princess," I tell her, smugly.

She shakes her head. "I don't even know why I'm here."

"I do. Because you want me. It's okay to admit it, I won't hold it against you. Well..."

She scoffs, "This was stupid. I had a moment of temporary insanity, I'm leaving."

"Wait." I reach out, and take hold of her arm as she starts to walk away. She narrows her eyes at me when I don't let go. I'm not holding her hard, but I don't rush to let go either. "One drink. You're already here."

Her eyes flick over to the mechanical bull, and she smiles. "I will if you try that out."

I drop her arm and ignore how I feel about not touching her and that I don't like it. Shaking my head, I respond, "No, if we're making a bet involving Bill then we're making it more exciting."

Her eyebrows shoot up. "Bill? The bull's name is Bill?"

I nod.

"Must come here often," she comments.

I just shrug. It's one of the places I frequent more often than others because I know none of the team will ever come here, and it reminds me of home in a weird way. Not L.A. home. Childhood home, back before anything involving my childhood was shitty. But I'm not telling her any of that.

"If I try out Bill, I want something more interesting," I tell her. "Like you inviting me back to your place."

She barks out a humorless laugh. "If you can last eight seconds on Bill you can negotiate something ridiculous like that."

"Baby Collee, I always last longer than eight seconds." I give her a wink that results in an eye roll from her. "So, if I last eight seconds, then you come home with me. And if I don't, what do you want?"

"You to leave me alone and never talk to me again," she answers easily.

I shake my head, "No, that can be what you get if *you* last eight seconds."

"I'm not getting on that thing."

"It's only fair, Princess."

She groans. "Fine. If I last eight seconds, then you leave me alone forever."

I smirk. She's not lasting on the bull so I'm confident enough to make the deal.

"Fine, and if you don't, then you give me your number. I'm tired of messaging you through DMs."

She cringes but agrees. And her reaction makes me chuckle, because she showed up here, so she can deny that she wants me all she wants, but her actions are showing a little differently.

"We have a deal then? If I don't last the full eight seconds, then I'll buy you a drink," I offer, putting my hand out for her to shake.

She hesitates for a moment before sliding her slim hand into mine and the warmth shoots up my entire arm the second her skin touches mine. I smile down at her, *let's do this, baby Collee.*

BRYNN

I hate how attractive Colton is.

I hate that I noticed it as soon as I caught sight of him at the bar when I walked in.

I hate that I'm even here.

I was bored, all of my friends were busy with their men returning from the road trip. Brent is busy, and my other siblings aren't talking to me. I have yet to make any other friends around here.

So yeah, in a weird desperation for *something* I actually showed up to the bar Colton told me to, around the time he told me to get here. And when I did, I saw his shaggy light brown hair under his black baseball cap. The white t-shirt stretched across his muscular torso like a second skin showing the tattoo sleeves on both his arms. He towers over everyone around him and the way his jeans hug his ass should be illegal.

But I'm pretending not to notice any of that and remember

who he is and that I hate him. Which doesn't change just because he's good looking. He's still an asshole.

An asshole that is currently making his way onto Bill, the mechanical bull, to try and win a bet with me. One I can't let happen.

I catch sight of the person who controls Bill and sneak my way over to him.

"Hey," I greet with a smile. "That's my friend about to go and we may have made a bit of a bet so I would *really* appreciate it if you could make sure he doesn't stay on for eight seconds."

The control guy chuckles, it's obvious this is a somewhat common request. "I got you covered; don't worry I'll send his ass flying."

I widened my smile, "You're the best."

Making my way back closer to the area Colton is currently preparing to mount the bull, I can't help but appreciate him from afar. It really is unfair that the universe decides to give a man that face and body, but his shitty personality.

Once he's situated, his eyes search for me and as soon as our gazes lock onto each other, his cocky smirk makes its appearance. My face drops the slight smile I had as I glare at him. He chuckles right before the movement starts.

It doesn't take long before the operator is true to his word and Colton is being thrown around, but his stupidly strong bicep flexes as he holds on with all his strength. With one hand. I start to get anxious as the seconds go by. It feels like the three that have passed have already been an eternity. Then, the movement really kicks up and I notice the slightest slip from him, and I know he's about to lose it.

It's been five seconds, though and he doesn't have much more to go. Suddenly, right as the clock turns to seven, Bill is whipped in the other direction so hard I think it's physically impossible for anyone to stay on and Colton flies onto the soft ground.

I laugh with my victory as he stands up, snatching his hat that flew off and securing it back onto his head. He looks pissed as he stalks toward me, but I'm continuing to laugh.

"No going home with me tonight, *hah,*" I gloat.

His stupid smirk is back. "Your turn, though Princess, then I'll buy you your drink."

I want to go back on my part of the deal, but then I remember if I stay on the entire time then Colton has to leave me alone forever. And I made friends with the operator. Even though I don't even know his name, I'm sure he'll go easy on me.

"Good luck," Colton says, his voice low, almost like a seduction. I shake it off as I get to Bill the bull.

"Alright, buddy, let's win this," I whisper to the fake animal before climbing on. I'm thankful for my height, though, because I'm pretty sure anyone shorter than me would need help and I refuse to ask for any.

He did, in fact, not go easy on me.

After what felt like a lifetime, I'm thrown off, flopping onto the inflated floor so hard I bounce a couple times. When I looked up at the clock, I was on for a whole two seconds.

When I approach Colton again, he's wearing the smug smile of victory while I glare at him.

"I'll take your number now," he says, expectantly.

I shake my head, "Drink first." I walk past him, beelining it to the bar, Colton following close behind.

"What're ya having, Princess? Let me guess." Colton looks me up and down while I just roll my eyes. "A sex on the beach?"

"You're a pig," I scoff.

"What? You just seem like a fruity drink type of girl."

"You don't know a single thing about me."

Before he can say anything else, I turn just as there's a commotion on the other end of the bar in the direction I'm facing. A pretty bartender in shorts, a tight tank top, and her long brown hair pulled in a ponytail is sitting on the bar while a guy stands in front of her just a few inches from her knees. They both have a cup of liquid in their hand, and I watch as the guy drinks his like a shot and instantly the bartender tosses the liquid from her cup onto his face and then slaps his cheek.

The group around them cheer while the guy celebrates what just happened and I'm still staring, completely confused on what I just witnessed.

There's heat at my back right before a deep voice is in my ear.

"That's a hurricane shot, and it's what I'm going to order next," Colton says.

I shrug him away, not liking the heat his body is permeating and how it's making me feel between my legs. "Have fun with that," I grumble before starting to walk away.

I'm stopped by a hand wrapped around my bicep. That damn heat shooting through my body starting from where his hand is on me. Turning around, I narrow my eyes at the stupid hockey player, annoyed that my own body seems to be betraying me.

"*You* are going to be the one to give it to me," he says, his eyes shining with mischief.

Mine shoot up in surprise. "You want me to throw water on you and then slap the shit out of you?"

He just smirks.

"Then you'll let me go home in peace?" I question.

He nods just once.

I feel like there has to be a catch here. Something is up, but with how much he's pissed me off lately I'm also not about to turn down the chance to feel my palm sting from it meeting his ridiculously, annoyingly handsome face.

"Fine." I fold my arms across my chest.

He pulls me back over to the bar, turning me so I'm facing it while he crowds me from behind, caging me in with his arms on either side of me while his body presses into mine. I try to push him away, but he's like a brick wall.

He flags down the bartender while I'm trying to find a way to possibly kick him in the balls in this position, but he has me pressed against the wood too tight. Speaking of wood, why can I–

"One hurricane shot, and my friend here will be the one giving it to me." He sounds so cocky, and I just roll my eyes.

The bartender just nods before handing over the two cups then looks at me, "Don't hurt him too bad, sweetheart." With a wink he goes back to helping other patrons.

Colton spins me around quickly and I see the look on his face isn't as playful as it was before. He looks almost angry, or annoyed, but it's not directed at me. The way his eyes narrow on the good-looking bartender that just gave us the shots and if I didn't know any better it almost looks like he's...jealous. But that wouldn't make sense because he knows there's *nothing* between us and there never will be.

"Hop on up, Princess." His gaze softens slightly looking back at me. Mine does the opposite.

I must not move fast enough for him because not even five seconds later his big hands are gripping my waist and pushing me up onto the bar. I yelp in surprise as he maneuvers me a bit too easily for my liking. And not because it makes me uncomfort-able, but because I don't like how it's making me feel in my lady bits. I'm a strong independent woman who *loathes* the man in front of me. My vagina doesn't get to react positively to a single thing he does.

Which is why I'm ignoring the slight throb and feeling of wetness that may or may not be present.

He also stands a lot closer to me than the other guy did with the bartender. While he wasn't touching her, Colton is standing between my legs, my knees grazing his hips. He takes off his baseball cap, shakes out his hair before putting it back on. Backwards.

I hate how good he looks.

"Ready?" he asks, his voice low and gravely.

"Are you?" I counter.

He smirks while lifting the cup with the shot up to his lips and downs it easily. As soon as he pulls the cup away, I'm throwing the water onto his face then immediately my hand connects to his cheek in a harsh, loud slap. My palm stings from the contact, but I won't lie, it felt pretty good to smack him.

Colton seems unaffected by any pain he may be feeling, which is a bit annoying to me because I slapped him hard. Before I can move or say anything, he reaches out, wrapping his hand around the back of my neck and yanks me forward while his mouth crashes onto mine.

I freeze. I can't believe this is happening. And I can't believe that it feels...*good*. When his tongue swipes against my lower lip, I'm ashamed to admit that I open, letting it sweep inside my mouth. He tastes like the alcohol he just drank. My head is spinning. My skin is buzzing, starting where his lips are on mine and where his hands are holding me by the back of my neck and my hip.

When he presses forward so I can feel the bulge of what I'm refusing to admit feels...substantial I start to realize what I'm doing. And *who* I'm doing it with. So, I suck his bottom lip into my mouth and bite down. Hard. I expect him to break apart at the sharp contact, but he doesn't. In fact, I feel the growl he lets out before deepening the kiss further.

I squeak in surprise at his reaction. And despite all the positive feelings I'm having, mostly in my pants, I need to end this. I push against his chest and our contact finally breaks. The look he's giving me is full of smugness and lust. The damn backwards hat and tight t-shirt aren't helping.

I hate him.

Sure, he's hot, but I *hate him.*

"What was that?" I snap, finally finding my voice.

"That was a kiss," he responds with a shrug.

I roll my eyes. "Why?"

"Because I wanted to. And I tend to do what I want."

"Well, I didn't want it. Let me down," I command since he's still standing too close and if I jump down then our bodies will be flush and that's the last thing I want right now. Or ever.

Instead of backing up like I wanted, Colton's hands are on my hips once again as he lifts me off the bar top, setting me back on my feet. I immediately put distance between us so I can breathe and work on slowing my heart rate down.

"I should go," I say, refusing to look at him because every

time I do my body betrays me more, and I need to get my head back on straight.

"You should stay." He smirks, like he knows every single battling thought I'm having.

"This has been…" my voice trails off because I don't even know how I want to finish the sentence and it only makes his smile widen. "I don't even know why I came here, bye Colton."

I push past his brick wall of a body, and he lets me as I make my way out of the bar. As soon as I get outside, the cool night air feels like a slap in the face as reality comes raining down on me as I process what actually just happened.

Colton kissed me.

It was the hottest kiss of my life.

And it's never *ever* going to happen again.

I'm getting a cat.

This wasn't the plan when I woke up today. The original plan was to pretend that last night never happened. And to decorate my apartment to make it feel a bit homier.

Well, on my quest to do the last part, I ended up at the pet store. I thought about maybe getting a little fish tank because I like the sound of running water and the pretty lights they can have. The idea of the peaceful ambiance for my place sounded nice.

And then I walked past the cats up for adoption. There're a couple litters of kittens who are all rambunctious little things. But it's not them that caught my eye. It was the corner kennel that had a fluffy black and white cat who is lying on a little bed that's tucked under a shelf. I look at the card on the front of her cage and see that she's five years old. Her name is Ellie and there's something that draws me to her.

The person working behind the kennels notices me. It's an older woman who pops her head out. "Did you want to meet any of them, darling?"

I look back at Ellie. "Yeah, I'd love to meet her."

The older woman gestures me into the room behind the kennels and I follow her.

"She's very sweet, but shy. We don't know much about her other than she was surrendered to a shelter and after six months she was set to be euthanized. Our rescue took her in about three months ago," the woman tells me while opening up the kennel.

My heart breaks at the thought of this sweet baby sitting in a cage like this for the last nine months. And who knows what her life was like prior to this.

I step up to the open cage. "Hi Ellie," I say softly to the sweet ball of fluff.

She looks at me and it may seem ridiculous, but it almost looks skeptical the way her large gold eyes lock onto me. I rest my hand on the edge of the cage, and she starts to get up, slowly, stretching her lanky body out as she carefully approaches me. That's when I notice she only has three legs, her back left one is missing, and I actually start to tear up. After sniffing my fingers, she drops her head onto my hand and rubs. I feel the vibration of her purring and I start to pet her.

Smiling as my fingers run through her soft fur, the purring gets louder as she continues to rub against my hand.

"I've never seen her take to anyone so quickly," the woman

says. I realize she might just be saying that because she wants me to adopt Ellie, but her words don't matter because I've already made up my mind.

"You want to come home with me, sweetie?"

I MAY HAVE GONE a bit overboard with buying things for my newest best friend. But I don't even care. I'm terrible at spending money on myself, but for other people it's my favorite. Which is why my niece is going to be extremely spoiled once she gets here because I refuse to hold back.

And my new child, Ellie, is about to be the most spoiled cat on the planet and I don't even care. I do, however, struggle bringing in all my purchases. She's in the kennel meowing as I carry in the giant box containing her cat tree and add it to the corner of my apartment where everything else is.

I open up the kennel once everything is inside. "Welcome home, Ellie."

She's cautious about coming out, so I just sit on the floor and watch her as she explores. The way she has to hobble around because of her missing leg just makes me fall more in love with her every second.

I start to set up everything for her, starting with the necessities of her litter box, food, and water. Then, move onto building the cat tree. I am not very handy, so after a couple arguments with myself that had Ellie questioning who she's living with I finally built it. I can only hope it's secure enough and that I didn't mess anything up.

Ellie immediately starts exploring her new area, meowing and purring loudly. When she finds a spot and rolls onto her back, I take a picture to send and share with everyone.

> Spencer: OMG she's so cute! I want to meet her!
>
> Chandler: I love her already!
>
> Brent: You got a cat?

I also sent the picture to Bryson and Bailey, but don't expect a response from them. Bryson might respond in three to five business days, but Bailey likely won't say anything.

> Brynn: Yeah, you all should come over to meet her. Well, maybe that's a lot. One or two at a time can come over.
>
> Brent: I'm already trying to stop Chandler from rushing out the door right this second.

I switched over to the text thread with her.

> Brynn: Don't let my dickhead brother stop you from living your life. Fuck the patriarchy!
>
> Chandler: Hah, this house is the opposite of the patriarchy. He is just concerned because at my appointment earlier the doctor put me on bedrest until I deliver. *eyeroll emoji*
>
> Brynn: Are you okay??
>
> Chandler: Oh yeah, I'm fine. She's fine. Just a precaution. Please send all the cat pictures, I'm bored already.
>
> Brynn: Done. And let me know if you need anything.

Chandler: I will, thank you.

And because I like to fuck with my brother, I text him again.

Brynn: Your girlfriend just told me how much of a buzzkill you are and that I'm her favorite Collee. Sorry not sorry.

Brent: I'm next to her right now.

Brynn: Probably why I'm her favorite, I don't hover and bother her. CHANDLER BLINK TWICE IF YOU NEED HELP.

Brent: You're a pest.

Brynn: Wow, bro, you shouldn't talk about yourself that way. I'm disappointed.

Brent: Go take care of your cat, she's probably already planning her escape from you.

Brynn: She loves me, thank you very much. I don't bore the shit out of her like you would.

He doesn't respond and I shrug it off. When Brent doesn't reply it's not the same as when it's Bryson and Bailey because I know I'll see him. I know he cares. I know at the end of the day, he would be there for me. He always has been.

"Come on, Ellie, let's figure out what to have for dinner." She doesn't move from her spot on the tree, but it's nice to be talking to more than just the empty walls around me.

And probably better than talking to a fish if I'm honest.

Which reminds me that getting Ellie kind of sidetracked my entire goal for the day of making my place homier. Though, she is doing that for me just by being here, so I don't even mind.

As I'm going through my fridge examining the options I can make for dinner my phone goes off. I expect it to be Brent again, but then I see it's a DM, not a text. Without thinking too much about it, I open the message and am immediately brought back to last night. The night I have been desperately trying to forget about. I feel like I was doing a pretty good job of it too.

> Colton: You know, you still owe me your number since you ran out before you gave it to me.

"Ellie, this is why we don't let asshole hockey players tempt us out for a drink and then kiss us."

She meows like she agrees, and I knew adopting her was the right decision.

Last night I let my loneliness get the best of me, but that won't be happening again. Nope, I have the best friend I could ever ask for in a three-legged feline. Plus, my human friends, who are usually busy, but that's okay. I can go make new friends. Yeah, that's what I should do.

My phone goes off once again.

> Colton: If you don't give it to me, I'll just have to get it from your brother. Might be kinda fun to tell him I got his baby sister to slap me across the face, then kiss me.

> Brynn: Please ask Brent for my number. I would love to see how that works out for you. Spoiler alert, you still won't get it.

Colton: Maybe not, but then you have to explain to him why you went out with me. Which I know you don't want. I'm cool being your dirty little secret, Princess.

I want to call his bluff, there's no way he would actually tell Brent about what happened and ask him for my number. That's a surefire way to start a fight.

Wait, that might be exactly what he wants. If I know anything about the asshole who won't leave me alone it's that he enjoys a fight. At least on the ice, but something tells me he would do the same off it as well.

And I really don't want Brent to know I had a temporary moment of insanity and actually met up with Colton. I could lie, but he's always been able to read me too easily.

Reluctantly I send him my phone number and then throw my phone onto my couch.

"And this is why you don't give hockey players an inch because they just push and push for more," I tell Ellie while pulling out some pasta to make prime girl dinner for myself. Buttered noodles.

Ellie purrs and settles into the soft cat bed I got her that I put on the couch so she can cuddle, but still have her own space.

"You're lucky you're a cat. There won't be any little player cats coming in here to bother you."

She makes a soft sound that I'm going to assume is her understanding. Or it's her falling asleep noise. Either way, I know this cat is on my side with this whole Colton situation. And I decide that when he texts me, I'm just going to block his number. This needs to end before it goes any further.

The fact that I can still remember how it felt to have his lips on mine, and how quickly my body responded to the dominating way his tongue invaded my mouth, I'd hate to think how it would react to anything more. Because I have a feeling my traitorous body and vagina would happily submit to the hot hockey player.

My mind, on the other hand, refuses.

P racticing while knowing what the captain's little sister's mouth tastes like makes me a bit more of an asshole than usual. I left Brynn alone for the most part the following day because I knew she wanted nothing to do with me and wanted to freak out in peace.

Eventually, I gave in and messaged her because she never gave me her number. As soon as she gave in, I saved it and texted her.

> Colton: Are you coming to the game tomorrow?

She doesn't reply while I heat up one of my premade meal preps and scarf it down. Just when I'm thinking she won't respond tonight my phone dings.

> Baby Collee: Yes, but I don't want to see you.

> Colton: I already told you, I'm okay being your dirty little secret. But you'll have to see me.

> Baby Collee: You know what I mean. Act like you don't know me. Because you don't.

> Colton: I know what it feels like to have your tongue in my mouth.

I know she is ignoring me again when she doesn't respond as quick. Fucking with her just gets better and better. She just riles me up and it only spurs me on. Part of me wanted her to refuse to give me her number because if she didn't think I would go to her brother, she was dead fucking wrong.

The thought of pissing him off enough to throw a punch at me is everything I want and more. I've rarely seen him fight on the ice, and I doubt he's done it off it. I'm sure he'd have the other two guys in that weird little relationship they have also jump me. McQuaid might give me a run for my money, but I could take Dumont.

I get to keep the information about us a secret for a bit longer though, which is probably better for me anyway. Especially because I want to know what her pussy feels like. I bet she's just as feisty in bed as she is when she talks to me.

Or maybe she turns into a good little girl who would beg for my cock. Either way is a win to me because I'll have baby Collee coming all over my dick. While she'll want to hate every single second of it, she'll hate me even more because I'll make her feel better than any other guy has. And then she will never be able to find anyone who measures up to me.

> Colton: I know the memory of our kiss made you hot for me. I hope you're touching yourself to the thought of it, Princess. I know I have *wink emoji*

Baby Collee: I haven't thought about you for a single second.

Baby Collee: And what kiss? I don't recall such a thing...

Colton: I'll be happy to spark your memory. We can start with giving you a repeat of it. I'll come over and remind you.

Baby Collee: I'm going to get a restraining order.

I bark out a laugh she can't hear.

Colton: I love it when you threaten me, Princess. Makes me so hard for you.

Baby Collee: You can take care of that by sticking it in a blender. Night, Wheeler.

I have another plan to take care of it. It includes my fist while I imagine it's her mouth instead. For a brief moment I think of getting a *real* mouth to take care of it. But that seems like a lot of work and I'm hard now. I know the second I finally sink into Brynn's warm mouth while she sucks me down her throat is going to be so fucking satisfying.

I hope she talks back to me while showing me what a good little slut she is for my cock. She'll beg for me. Beg for everything I want to give her and more. *Fuck* I just know she's going to take me so well.

My hand's already wrapped around my cock and I'm stroking it to the thought of her. It brings me to the edge almost too quickly and I'm coming with a groan, wishing I was spilling inside her throat instead of just onto my abs.

There's always tomorrow, after the game. She may want to act like we don't know each other, but that's not going to happen.

———

MORNING SKATE GOES how it always does before a game. Some drills and running plays before watching some game film to prepare for our opponents then head home to prep for the game before I go to the arena.

As usual, I don't talk to any of the guys until I'm forced to. I can tell how sick they are of me, and I don't give a fuck. We've also been playing like shit, and I know they blame me. I'm not the only player on the team and they all suck.

Coach has me on the second line tonight with Mann and Jones. Simple enough, they don't piss me off as much as some of the others. Mann is pretty quiet, and Jones just glares at me.

During our first shift, Mann passes the puck to me as we race into Nashville's zone, and I'm forced to pass it back when I see one of their players gunning it for me. Mann shoots and scores, getting the first goal of the game.

As we go back to the bench after his celly, he leans toward me, "Good play, Wheeler."

I nod at him, but don't say anything. It doesn't matter anyway. We're up and that's all that counts.

Nashville wins the next face off and I'm instantly annoyed again. They keep taking shots and our defense is working hard, but the shift is going on too long and they're getting tired. I'm getting antsy to get back out there. I see so many openings to steal the puck that aren't taken, which only makes me even more pissed off.

As soon as there's a chance for lines to switch, we do and I'm flying back out, immediately checking another player into the boards and then the whistle blows.

"What the fuck?" I shout, slapping my stick against the ice.

"Boarding, two minutes," the ref calls.

"Fucking bullshit, I barely hit him!"

I'm being directed to the penalty box but refuse to shut up because this is a shit call.

"Are you blind? Because you know that call was complete horse shit."

"Keep talking and you'll get another two for unsportsmanlike conduct," the ref tells me.

"Fucking do it, I'm sure Nashville will suck your dick a little extra to give me two fucking penalties."

I'm given four minutes for the two penalties. I'm fuming while in the box. Sometimes I wish I could drop gloves with the fucking refs. They can make or break a game and this call was complete bullshit.

The first two minutes were killed off, but of course, they still end up scoring on the power play and I can't help but slam my stick on the floor screaming, "What the fuck!"

I race out of the box and snatch the puck from Nashville in a move that would make me impressed if it was anyone else. But it's me, and I know how to play fucking hockey. Suddenly, I'm knocked hard in the shoulder from behind. The hit takes me by surprise so I'm unable to stop myself from flying onto the ice and slamming into the boards. Pain shoots up my shoulder, but I don't let it hold me back as I shoot up to confront the guy.

"The fuck is your problem?" I shove him as soon as I'm standing.

"You acting like a bitch about an obvious call." He shoves me back.

"Talk about being a bitch, how about you drop your gloves and I'll show you who's the bitch here."

I shake mine off onto the ice and latch onto his jersey, clocking him in the chin so hard his helmet goes flying instantly.

"Still think I'm a bitch?" I snap, punching him again before he's able to latch onto my jersey.

We exchange blows, he gets a couple that barely graze me before we're falling onto the ice, I'm on him raining down hits until I'm pulled off.

"Bin," the ref barks at both of us.

I taste the tinge of copper on my tongue and lick my bottom lip to find it's split. *Oh well.* I don't get to pick up any of my shit as I'm herded to the penalty box once again. I shake out my sweat slicked hair so it doesn't stick to my face. Collee skates over to where I'm going to have to spend the next five minutes and hands over my gear.

"You proud of how this game is going for you?" he asks calmly. Or maybe because his voice is so fucking deep, he just always sounds calm.

I want to say something about how I feel like it's going well trying to get his sister into my bed, but I bite my tongue. I'm keeping that shit to myself a little while longer.

"Yeah, I am," I say instead.

He looks like he's about to say something else, and I raise my eyebrow waiting for it. Nothing comes out and he skates away so they can continue the game. I scoff at his back. My knuckles are starting to burn and when I look down, they are split. I stretch my hand out a couple times and rotate my shoulder, wincing at the slight pinch of pain, but shake it off. I grab a rag and start wiping them before putting my gloves back on.

Oh well, I'll deal with it after the game. Playing with busted knuckles and a sore shoulder isn't anything new. Every guy knows what it's like. Play through the pain that's what I had a coach tell me when I was in high school. He didn't have to tell me twice. I liked playing through the pain, in fact I think it makes me play even better. Something primal about it and just makes me want to kick ass.

After my penalty is done, I skate to the bench. Coach comes up behind me and leans down and whispers so only I can hear, "Pull one more fucking thing and you're out."

I bite the inside of my cheek to prevent myself from snapping something about him begging management to send me somewhere else. Instead, I mumble, "Yes, Coach."

That's twice tonight I've stopped myself from saying something I know I shouldn't. That must be a new record for me. I deserve a reward. I know the kind I want. She has long legs, blonde hair, and green eyes that look at me like they want to rip me apart. But she won't be the one doing that. I want to fuck her so hard she can't walk tomorrow.

Shit, I shake the thoughts away because getting hard right now is not in the cards. Winning this fucking game is. Though, the rest of these assholes are making that less and less likely.

———

FUCK THIS SEASON. Fuck this team. Fuck that game. We lost, yet again. I'm almost forgetting what it feels like to even win. I go through my post-game routine which is to ignore every one of these motherfuckers while I shower and get out of here. Except, when I'm leaving the locker room, I keep an eye out for one particular woman and when I see her, I'm surprised to see she's alone.

Of course, I take advantage of that, approaching her confidently. "Waiting for me, Princess?"

Her gaze snaps up to mine and narrows. This is my favorite way she looks at me. A little pissed off. A little bitchy.

"Gross. No, I'm waiting for my brother."

"Where are the others?" She knows who I'm asking about.

"Chandler is on bedrest; Spencer is at home in the zone and Audrey is—why am I telling you this? Get lost."

I chuckle. "Fine, but only because one fight was enough for

me tonight. I don't need to kick your brother's ass in front of you yet."

"More like you don't need to lose two fights in one night."

"Did you *watch* the game? I won that fight, it wasn't even close."

She shrugs. Fucking *shrugs*.

"Baby Collee, you are just *asking* for a punishment, you know that?"

She gasps almost too quiet for me to hear, and I see the slight tinge of pink that appears on her cheeks.

"Seems like you might like the sound of that," I taunt.

Brynn opens her mouth to say something, but then her eyes catch on something behind me, and she snaps it shut.

"Why do I always find you talking to my sister?" Collee asks.

"Because she always wants to talk to me when I'm just trying to head home." I wink at her.

Her eyes roll, and fuck I want to keep track of each time she does that and make sure once I get her in my bed, she gets her ass spanked for every fucking time.

Collee gets in my face, and since he's only an inch taller than me we're basically at eye level.

"Leave my fucking sister alone, got it?" he says darkly, and I think it's as close to pissed off as I've seen him.

It makes me smile.

"Aye aye, Captain."

I push past him, nodding at Brynn as I head out. As soon as I get to my car, I pull out my phone and send her a text before driving home.

> Colton: Just wait until big brother finds out his baby sister wants to fuck his big bad teammate.

"**I** don't like him," Brent mumbles as Colton walks away.

"Yeah, well, I think that's why he wants to get a rise out of you." I pat his arm.

"You'd tell me if he was bothering you and I need to say something to him, right?"

"Nope, definitely not. Stop worrying about me and go home to your baby mama." I wave him off as I go to the parking garage to head home for the night. It wasn't the same going to a game without my friends. It reminded me of when Brent would drag me to his games because no one else could watch me since Bryson and Bailey were doing their own things and Brandon couldn't be trusted.

Except now his games are louder. Obviously being the NHL and not just a high school hockey game.

After I get home, I check my phone and see a text from Colton.

Colton: Just wait until big brother finds out his baby sister wants to fuck his big bad teammate.

Brynn: Don't you have a whole slew of puck bunnies to bother instead of me?

Colton: They don't get bothered by me. They love the attention I give them. Especially with my mouth.

Brynn: Gross.

Colton: I can come over and show you.

Brynn: Find someone else.

I'm done entertaining him for the night, so I plug my phone in and put it on silent, so I don't have to deal with him anymore.

———

THE CONSTANT BUZZING wakes me up. Blindly, I try to get it to stop and once it does my arm drops like dead weight from exhaustion. Only the damn sound starts up once again. Groaning, I grab my phone, ready to launch it across the room when I see it's Brent calling me. Him calling in the middle of the night has me instantly on edge that something is wrong.

"Hello?" I answer, panicked.

"Sorry to wake you up," his annoyingly calm voice says.

"What's wrong?" I'm already getting out of bed because my heart rate is too high to just sit still.

"Chandler is in labor," he says it in the same tone he would tell me the weather.

"Oh my god, what? What hospital, I'm coming." I'm already pulling on some jeans and tripping over the legs as I attempt to pull them up while balancing my phone on my shoulder.

"You don't have to; I can let you know once she's here."

"Hah, hilarious, bro. I'm going to be there, and you can't stop me."

He sighs, I know he would normally argue with me, but clearly is too preoccupied to do that, so he tells me what hospital and I'm out to my car in record time. I may break a couple traffic laws as I get to the hospital much faster than my GPS thought. The estimated time of arrival on those things is a challenge anyway.

The receptionist gives me a look when I tell her I'm there for a Chandler Hart. For a second I think she's going to give me a hard time, but she buzzes me up and I see Audrey and Charlie in the waiting room.

"Hey," I greet, trying not to show how out of breath I am from how quickly I rushed up here.

"Hey." Audrey gets up to give me a hug. "They won't let anyone else in the room. Matt had to throw quite the bitch fit for them to allow all three of them."

"Ah, that must explain the look the receptionist gave me." I nod in understanding, sitting in an empty chair across from them.

Audrey laughs. "Yeah, it was pretty funny, I'm glad I got to see it. Sorry, everyone was trying to get ahold of you, but you must sleep like the dead."

"I guess so, my phone volume wasn't on because I thought we had more time before this happened."

"I think everyone did. She's two weeks early but look at her dads. I'm sure she's run out of room in there."

I nod with a light chuckle. "Good point."

The three of us wait in the cold lobby for any update. I regret not grabbing a thicker jacket, but I wasn't thinking much beyond getting here. I haven't had much one-on-one time with Audrey before. I've always liked her, she's confident and spunky which doesn't seem to change even in the middle of the night.

Charlie doesn't say much, but he looks at Audrey while she talks like she hangs the sun, moon, and the stars. That damn pang in my chest hits when I see it. The love in his eyes would scream if it had a voice.

The sun is starting to peak out when Brent walks into the family waiting area. We all stand, immediately anxious to see what he says because his face gives nothing away.

"Who wants to meet Evie?" His mouth turns up in a small smile when he says his new daughter's name.

"Me!" Audrey and I yell at the same time.

"It can only be one at a time, we've already pissed off the nurses enough with our situation," he tells us.

My shoulders drop because Audrey is Chandler's best friend, so I'm sure she's going to go first. It's fine though, I understand.

"Go ahead, Brynn, she's your niece," Audrey encourages.

"Really?"

"Of course."

I follow Brent back to the room, and as soon as we enter my eyes find Chandler lying on the hospital bed with a bundle wrapped in her arms. Vince and Matt are hovering close by, but I don't pay much attention to them, all my focus is on my brand-new niece.

"Hi Aunty Brynn," Chandler says.

Tears already start to well in my eyes as I approach and see the little girl that has just joined our family.

"She's so tiny," I say, trying to joke so the tears don't fall.

"Didn't feel so tiny to me," Chandler jokes back. "Want to hold her?"

I don't know why the simple question has me panicking. I've never held a baby before; she looks so delicate I don't want to accidentally hurt her.

"Are you sure?" I ask softly.

"Of course," Chandler smiles, lifting her slightly so I can get my arms underneath hers and we don't disturb her sleeping form.

I faintly notice Vince and Matt shift more in my direction,

like they need to be within reach of Evie at all times. I don't think I've ever seen those two not bickering over something and it's all because of this little baby in my arms. Brent goes to Chandler, and I see him press a kiss to the top of her head while whispering something in her ear I can't hear.

All my focus is on Evie anyway. She's sleeping and her face is so perfect with chubby cheeks and dark hair. Her lips are slightly pursed like she's pouting already. I'm so happy for her and the family she has been born into. There won't ever be a shortage of love in her life. She'll be shown it every single day by so many people.

Love surrounds her and always will.

She's the luckiest little girl in the world.

"I already love you so much," I whisper to her while silently making a vow that she'll never ever experience any pain. Which might be a ridiculous thing to promise, but I don't care. She's perfect and deserves to have the perfect life.

The Collee past won't taint her in any way. When I look up at my brother, I can see the same promise written all over his face.

We can't control our past, but we can make a better future and I know that's exactly what Evie is going to get. An amazing loving mom and three dads who will protect her in every single way possible. Aunts that will spoil her rotten. And every single one of us showing her unconditional love.

Nothing else matters in this moment except her and I'm so glad I got to be a part of it.

Which is why when I finally leave the hospital by midday, because Chandler wanted to take a nap I walk into my dark and quiet apartment and the loneliness hits me. I collapse onto my bed and Ellie immediately joins me, curling up to my side like she can tell I need her.

I try not to feel too sorry for myself as my eyelids drop and the adrenaline rush of the night fades, but it's hard to stop my spiraling thoughts from taking over as I drift off. This will always be my life. Coming home to just my cat, always being the aunt and the friend to everyone. I'll just have to accept that at some point.

I f I have to hear Dumont bitching about how he wants to get back to Chandler one more time I'm going to punch him in the fucking face.

I guess she had their kid the other day and now we are on a road trip for the next five days. The NHL doesn't give a shit about babies being born during the season, we don't get time off so he just has to suck it the fuck up. Collee isn't talking about it, which isn't surprising. He's ignoring me a little more, which I enjoy. McQuaid even acts like he wants to get back which is weird for him.

I drown everyone out with my headphones on while we fly to our next destination, Toronto. I pull out my phone to change the song and find myself looking at my text chain with Brynn where my last few texts have gone unanswered. It annoys me, I like our interactions, getting her pissed off is one of the few things that brings me joy outside of hockey.

If she doesn't respond the entire time I'm gone, then I'm stepping it up once we get back and I know exactly how I'm going to do it. She likes making bets, so I have one in mind. But that will have to wait.

Once we get to the hotel, I hear some of the guys talk about wanting to go out. Of course, none of them tell me directly and I'm not about to tag along where I'm not wanted. I think about going out alone, but I need to be on top of my game tomorrow and risking a hangover isn't worth it.

Instead, once I get into my hotel room and strip down to just my boxers, I decide it's time to fuck with the princess a bit more.

I take a picture of my bare chest down to the bulge in my boxers and send it to her along with a message.

> Colton: This could be your view if you'd just give us both what we want.

> Baby Collee: I now have to bleach my eyes and throw my phone out the window.

> Colton: Quit lying to me, I know you saved it. Probably will make it your background. Now it's your turn.

> Baby Collee: NEVER HAPPENING.

> Colton: I can't wait to have you underneath me, Princess.

She doesn't respond again, and I think about calling her, but decide to leave her alone. For now.

————

THIS TEAM FUCKING SUCKS.

I've known this, obviously, but I feel like it's gotten so much worse.

This game against Toronto started off strong but went downhill during the first power play they got when McQuaid got an interference call. I slammed my stick against the boards when that fucking buzzer went off signaling the goal. I'm shocked it didn't break, part of me wanted it to.

"Keep your shit together, Wheeler, or we will end up with another fucking penalty thanks to you," Coach's stern tone comes from behind me.

I mumble a, "yes Coach."

During the second period, Collee ends up getting a goal that ties us up and once the third period starts it's a race to see who can get a goal first to win the game. My shifts go by in a blur as I do my best to ignore everything that isn't the puck and my stick. I get close to scoring, but the damn puck hits the cross bar instead of going into the net.

This time I do break my stick when I slam it down.

With only thirty seconds left of the game, by some fucking miracle, Dumont ends up scoring. When the next play starts, Toronto pulls their goalie for the last few seconds and its high pressure six against five while we do our best to run out the clock.

The final buzzer never sounded so sweet, and we actually won a fucking game.

It's about time.

After we all get on the bus, I hear some of the team talk about going out to celebrate, and while I don't really want to join them, I do want to go out since it's been too long.

"I'm in," I say, which results in a few odd looks.

"Alright, guess Wheeler is joining us too," Jones says, shaking his head like he can't believe it.

I'm glad I won't have to deal with Collee because he decides not to come out. Dumont says something about FaceTiming Chandler. McQuaid doesn't say anything, but I doubt he's coming out and Colver is already on the phone with who I can assume is Spencer while we're on the bus so I'm sure he's not joining.

Which is all for the best since those fuckers would be the reason anything about me would get back to Brynn and she doesn't need any other reason not to like me. Even if I decide to hook up with someone it's none of her business. It's not like she will and it's been too fucking long. My dick hates the lack of action he's not getting and is sick of my hand.

———

I MUST BE FUCKING BROKEN. Defective. Sick. Something.

There isn't a lack of beautiful women at the bar we are at, and a few of the other guys already have someone in their lap, or under their arm. Yet, for me, anyone who's shown interest in me, which is a lot, I think of a reason to say no.

My eyes catch on a tall blonde, but when she turns around and isn't Brynn my interest disappears. It's fucking annoying. She doesn't own me or my thoughts and yet, I can't fake interest in anyone else because when I think of how they would look next to her it's no competition. Plus, I know they won't spar with me like she does. I need that back and forth because apparently that's what fucking does it for me these days.

Which is why I pull out my phone to text her because I need that hit of a fight from her.

> **Colton:** I heard you were thinking of me, so here I am.

> **Baby Collee:** The hex I was putting on you must be working then if you could feel it.

> **Colton:** Sounds kinky, can this hex involve some rope for me to tie you up?

> **Baby Collee:** Nope. Not into that.

I smirk at the screen. Seems like she may be ready to play along. This is the first time she hasn't immediately told me to stop or go away. *Interesting.*

> **Colton:** What are you into then?

> **Baby Collee:** Nice guys. Anyone who isn't a hockey player.

> **Colton:** And I'm into dirty little liars.

> **Baby Collee:** Bet you have your pick of them at that bar you're at. Have a good time. Wear protection.

How the fuck does she know where I am?

> **Colton:** You stalking me, Princess? I could get into that. I'm glad you care about me wearing protection, but no need to be jealous. The only woman I'll be fucking in the near future is you.

Baby Collee: Guess you'll be celibate the rest of your life, then.

Colton: We'll see about that.

I pay my tab and head back to the hotel, done with the bar scene for the night. I also have the desperate need to do something about my rock-hard cock. My hand will have to do for yet another night, but once I'm back in Denver that's going to change.

———

AFTER ANOTHER GAME, I'm bored and not wanting to go out with the guys and be disappointed in my lack of interest for anyone else. Which is why on the bus I pull out my phone to mess with a certain little blonde.

Colton: What are you thinking about?

I'm impressed how quickly she responds.

Baby Collee: Top ten most painful ways to die. Want to let me try some out on you?

Colton: I'll let you try a lot of things on me, Princess, just say the word.

Baby Collee: Pretty sure we could only get through one of these...

Colton: Make it count then, Princess.

Putting my phone down for the night, I climb into bed and fall asleep thinking about the woman who makes me hard even when she's threatening my life.

THE REST of the road trip was uneventful. Especially since we lost the other two games we played, and it feels like the win in Toronto was a fluke. I fucking hate losing, and I'm determined to win the first game of this home stand.

To make sure of it, I give myself some motivation, which comes in the form of a single text to Brynn. She hasn't ignored me as much, because I know she likes fighting with me just as much as I do. But I'm done with the texting. I replay the kiss in my head more than I should and I need more. I need to touch her. I need to feel her. I need to see how she comes apart. I need to see what it is she comes apart for.

I bet the little princess is a dirty fucking slut in the bedroom and I'll give her exactly what she needs.

It's time for another bet, this one is my motivation to win the game tonight, and I'm going to make sure it happens.

> Colton: If I get a hat trick tonight, I'm coming over.

I scoff at the text from Colton, refusing to reply. The chances of that happening are so slim I'm not even worried about it. I'm not going to the game tonight; I'm doing some work to update Spencer's social media and send some emails telling everyone on her current status. Still deep in her creative cave.

While the guys were gone, I spent a lot of time with Chandler, helping her with Evie. Usually that consisted of me watching her while Chan got some sleep. Newborns are brutal, but they are so cute that it's all worth it.

Ellie has been great company to me, and I swear she can tell when I start to get into my head a bit too much and start to think about how alone I am. I tried to reach out to Bailey and Bryson again. Bailey has resorted to ignoring me completely, and Bryson is always too busy.

It's hard not to feel the sting of being unwanted. Especially from my own family.

Then, the devil himself appears on my phone screen and makes it clear how much he wants me. At least in the physical sense. And I engage, instead of ignoring him like I should. Because at the end of the day it feels good to get some sort of attention. Even if I hate who it's coming from.

But a hat trick is hard to get, so I'm sure it's not going to happen, and there's no point in worrying about it.

"Right, Ellie?" I ask like she can read my mind.

She doesn't acknowledge me since she's curled up in her fluffy bed next to my desk, which is her favorite spot.

Pushing all thoughts aside in regard to the game later, I put my headphones on and jump into work.

I find anything and everything to do to keep myself distracted well into the evening when the game is starting. Keeping my music turned up, I take a couple breaks to dance around my apartment, which results in Ellie staring at me like she's questioning what's wrong with me.

Eventually, I run out of things to do and have been mind-lessly scrolling and the music isn't hitting as hard as it was. My ears are sweaty from my over the ear headphones and my stomach is growling. I feed Ellie while I heat up the leftovers from the takeout I got yesterday.

Staring at the black TV, I shake my head. Refusing to turn on the game. I don't need to see anything.

I end up eating in silence, other than Ellie's soft crunching of her food. After I finish cleaning up, I stare at the TV once again.

"No, nope. Not going to do it."

Another five minutes goes by, and I find myself turning it on. I'm just going to check really quickly. Ease my mind so I can go to bed peacefully. My eyes fly to the score in the top left corner of the screen, and I see the Dragons have two goals. I let out a sigh of relief because I know there's no way *both* those goals were by Colton. And because the game is going to be over in another ten minutes, I think I'm in the clear.

Just as I think that, I see the familiar player skate toward the opponents' zone and the puck goes flying into the net. The announcement makes my stomach drop.

"Wheeler with a hat trick!"

My jaw drops, still refusing to believe it until I see the hats being thrown onto the ice. I turn off the TV, throwing the remote down. Forget what he said, I'm going to bed.

"Come on, Ellie."

I ignore everything as I do my nightly routine, taking my time in the shower, letting the steam seep into my pores while the scent from my body wash surrounds me. After, I even put on a face mask because I'm having prime self-care time.

When I climb into bed, where Ellie is already curled up in her corner, I plug my phone in. It lights up with the single notification I missed and my jaw drops, heart races, and panic ensues. Three words. Three simple words that have me both angry and excited. I'm not sure which is worse.

Colton: On my way.

Chapter Eighteen

WHEELER

24

I remember her complex from the night I tried to be a nice guy and make sure she got home safe. I know she didn't see it that way, but whatever. I watched the elevator stop at the fifth floor that night, so I know that's where her apartment is.

Once I arrive, I don't hesitate to pound my fist against what I think is Brynn's door, if the doormat with a B on it is anything to go by. I'm pretty sure she's going to leave me standing out here for a while. Or ignore me all together. But I'm stubborn as fuck and I know she's awake.

I also know she wants me, even if she refuses to admit it. And tonight, I plan to prove it to her.

After a minute I knock again, louder this time.

Right before I'm about to knock a third time the door swings open. Her blonde hair blows back from the force of it while her eyes stare daggers at me. Without giving her the chance to slam the door in my face I storm inside, kicking the door closed behind me once I'm in.

She backs up and continues to keep her narrowed eyes on me.

"I got a hat trick," I tell her. Obviously, she knows, but I want to make it clear.

"Yup," is all she says.

"You going to congratulate me?"

"Nope."

"Aw, come on, princess, I know you were here secretly hoping I would so I would come over."

"I would love to spend a day in your head just to see how many delusions are really up there."

"If you didn't want me here, you wouldn't have opened the door." I raise my eyebrow at her.

"You just would've kept knocking."

"You could have called the cops to have me removed."

"Still could."

"You won't."

She rolls her lips between her teeth and then sighs, her shoulders deflating. A black and white hobbling fluff ball catches my attention as it comes toward me, meows, and then rubs herself along my leg.

Brynn's gaze falls to her cat and she glares. "Traitor."

I lean down and pet the little three-legged creature while she purrs loudly. "You know." I stand back up. "I know this isn't the only pussy in this apartment that wants me."

"You wish," Brynn snaps.

I take a step toward her, the cat hobbling off somewhere as if the tension is so thick she can feel it.

"What do you want, Colton?"

I take a step toward her. "You know exactly what I want. And it's the same thing as you."

"You want you to run off somewhere far, far away, never to be heard from again?"

Another step.

"You'd miss me."

"Not even a little bit."

Step.

"Tell me you want me. You have since that kiss."

"Want you to go away."

Step.

"Tell me to leave," I taunt.

She looks behind me at the front door but doesn't say anything.

Another step. This one has her back pressed against a wall while our chests are inches apart. Hers is rising and falling with quick breaths, and yet, she still doesn't say anything.

I close the short distance between our bodies, leaning down so our lips are almost touching, our breath mingling in the air between us. I give her one last opportunity to tell me to leave. To lie about not wanting this, but all she says is, "I hate you." Right before our mouths crash together in a kiss that practically lights me on fire.

Brynn moans against my mouth, and I take advantage of her parted lips, shoving my tongue into her mouth. Her hands fly up to my shirt, gripping the fabric in her fists and I can feel how she wants to keep fighting me, but doesn't push me away. Her tongue battles with mine as I consume her. I want more.

My hands grip her ass, pulling her hips flush against me so she can feel how hard I already am for her. She gasps into my mouth as I grind against her. My teeth sink into her bottom lip and I shove my leg between her thighs, feeling how much she wants me through the fabric between us.

I move one of my hands up to her throat, collaring it there, but not cutting off any of her air. My mouth trails across her cheek toward her ear as she presses against my leg, moving against me to get some friction like the filthy little slut I knew she would be for me.

"Such a little liar, Princess. You're grinding that hot little cunt against me like you're dying to be fucked."

"Don't talk so much," she breathes.

I nip at her earlobe, and she yelps but presses herself harder against me again.

"Hm, you like a little pain? What else do you like?"

"You to shut up," she snaps, but her movements haven't stopped, and I can recognize that she's chasing her orgasm. Too bad, she's not going to get that yet.

I chuckle, my breath fanning against her sensitive skin as I look at her, removing my thumb from it's spot on her throat and rubbing it along her bottom lip pulling it down slightly when my eyes catch on something. I pull her lip down to reveal a tattoo hidden there that makes my smile widen.

Two words etched into the skin of her inner lip in black. *Good girl.* If I wasn't hard before I sure as shit am now. "No, I think you'd like to be told what to do. I bet you're a submissive little slut, aren't you?"

She gasps and grinds harder. My smile widens.

I knew it.

She's getting closer to her release, and I can feel it with the way her breathing speeds up under my palm and her rubbing against my leg becomes harder and faster. Instead of letting her get what she wants, I move back to cupping her ass and lifting her up into my arms. She screeches in annoyance.

"Only good girls get to come, and you've been a bad lying little brat. So, you can come when I let you, got it?"

She whimpers, and bites my lip like I did to her, but she may have drawn blood, yet it doesn't stop her from kissing me hard. It certainly doesn't stop me from carrying her to the bed and dropping her onto it. She bounces and glares at me while rising up onto her elbows.

I reach behind my neck to pull my shirt off. Brynn's eyes track the movement, especially as she takes in my muscled torso. I work hard for this body, and I know I look fucking good. The tattoos on my arms stretch onto my pecs so the black and white art decorate my skin. She takes me in, eyes bouncing around, and I let her get her fill.

"I like you like this," I tell her, which has her stopping her exploration so her eyes snap up to mine. "Yeah, you're so much better to be around when you're not talking."

"What the fuck ever," she scoffs.

I yank her to the edge of the bed by her ankles and she yelps as she collapses. I waste no time pulling off her pants, but leaving her panties in place, the nude color thong that I can see is soaked already.

"Let's see how you sound screaming and begging for me to let you come." I dip my head to taste her, but she stops me with a foot on my bare shoulder.

Looking up, I give her a questioning look because I thought we were done with the lies for tonight.

"This is only happening once. I still can't stand you and this means *nothing,*" she says sternly.

I smile. "Whatever you say, Princess."

Then, I latch my mouth onto her through the soft fabric. She gasps and falls back at the initial contact. She's right, this means nothing, but she's wrong about this only happening once. Because I haven't had my mouth on her fully yet and I know this is happening again. She will be begging for it after I give her the best orgasms of her life.

Too bad she hasn't earned them yet.

But I'm sure as shit going to enjoy myself eating her like she's my last meal.

With a single finger, I move the fabric to the side to expose her dripping core to me. I'm salivating as I take in the view. She's not fighting back anymore. In fact, she wiggles her hips slightly, silently begging me to do something.

And I do. Leaning forward, I latch my mouth onto her and suck her needy clit into my mouth. She cries out, her thighs clamping around my head, trapping me in place. I press against her inner thighs, pushing them open wide and looking up.

"Keep these open, Princess. I don't want to be interrupted during my meal again."

She whimpers and I know I have her right where I want her because she's not fighting back anymore. I slide her panties off so I can have full access to her delicious cunt and then go back to the only place I want to be right now.

It doesn't take long to figure out what Brynn likes the best. She's gripping the sheets, moaning and grinding herself against my face, especially when I flick her clit with my tongue. She almost goes off when I suck it into my mouth.

I pull back when I can tell she's on the brink of her orgasm.

She cries out in frustration, rising up to look at me. "Thought you didn't want to be interrupted. Why the fuck are you stopping?"

"I told you; only good girls get to come. And I want you begging for it."

"I will never beg you for anything."

I nip the inside of her leg and she whimpers. "Naughty Princess, guess you don't get to come yet."

I don't let her retort before I have my mouth on her once again. She falls back onto the bed with a moan. Her fingers find my hair and yank. The bite of pain has me even harder. I've wanted to fuck her since before I stepped foot inside her apartment. I'm hard as a rock and wanting to dive into her, but I also don't want to take my mouth off her.

Doubling my efforts, I bring her to the brink once again before pulling back. She cries out in frustration and it's sexy as fuck to see her so pissed off.

"Make me come," she demands.

"Ask nicely."

"No."

"Okay." I go back to having my mouth on her and this time I push a finger inside her tight channel.

My cock is dying to feel her tightness. I'm rutting against the bed to get some relief as I suck her clit into my mouth and finger her, rubbing her inner walls as she cries out.

Finally, she begs.

"Please, make me come, *please* don't stop. Oh my *God.*"

"Who is going to make you come?" I ask roughly. "Say my fucking name."

"Agh, *you.*" She's so close I can feel it, but I want her to admit who's doing this to her, who's making her feel this way. Who the fuck she's begging to let her come.

"Say my name, Princess, or I stop again."

"Fuck you." I go to pull back, but she grips my hair tightly, pulling me against her pussy and refusing to let up. "Colton. Please make me come, *please.*"

I don't stop this time and she goes off like a rocket, I feel her tighten around my finger, the pulsing of her orgasm as she cries and writhes against my face.

When I pull back, I wipe her release from my mouth and look down at her, lying on the bed sated, flushed, out of breath, and sexy as fuck.

"That was better. Now, you're going to beg to come on my cock."

I stand up and start to unbuckle my pants while Brynn stares up at me with a hazy look from her orgasm, but I can see the lingering hatred for me still simmering below the surface and I know she's going to get right back to putting up a fight. Which is good because I like it.

She smirks, sitting up onto her elbows, her eyes tracking my hands as I push down my slacks, leaving my boxers on for now.

"More like you'll have to beg for my pussy," she sasses.

Grinning, I descend on her, taking both her wrists in one of my hands and pinning them above her head. "I don't beg, Princess." I press my hardness against her exposed core, and she gasps at the feeling. "You can feel how badly I want you. I tasted how badly you want me. So, I'm going to fuck you so good you'll feel me for the next week. And when you can't feel me anymore, you'll be back. And *then* you'll beg."

I expect her to argue, but instead she says, "Prove it."

My mouth is on hers; we're all tongues and teeth as my hips thrust against her and if I didn't have my underwear on I would be inside her already. With my free hand, I push up her shirt and find she's not wearing a bra when I take one of her perfectly sized tits into my hand and pinch her nipple. She cries out and I move my mouth over to the other one, sucking it into my mouth.

She bucks up against me, her mewls and heavy breathing mixing with my groans as I give each nipple equal attention. I push her shirt all the way up over her head, but it's trapped because I won't let up on her wrists yet.

I continue switching between each nipple, while grinding harder and harder against her. She meets my movements. I pull back my mouth with a pop.

"Ask nicely for my cock to fuck you, Baby Collee."

She clamps her lips between her teeth but doesn't say anything.

I take one of her wet nipples into my mouth again and bite down hard enough she squeals, and I soothe the sting with my tongue.

"Ask for my cock," I demand, trailing my tongue up her chest, her neck to her jaw, hovering my lips over hers.

She tries to arch up to capture them, but I pull back and push down to keep her pinned underneath me. She lets out the cutest little growl of frustration. I thrust against her, and she tightens her legs on my hips trying to keep me in place.

"Ask. Me. To. Fuck. You."

"Fuck me," she practically whispers. I want to make her ask louder, but I can do that next time. I'm too hard and desperate for her to waste another second when she's given me the green light.

I let go of her wrists to pull her shirt completely off so she's bare and exposed to me. I barely have any time to take her in because I need to be inside her. I need to feel her. Flipping her onto her stomach she lets out a surprised sound at the sudden movement.

"Spread your legs," I tell her as I push my boxers off completely. I quickly grab a condom from my wallet in my discarded pants.

She listens for once and gets on her knees, spreading them and arching her back to extenuate her perky little ass and that dripping pussy.

"Fuck," I grit out, sheathing myself with the condom. My eyes don't leave her beautiful body, spread and waiting for me like a wet dream. "Next time I'm going to see how submissive you can be for me, Princess. I'll bet you'll love to give me complete control of this body."

I kneel behind her on the bed, my hand is between her shoulder blades while I line up at her entrance, swiping my cock through her folds, getting it nice and wet. She whimpers, wiggling her hips trying to push back, but I hold her steady.

"Knew you would beg for me," I tell her right as I push inside, being completely surrounded by her warm tightness. "So fucking tight."

She moans and I lean over her back, pushing her hips into the mattress with mine, holding my weight off her with my elbows. I'm fully seated inside her warmth and give her a moment to adjust to my size, and to give myself a second because I'm way too close to coming already.

She turns her head slightly to look back at me. "You going to fuck me, or not?"

I bite her shoulder, pull my hips back, and then drive forward, hard. She cries out and I continue to fuck her into the mattress. She feels so good, too fucking good, and her moans have me desperate to make her come again.

Covering her body with mine as I keep the punishing rhythm I've set I ask, "You still hate me?"

"Yes," she moans as I pull back slightly and slap my palm against her ass. Her cry is muffled against the bed as she drops her face against it.

"You may hate me, Princess, but your cunt doesn't. Fucking takes me so well, such a perfect little slut for me."

Taking a hold of her hips, I move back enough to flip her onto her back, yanking her down to the end of the bed where I'm now standing and impaling her on my cock again. I hold the inside of her thighs, so she's spread for me to watch how we look together.

Her arms flail, searching for anything to hold on to and I can see how close she is, which she better be because I'm about to lose it myself. I rub her clit and she arches up. "Come for me, you know you want to let go for me."

"Fuck you," she cries as her pussy clamps down on me as she comes.

I pound into her, and it doesn't take long before I'm joining her, groaning as I release into the condom. I fall forward, catching myself with my arms braced on either side of her head as she drains every bit of my orgasm from me.

As we come down the only sound in the room is our heavy

breathing, I don't want to move yet. Brynn's eyes meet mine when the lust haze has started to fade and her hatred for me is still there, but maybe a little less.

I'm almost determined to try for round two, when she looks down between our naked bodies where I'm still inside her, then back up to my eyes and says, "Get out."

I'm losing it.

No, scratch that, I've officially lost it.

I'm holding onto the tiny little shred of sanity I have which is why I tell Colton to get out while he's still buried deep inside me and I'm recovering from the hottest sex of my life. I need him to leave because if he doesn't then this may happen again. I may want it to happen more than once, and I told him that was going to be it.

He didn't agree, but I don't care, it needs to just be this one time. One stupid blip of a mistake that we can both move on from now that we've gotten it out of our systems.

Except it's not out of my system, not by a long shot.

The comment he said about me being completely submissive did so many things to my body I can't even explain. Probably because that is what I truly want in the bedroom, to be completely dominated and he knew that instantly.

Which is why it can't happen.

None of this will happen again.

He still hasn't moved, so this time I push his chest when I say, "Get out."

Colton lifts off me and I watch as he removes the condom from his dick that already looks half hard again, which is impressive. But no, I can't think anything about him is impressive. Even though I felt that thing and it *is*. He may be cocky, but he sure as shit has the equipment to back it up and that's just not fair.

"You're brutal, Baby Collee. Kicking me out before we've had the chance to cuddle."

I grapple for my blanket to cover myself because now that we aren't in the heat of the moment, I feel more vulnerable than I did before. My body is still humming, and my mind is completely mush, but I don't want him to know that he has fucked me into oblivion.

"There's not a chance in hell you cuddle," I murmur, shifting and hiding my wince because I'm already sore.

He's pulled up his underwear and pants, but hasn't buckled them so they're just resting on his hips, with his shirt still off showing off his sculpted and inked skin. My hands itch to touch him more, but I clench my fists to fight the urge.

It's only intensified when he leans forward, his fists press into the bed by my hips as his face inches closer to mine. I lean back slightly trying to keep the distance between us because I don't trust myself anymore around him.

"I'll leave tonight, but I know you're going to be a good girl for me and call me back when that needy little pussy of yours needs me again. Because you and I both know this wasn't just a one-time thing."

For a second I think he's going to kiss me, and I know if he does that I will fall back into his trap once again and likely let him fuck me into a coma. Instead, he pulls back with a smirk like he knows exactly what I'm thinking. I haven't made any move to get dressed, even once he is.

"See you soon," he winks, finally leaving my room.

I'm frozen until I hear the front door closed a few moments later, which is when I drop my head into my hands and groan loudly. Ellie takes that as her cue to come out of hiding and jumps onto the bed with me.

"I'm sorry you had to experience that; you probably hate me just as much as I hate myself."

She nudges my hand, signaling she wants pets and I oblige. Her purring starts instantly and I'm glad she doesn't hate me. Too bad I still hate myself.

———

BY THE NEXT MORNING. I still hate myself. Add in the fact that my body still hurts, reminding me over and over of everything that happened last night. My memories replaying also isn't helping.

Colton didn't text me after he left, and I took that as a positive that maybe he was happy he finally got what he wanted and was going to leave me alone. One and done. Hit it and quit it. And all those cliché one night stand sayings that I'm sure he's all too familiar with.

Unfortunately, as I'm feeding Ellie her breakfast my phone goes off and when I see it's him, I look up at the ceiling and speak to the universe or whoever would be listening to me.

"Why me?"

Yes, why is the extremely hot, big dicked, amazing hockey player obsessed with you?

My consciousness nearly taunts. But I don't do this. I don't get involved with hockey players. Surprisingly, he's the first I've ever slept with. All the rest that have tried, and there have been several, have been scared away by my brother before it got that far.

Other sports have been fair game, though they are all the same to me. Douchey, and annoying. Though, it took a couple experiments to learn that before I finally accepted it.

Colton: You ready for me again?

I ignore his message and notice I have one from Chandler inviting me over to see Evie if I'm available. Even if I wasn't, I would make time to go see my niece. After I text her that I'll be over in about thirty minutes I text Spencer because I know I'm going to need to confide in someone and I love Chandler, but she can't know. I would go to Audrey, but she will definitely tell Chandler. Plus, Spence is my best friend and I feel like we haven't been as close since moving to Denver because she's been so holed up with writing.

Which I get, obviously we were around each other every day while she was on tour, so I think I'm just having a hard time adjusting.

> Brynn: SOS need a girl meeting ASAP.

Spencer: My place or yours?

I can't have Jared knowing either because I need to make sure this doesn't get back to my brother. I know she won't tell him if I ask her not to, but I can't run the risk of him over-hearing either.

> Brynn: Mine. I'm going to visit with Evie right now, but later today, okay?

Spencer: I'll be there, but are you okay?

> Brynn: I will be.

No point in lying. I will be after I have a thorough bitch session with her.

I take a quick shower because I was too worn-out last night to do that, and I can still feel Colton's sweat on me. I want to scrub the entire top layer of my skin off so it can be like he never touched me, but the persistent ache between my legs makes that impossible.

Once I'm done, I throw my hair up in a ponytail and pull on a pair of leggings and a hoodie and head to see my niece.

Chandler offers to let me hold Evie the second I'm in the door, and after I settle on the couch, I happily take the little bundle who falls asleep on me almost instantly. Vince and Matt hover close by but are trying to act like they aren't. Brent sits across the room watching me, his posture seems calm, clearly him and Chandler are the only ones that trust me.

Of course, the second Brent looked at me I felt like he could tell what I was up to last night. Which is ridiculous, he doesn't know. Yet, it feels like I have a scarlet letter on my chest, or a billboard on my forehead that says, "I fucked Colton."

"How are you doing?" I ask Chandler to distract from my thoughts or I feel like I'll blurt out my transgressions to the whole room.

"Good, actually. It's pretty nice to have these three around to help, I don't know how anyone does it with just two parents."

I bite back a laugh to not jostle the sleeping baby in my arms. "You are pretty lucky. Until they all have to leave for their away games."

She sighs, "True, that's the downside. But I have you, Em and Audrey so I still have the help."

Em is Vince's sister, and I know she's just as smitten with the little girl as I am, even though she has two daughters of her own. Even Audrey, who I'm pretty sure never wants kids, loves Evie.

"What about you guys, how are you liking the dad life?" I ask Vince and Matt.

"It's the greatest thing I've ever been a part of," Vince answers with a wide smile. He's so attractive, when I first met him, I considered making an exception to my "no hockey player" rule for him because he seemed sweet. Too bad I did that for an asshole.

"It'll be even better when we can get her on some skates in about two months," Matt says confidently.

All heads swing toward him.

"You think she can skate at three months?" Chandler asks, shocked.

He shrugs. "Yeah, don't they walk by then?"

"Uh no," she responds.

"What? So, when does she get fun?" Matt seems genuinely shocked, and I just stare at him with my mouth dropped.

"Probably the same time you get a brain," Vince mumbles.

"Oh, because it's my fault she's the first baby I've been around? Not all of us have had the perfect little family," Matt snaps.

My gaze drops down to Evie because even though he didn't mean me, I can't help but feel his words hit me in the chest.

"Knock it off," Brent scolds, sternly. For some reason it takes me back to when we were all younger and Bryson and Brandon would get into it like they always would, and Brent would be the one that would have to get them to stop.

That would usually lead to Brandon lashing out at Brent, like he always did, especially once he started using drugs. None of us knew at the time that's what was happening, but looking back all the signs were there.

Maybe Brent knew back then, but he never said anything to

any of us. He was always trying to protect Bailey and me from the negatives that surrounded us on a daily basis.

"You think you're so much better than the rest of us because you got that stupid fucking scholarship to join that lame ass hockey team?" Brandon *screams at Brent.*

"I'm on that hockey team to work on getting a better future for all *of us. I'm going to go pro, then we don't have to worry about anything anymore," Brent argues calmly.*

"You're not going to go fucking pro, you're just wasting your time and doing whatever you can to get the fuck out of here and leave us," Brandon sniffs.

"You're not going to talk like that in front of them, so you either knock it off or leave and come back when you're calm," Brent tells him, his voice has gotten a lot deeper.

"What the fuck ever." Brandon stomps away from Brent, stopping in front of Bailey and me who are standing in the corner of the kitchen, where we huddled when the argument between him and Brandon first started. "When he leaves and forgets all about us, I'll be the one taking care of us and I'll do a better fucking job that he ever would."

"Out," Brent yells, making us jump.

Brandon leaves out the side door, sniffling as he goes. Brent drops closer to our level, "You guys, okay?"

We both nod, but I'm just doing it so everyone stops fighting. I don't like the yelling and fighting. Not between my siblings. My parents. I just want one day where there isn't someone yelling.

"Brynn, are you okay?" Brent's voice breaks me out of the

memory I slipped into. I still feel the tears prick the corners of my eyes and I feel like I need to get away.

"Yeah, sorry, I forgot I need to go meet Spencer, who wants the baby?" I try to keep my voice light, but I know my brother doesn't buy it.

Vince happily takes Evie from my arms, and I'm impressed we don't even wake her during the transition. I say my quick goodbyes, managing to make it to my car before breaking down completely. Everything feels like it's catching up to me, last night with Colton, the memories of the past. I let the tears fall as I let the emotions take over, letting my façade drop as I fully embrace the shit show that is my life.

I managed to pull myself together enough to drive home. Once there, Ellie greets me and I swear this cat knows how badly I need her at times. I know I want my best friend more than before, just for the distraction alone, so I text her letting her know I'm home and she can come over.

While waiting for Spencer to get here, I do everything in my power to push the memory of my breakdown out of my mind because that's not me. No, Brynn Collee doesn't break down over her shit childhood anymore.

Spencer shows up with her distinct red hair in a bun at the base of her skull and tucked under a baseball cap, a baggie hoodie I assume is Jared's and some jeans. Luckily, here in Denver she doesn't have as much of a problem with fans and paparazzi, but you can never be too careful.

She comes in, and we settle on my couch. I tuck my feet underneath me and chew on my bottom lip until I remember how it felt to have Colton's teeth sinking into it and stop.

"What's going on?" Spencer asks when I still haven't said anything.

"I...um...okay, no telling Jared. No telling *anyone*. I'm calling best friend code on this one."

"Done. Tell me." She leans forward slightly, just waiting.

"So...I may have....and I don't know why...I was just....and then...so I..."

"Brynn, spit it out, that's not telling me anything."

"I slept with Colton." I drop my face into my hands immediately.

The silence is deafening. I just wait for a reaction, but I swear neither of us is even breathing.

"Colton...Wheeler?" she asks cautiously.

I just nod.

"What the fuck?"

"I know! I mean I don't, he is *such* an asshole, and this doesn't change that, it just...happened."

"Start from the beginning. Now."

I wince not wanting to tell her about how I willingly met up with him at a bar because I was lonely. I give her the short version and say we just happened to be at the same place when one thing led to another, and we kissed.

"So, what you were drunk and then fucked him?" she asks, like it's not a big deal.

I shake my head slowly. "Uh, no. That happened a couple weeks ago. The sex happened last night."

"So..."

I sigh. "He said if he got a hat trick then he was coming over." I swing my gaze over at her because I'm sure she saw the game and knows how that worked out.

She rolls her lips in between her teeth, and I can tell she's trying to stifle a laugh.

"It's not funny," I scold.

"No, it's not, but I will admit that was smooth of him."

"We hate him, Spence, come on."

She nods. "I know we do, we really do, so then what happened because you didn't have to let him in."

"I mean no, I didn't, but I opened the door to tell him to go away, and he pushed his way inside. Ellie is a traitor, then things just...happened."

"So, it was your cat's fault?" she teases.

"Partly, yeah."

She waits for me to say more, but I don't.

"And?" she finally prods.

"And what?"

"And how was it?"

"We aren't talking about that because it doesn't matter. I told him it was only happening once, and I figured that's all he wanted, but he texted me today asking if I was ready for him again."

This time she doesn't hold back her bark of laughter and I scowl. "Damn, he's down bad for you, isn't he?"

"No, he just wants to piss off Brent."

"And he wants to do that by secretly fucking you?" She raises an eyebrow at me.

"Well...yeah, I guess."

"And what about you?"

"What about me?"

"Do you want to continue secretly fucking him?"

I cringe, but don't say anything. My knee jerk reaction is to say, "fuck no." But I don't. I can't because as much as I hate him, I can't deny how good everything felt, and there's no fear of any feelings getting involved. It's honestly the perfect no strings attached situation since there could never ever be strings. I can hate him and still fuck him.

"Maybe," I answer finally.

"If it feels good, then why not. I mean you haven't been with anyone that I know of for a hot minute."

"I haven't."

"So, if it doesn't hurt anyone, then why not?"

I narrow my eyes at her. "You're not going to tell me this is a terrible idea?"

She shrugs. "You're a big girl. You know it's a terrible idea, but I know you can handle yourself. Plus, he's persistent and could use you putting him in his place a bit."

I don't dare tell her I think I'll be the one being put in my place if Colton actually backs up the things he said to me last night. Especially about me being submissive.

"Promise you won't say anything to Jared?" I ask, needing her to confirm.

"Promise, this stays between us completely."

"Perfect. I also need you to promise that when this all blows up in my face, you'll be there for me?"

"I'll always be here for you, just like you've always been there for me."

We link pinkies, sealing the promise. Because no matter what, I know there isn't a world where this doesn't completely blow up in my face.

Chapter Twenty-One

WHEELER

24

I
f I thought it was fun to know what it was like to kiss Brynn behind her brother's back, it's nothing compared to knowing how she really tastes. What she looks like when she comes. What she sounds like when I fuck her. Yeah, I'm fucking sick and I don't even care.

It's been three weeks since it happened, and she's been doing everything to avoid me which is starting to piss me off. I like the chase, but I don't like being ignored. Which is exactly what has been happening. She doesn't respond to any of my texts, sends my calls to voicemail and the two times I've attempted to see her after the games she left before I came out of the locker room. Or maybe she avoided coming to the games altogether, but I wouldn't know since she's fucking ignoring me.

It's been tempting to show up at her door, but I don't need her running away even more. Someone else might be worried about her running to her brother, but that's not even on my mind because I would love it if she did. I'm still itching to fight that fucker.

We're about to leave for an away game in Arizona before coming back to face Vegas, then it's Thanksgiving before we're back on the road for another week. And I'm running out of patience.

> Colton: If you don't say something to me, I'm going to tell your brother exactly what I plan to do to you when I see you next.

I finish packing my bag for the trip tomorrow and toss it by the front door just as my phone chimes.

> Baby Collee: I already told you there will never be a next time.

I smile at the screen.

> Colton: Finally done ignoring me, and I told you there will be.

> Baby Collee: I've been busy. You were beginning to seem desperate. Consider this me throwing you a bone. Go fetch, doggy.

> Colton: There's only one bone around here, and I won't be the one fetching it.

> Colton: How much has your pussy missed me?

> Colton: Your cat, I mean, of course.

> Baby Collee: She forgot all about you.

> Baby Collee: And before you ask, so did the other pussy.

> Colton: Perfect, sounds like I need to come over again, then.

> Colton: Once we get back from Arizona.

She doesn't respond, which means she isn't outright denying me anymore. Just ignoring me. But I'm done waiting to touch her again.

———

As I'm getting ready for the game, I reach out to Brynn again because something about talking to her can get me riled up in a way that helps my game performance. It might be the sexual frustration, or just the frustration in general. Either way, it works, and I play better with a little motivation.

> Colton: You going to be ready for me again tomorrow, Princess?

> Baby Collee: Maybe if you get a hat trick again. Or a hat trick each period. That would impress me.

> Colton: Nah, that was a one-time deal. Hat trick or not I'll be seeing you.

Regardless, I'm still trying to get as many goals as possible, but that's for myself every game, no matter what.

> Colton: And when I do. It'll be you on your knees, naked, waiting for me. I know you want to be a good girl for me.

> Baby Collee: In your dreams, Wheeler.

Smirking, I put my phone away. That does it. There's the motivation. The visual of her doing exactly what I want, on her knees, waiting for me in my bedroom when I get home. I'd take my time before giving her any attention, just letting the anticipation build, not saying anything to acknowledge her in any way. And when I sit on the edge of my bed and tell her to crawl over to me, she will want to fight, but ultimately gives us both what we want. And that's when she will take my cock out of my pants, parting her plump lips, about to take me in—

"Wheeler, you going to join the team at all?" Captain Collee's voice obliterates my fantasy about his sister. I can't help the smile on my face knowing what I do.

"Not like I have a fucking choice," I mumble before joining the stupid pregame ritual bullshit I'm roped into. I still don't feel like these guys are my team, they all hate me, and the feeling is mutual. But having this secret over all of them makes it more tolerable.

———

EXCEPT NOW WE are losing once again.

This shit is getting old and when I pass the puck to Jones, his shot goes so wide I'm pretty sure he wasn't even aiming for the fucking net.

"What the fuck was that?" I yell at him as we skate toward the bench.

"Shitty shot, like you never have those," he snaps back.

"No, because I'm never aiming for the boards like you just fucking did."

"Shut up, and lay off," McQuaid butts in.

"Oh, what? Is he also fucking your girlfriend, so you have to defend him being a shitty player?"

"Motherfucker," McQuaid shoves me, and I shove him back, gripping each other's jerseys. There's yelling and a whistle as we're pulled apart at the bench.

"What the fuck?" Coach yells.

"This piece of shit doesn't even want to be here; you should take him off the lines altogether." McQuaid shakes his head, fixing his helmet that I fucked up on his head.

"I'm going to lock you all in the fucking rink to work out your issues if you don't knock it the fuck off." Coach glares at both of us.

The ref skates over and points to both myself and McQuaid. "Both of you to the box, delay of game."

"What the fuck?"

"Fucking kidding me!"

We both scream.

"Now, or be ejected," the ref threatens.

We both skate over to the box. I'm aware this probably has never happened during a game before and part of me is proud of that. The other part is concerned that we may kill each other in the penalty box for two minutes. The moderator is a middle-aged guy that isn't even six foot, there's no way he would be able to break up a fight between us.

"You happy about this?" McQuaid spits out as we sit as far apart as we can.

"You didn't need to get involved, and yet that's always what you seem to do, isn't it?"

"You don't fucking know me. You don't know any of us and you clearly don't want to."

"I don't. At all. I don't give a fuck about any of you."

"Yeah? What about Brent's sister? You give a fuck about her?"

My eyes shoot up to his and see the smug look he's giving me.

"I'm not fucking blind, no one is, and you're obvious as shit that you want her. Terrible fucking idea, but if you want to get murdered that's on you." He shrugs like he doesn't care.

I bite my tongue and I know my lip curls up at what he doesn't know. The temptation to tell him is so strong, but luckily for both of us the moderator gives us a ten second warning so we both shoot up, putting our helmets back on and get into position to shoot out of the box as soon as the door is opened.

"For someone who thinks I should mind my own business, maybe you should do the same," is all I say before flying out onto the ice and joining the play. Managing to snag the puck, I'm unguarded as I skate to the other zone, fake out the goalie, shoot and it goes flying into the net.

I drop to my knee, pumping my fist in a celly as I circle around back to the bench. The team bumps my fist as I skate by because that's what you do, but I can see the look of disdain on all their faces.

Collee is at the end and the first person I have to pass as I go to sit on the bench.

"You may be a decent player, but you need to fix your personality," he says before jumping onto the ice and getting into place for another play to start.

Chapter Twenty-Two

BRYNN

"What do you think that was about?" Chandler asks quietly as Evie sleeps on her while we watch the game on an extremely low volume.

I shrug. "Colton probably made some dickhead comment."

Chandler's eyes swing over to me. "And how's that going?"

My heart rate kicks up before I remember that she doesn't know about anything happening.

"The same, annoying and I'm ignoring him." *After I let him fuck me into oblivion.*

"You really don't want to give it a try just once?" Audrey asks from the other side of me.

Just once. Those words are haunting me and have been for the last three weeks. I keep trying to convince both of us that's all that was going to be, but he's determined and I'm losing my resolve. I really have been busy preparing for the holidays, making sure everyone involved in Spencer's professional life is appeased for now until after the first of the year so I can enjoy some peace.

Not like I have some special family plans or anything.

I don't even know if Bryson is going to join us this year.

I'm sure Bailey won't.

"No, I don't," I finally say, shaking my head.

Spencer is curled up in a chair across the room and I'm impressed her face doesn't give anything away when I look over at her. She just gives me a small smile but doesn't say anything.

Somehow, the guys end up winning by one when Brent scores a goal within the last ten seconds of the game, avoiding overtime and securing one of their rare wins this season. We celebrate quietly, but Evie wakes up anyway, though she's such a good baby she hardly cries and just whines a little, which Chandler says is because she needs food.

We all take that as our cue to head out and go home.

Ellie greets me as soon as I get home and immediately goes to her food bowl, silently begging me to fill it. The sound of her quiet crunches are the only noise in the small apartment as I turn on the shower right before my phone rings.

I look down and groan. I don't know who I expected, truly anyone calling me is a shock. But the fact that it's Colton isn't entirely surprising since he's tried a couple of times while I've been ignoring him, and I always send it to voicemail.

Though, I am curious about what happened with Matt tonight and that's the excuse I give myself as to why I answer this time.

"Hey Baby Collee," his deep voice greets, and I'm instantly reminded of that same voice saying dirty things while deep inside me.

"What do you want?" I ask to avoid thinking of the thoughts that should fill me with shame, but just end up turning me on.

"To talk to you, know what you're doing, making sure you're thinking of me."

"Whatever, about to take a shower, and nope."

I hear his voice perk up a bit when he says, "A shower? Show me."

"Absolutely fucking not."

"Come on, you've been ignoring me and if I was in Denver I'd already be inside you again, so this will just have to do for now."

"You're gross."

"You don't believe that."

I should hang up. I know that, but that damn little part of me that likes the attention he's giving me is stopping me. I've been able to suppress it while avoiding him, but with his voice in my ear, reminding me of us together, I can't. How it could happen again. How I could have a little fun with him...

"Tell me something first," I blurt.

"What do you want to know?"

"What happened with Matt during the game?"

He doesn't answer right away and I'm curious if I finally found a way to shut him up.

"I was annoyed with Jones missing a clear shot and was laying into him when McQuaid decided to stick his nose in it." He still sounds a little irritated and I don't know why I feel like he's not telling me the full story, but I accept it for now.

"Fine," I say softly. "On one condition."

I hear shuffling on the other end of the phone. "Anything."

"You don't talk. Only watch." I can't believe I'm going to do this. I can't believe any of this. Someone give me a lobotomy, I've lost it.

"I'll agree to that with a condition of my own," he concedes.

"What?"

"When I get back, you do what I want."

I groan inwardly, throwing my head back, closing my eyes, taking a deep breath, and already knowing I'm going to regret the words that are about to come out of my mouth, but unable to stop them anyway.

"Fine. Your no talking starts now."

My phone alerts that he's trying to switch to a video call and with one more deep breath I answer. Knowing this is a mistake, knowing agreeing to what I just did was probably a bigger mistake. Yet, never being so turned on in my life and liking the idea of having his eyes on me, unable to say anything to me and getting to tease him however I want.

Yeah, this might be kind of fun.

It makes me think of how Audrey does this for a living, but for more than just one person at a time. I know how she and Charlie really met, and I wonder if this is how it felt, except they didn't know who the other person was.

There's something sexy about it, a power I've never felt before as I set my phone on the counter and watch his eyes as they take me in. His bare chest rising and falling with deep breaths as I try not to drool over the cut muscles I can see.

His shaggy hair looks like it did the night we fucked when I messed it up with my hands, his eyes are dark with desire as he watches me.

The bathroom is already steaming from the hot water. I'm too busy staring at Colton when I notice he raises his eyebrows and opens his mouth to start to say something, but I stop him.

"No. Talking."

He smiles widely, but does what I say which I didn't really expect from him. I set my phone on the counter, the shower in view, the glass is frosted so his visibility is going to be obstructed, just like I prefer.

I step away from my phone to feel the water temperature to

make sure it's not too hot, after a slight adjustment I step back and start removing my clothes. My back to my phone. Colton clears his throat and I turn to look over my bare shoulder to glare at him.

He gestures for me to turn around.

"No giving instructions of any kind," I tell him.

"That wasn't the rule, Princess."

"You suck at following them anyway apparently. I'm hanging up." I stride forward with my arm banded around my chest.

"No, I'm done. I'll behave." The smile he sends my way makes me believe it's yet another lie, but I'm just going to pretend like he's not here.

Which is what I do as I finish stripping off my clothes, still keeping my back to him. I think I hear him make some frustrated noises, but I don't acknowledge it. He gets a side view as I step into the shower before my body is distorted to his view. And same with mine because I can't see my phone from here either.

Closing my eyes I rinse my hair and can't deny the heady feeling of doing this with him. I've never done anything like this before and it being with someone so forbidden is adding to the moment in a way I would've never expected.

Which is why when my hand finds its way between my legs, feeling how wet I am, I let out a loud moan as my fingers press against my clit. He may not be able to see me, but I know he can hear me.

I rub a couple circles over the bundle of nerves, not trying to bite back any of my sounds. I think I hear a faint "fuck" come from him, but it only adds to the feeling I have building. My mind wanders to how he's reacting. Is he touching himself? I imagine what he looks like with his hands stroking that thick cock. The way his muscles would look bunching as he pumps himself all because of me.

The fantasy morphs to how it felt when we slept together, like it does even when I try to prevent it. I just can't. I continue to rub myself thinking of how it felt when it was his mouth on me. And now I know he's watching but can't see much. I lean forward to press my chest against the glass which I know makes it so he can see my nipples a bit clearer. He may say something else, but my orgasm is too close for me to focus on anything that isn't the pleasure that's about to consume me.

"*Ah*, oh God, *yes*," I moan, pushing a finger inside myself that doesn't even come close to comparing how it felt to have him inside me. I bite back moaning his name because the tiny bit of self-preservation I have makes sure I don't give him that.

I could be fantasizing about anyone else right now.

My orgasm hits me hard and fast as I gasp out as the sensation takes over my body. I place my hand on the glass to help support myself as my knees wobble from the onslaught of pleasure.

When I'm able to compose myself, I end up rushing through the rest of my shower and convince myself Colton won't still be on FaceTime.

After I've finished, I grab my towel and wrap it around myself before stepping out. My eyes zero in on my phone screen instantly. It's fogged a bit with condensation, but I can see him still there, staring and smirking that infuriating smirk.

"Satisfied?" I ask with an impressively level tone.

"Not even a little bit. I'll see you soon." He hangs up before I can say anything else.

I'm standing here in my steamed-up bathroom with the worry about what I may have just started.

I have a text from my mom once I get off the plane after landing in Denver. Part of me wants to chuck the device onto the tarmac and let a plane run it over. I know what she is going to ask, she wants me to come home for Thanksgiving. I used to, back at the beginning of my career. I'd fly back to the small town just outside of Calgary where I'm from. Canadian Thanksgiving is a different day than America's, but since we always have the holiday off, I would go home then.

Back when I thought I could actually impress my parents by having made it. Being in the NHL. The dream I wanted more than anything.

But it didn't matter. Nothing I did ever mattered to them after Josh was gone. I'm just the son they have left. The one they don't care to acknowledge because once Josh was gone, he took every bit of their souls with them. And nothing I could do could help.

So, two years ago I stopped going home at all. It's not my home anymore. My mom still tries, acting like she cares if I'm there, though I know it's not true. Which is why the text pisses me off because I know she doesn't care, and this year wouldn't be any different.

And also, why I leave her on read without saying anything.

Instead of going straight home, I go to the rink to workout in the gym to rid myself of the sudden annoyance I have thinking about everything. Though I would rather take out my aggression in another way, preferably a certain blonde with the roundest ass, longest legs, and perky tits. I know that wouldn't work out well. I have a plan to see her tomorrow and I *will* have her underneath me again after the game.

————

I HATE to admit that this game is going better than the other ones this season. We're up two going into the third period and I haven't gotten into any fights with anyone on the Dragons. I've almost gotten into one against Vegas, but that was broken up before anything could escalate.

Finishing another shift on the ice, my hair is wet with sweat as I sit on the bench for a break, spraying water into my mouth and then spitting it onto the ground before repeating the action, drinking the cool liquid this time.

Vegas almost scores, but Colver is able to stop the puck before smothering it to stop the play. Coach sends me back onto the ice for the next face off. I get into position and the other defenseman starts chirping.

"You going to get into another fight with your own teammate again, Wheeler?" he asks, pushing against my shoulder a bit harder than necessary for the position we are in.

I push back. "Nah, I think the next fight I get into will be some asshole who chirps at me. And I'll make sure to draw some blood this time."

The puck drops, starting the play and he gets one more solid shove in before we take off. Vegas got possession of the puck so I'm having to get into a defensive position to try and snag the puck before it has a chance to get to Colver again.

I manage to snag it, skating to the opposite zone, the chirper right on my ass, smacking his stick against my legs, but then it lunges a bit too long in front of my legs and sends me flying forward as I lose my balance. The whistle blows calling the penalty, but I'm already up and getting into his face.

We're pushed apart, and I'm sent back to the bench.

"Fucking prick," I mumble to no one in particular.

"Solid play, Wheeler, you had that shit before he tripped you," Collee praises before taking his place on the ice.

I'm shocked he gave me any sort of compliment. I'm sure he feels required as the captain, so I don't take it too seriously.

We end up winning the game and the energy of the locker room is electric. Cheers about a celebration are all over.

"We're all going out. Every one of you, call your girlfriends and wives, we're celebrating, motherfuckers," a forward, Jenkins, announces.

"You all have fun, you deserve it and enjoy your holiday, but you better be ready for practice first thing Saturday morning," Collee tells everyone.

"No fucking way, Cap, you're coming out," Jenkins calls.

"I have a girl with a baby at home, you all enjoy."

"Whatever, Chandler will understand, just for a little," Jenkins tries.

"Yeah, come on," Jones joins in.

Collee glances at McQuaid and Dumont. McQuaid nods because I can tell he wants to join the guys. Dumont looks as unsure and is already on his phone, probably already asking for permission to take his balls for a walk.

I get in the shower before I hear the rest of the convincing. After I'm done, while drying my hair with a towel, I text Brynn.

> Colton: You're coming out with the guys, Baby Collee, to celebrate our win. Then, you're paying up on your part of the deal.

> Baby Collee: Are you nuts? Is my brother going?

> Colton: Doesn't matter. You're going to do what I say. We had a deal.

> Baby Collee: I hate you.

So she says.

———

KEEPING my distance from the rest of the team, I go right up to the bar to get a drink and watch for Brynn. She never said she would come, but I know she will. My eyes find her brother who's watching over a couple of the guys who're already acting a little rowdy and looking like he's going to scold them.

Rolling my eyes, I turn back to the bar to get my drink.

"No hurricane shot again?" A familiar voice asks from next to me.

I smirk, turning toward the source. "You offering, Princess?"

"To throw a drink in your face and slap you? Gladly."

Leaning down to her ear, "You can slap me again when I'm buried deep inside you later. I like it rough."

Her breath hitches as I pull back and see her scowl. I know she doesn't mean it.

"I don't know why you wanted me to come here, this isn't very secret when your entire team is here."

"Or is it? You came here because of your brother, not me." I smile.

"Hm, good point." She turns her back to the bar, resting her elbows on it and looking out. "You know, you have a lot of hot teammates that I could go home with if I wanted."

"Fuck that, you don't sleep with hockey players," I snap.

Her eyebrows shoot up as she looks at me. "I don't? Great, then I'll have my bed all to myself tonight."

She starts to walk away, but I grab her waist, turning her to face me, our bodies pressed together. Mine immediately reacting to hers.

"None of these other assholes get to touch you. And you will be coming home with me at the end of the night. So, flirt with whoever you want, tease whoever you want, do whatever you want, but it'll be my name you're screaming at the end of the night. Now, go see your brother, Baby Collee." I turn her around and tap her on the ass which has her turning back to glare at me.

And instead of fighting me about what I just said she walks toward Captain, and I smirk into my beer. Yeah, she's going to be a good little slut for just me tonight, I'll make sure of it.

Chapter Twenty-Four

BRYNN

I feel Colton's eyes on me constantly. It's almost like a horror movie where the music is teasing the killer who's about to jump out at you. But Colton isn't a killer, just an asshole. An asshole who is too handsome for his own good, and makes my body crave his in a way I've never experienced before.

But still, an asshole.

I don't drink much, but I'm being extra careful tonight because I know how easily I'm willing to give into him sober. I'm scared to see what I would let him get away with when I'm drunk.

"Come on, Cap, one more," one of their teammates says to Brent when he tries to leave for like the fifth time.

Brent questioned why I was here, of course, but I mostly distracted him with my wit and completely not suspicious response. "Don't question me, I don't ask your reasonings for everything."

"Guys, I really need to get home, you let Dumont leave," Brent says. McQuaid is still here, but I'm pretty sure he's distracted sexting Chandler by the look on his face.

"That's because he was complaining and bitching and I didn't want to hear it anymore, but you're our captain," the same player says, slapping him on the shoulder.

"*One* more. Then I'm leaving," Brent relents right before his teammates throw an arm around his shoulder and usher him over to the bar, leaving me in the booth by myself.

I chuckle into my last drink that I've been nursing when a warm body saddles up next to me, and I immediately know who it is based on the woodsy smell and air of jerk that has surrounded me.

"Haven't seen you show any interest in any other guys tonight, guess you are saving yourself for me. I'm flattered, Princess."

Rolling my eyes over to him I meet his cocky stare. "And what if I did? You told me to go tease and flirt with whoever I want. What if I did go home with one of them? Would you throw me over your shoulder and beat on your chest like a caveman?" I'm glad the little bit of alcohol has made its way into my system and given me some sort of bravado to say something to him this time. I'm sick of being struck silent.

"Want to try it and see what happens?" Colton taunts.

I narrow my eyes, about to say yes when his hand lands on my thigh, pushing up the fabric of my t-shirt dress just slightly. I went for comfort when I threw on the simple dress and boots that end just above my knee. It's cold outside, but I ditched my jean jacket because the bar is stifling. Even more so with Colton's presence.

Now his large, rough hand has taken space on my bare thigh. I want to hate it. I want to push him away, but I don't. Instead, I finish my watered down drink in a single gulp without my eyes leaving his. That's when his fingers start moving along my skin, just barely. It's so subtle I'm not sure if I'm just imagining it.

He leans closer to me, his lips so close to my ear they graze my skin as he speaks, "What about if I made you come right here right now in front of all of these people? Then what would you do?"

"You wouldn't. Your team is here. My *brother* is here."

His hand moves up higher, the tips of his fingers are less than an inch from the hem of my panties. My breath hitches at the slight contact. *He really wouldn't...would he?*

"I don't mind an audience, Princess. And I really don't care who that audience is."

I need to stop him. I have to. This is ridiculous, he can't be serious right now. He can't—

My thoughts stop as the tip of one of his fingers slides under the hem of my panties and a low groan leaves his lips when I know exactly what he finds. I go to cross my legs to remove his hand, but he stops me by pressing his palm harder against me.

"You're so wet for me already, Baby Collee. Seems like you enjoy the idea of coming in front of everyone too." He drops his voice even quieter, speaking against my skin, "Looks like you're just as sick as I am and don't care who's around."

I want to tell him he's wrong, but it's hard to deny the very obvious reaction my body is giving him right now. How the smallest touch from him is making me feel already. Fuck this guy. And fuck him for how he knows how to work my body.

He moves higher, dipping his finger into my underwear, rubbing along my slit. My hips buck slightly, trying to get him to touch where I really want him to. He chuckles and it makes me want to slap him.

"Such a needy slut for my hand already, aren't you? Or is it my cock you're wanting to fill up this desperate pussy?" He pushes a thick finger inside me, and I gasp, reaching out to grab the table in front of us.

My eyes dart around the bar to see if anyone is paying attention to us. I'm sure we're going to get caught, but then he removes his hand and I take in a deep breath just as I see where the rest of his team is, including Brent. They're all huddled around the bar and not paying any attention to us or in our direction at all.

I turn to look at Colton, to tell him off once again, but don't get the chance before I'm lifted off my seat and into his lap, straddling his hips. I try to scramble away, but he keeps me planted with a firm grip on my hips.

"You're not leaving this fucking spot until you soak my hand with your cum. So, if you want to move then you better do it fast." He gives me a mischievous look.

"We're going to get caught you idiot," I snap, but even I can tell I'm lacking venom in my tone because I'm so unbearably turned on.

Colton looks around for a second before seeing a Dragons hoodie and yanking it over my head. It must be one of the guys' because it's huge on me. He scowls at the clothing he just put on my body.

"When we get back to my place, you're going to pay for having to wear some other guy's hoodie."

I go to retort, but his hand is back into my panties, starting to rub at my clit. I moan, falling forward against this chest. I'm already getting overheated from the thick fabric over my body and the hood over my head that obscures me from view. It also hides everything around me from my view, making me almost forget we're still in public. And that my brother is just across the open space while his teammate is finger fucking me in some booth in the middle of a bar.

I've officially lost my mind. I'm no longer Brynn Collee, I'm another person who has taken over my body. That feeling is only intensified as Colton proceeds to push two fingers inside me, I'm so wet there's hardly any resistance. My hips move against him, grinding myself against his hand and feeling the erection he has no shot of hiding.

"Look at what a dirty little slut you are rubbing yourself against me in public. Such a good fucking girl who wants to come, aren't you?" he growls, grabbing the back of my neck with his free hand while working me with his other one.

I whimper, dropping my head down so it looks like I'm just some random girl making out with him, but our lips aren't even touching. I try to keep my movements subtle enough, but it's driving me insane how badly I want to come. His fingers pump, curling to rub against the sensitive spot inside me while I try to get some friction on my clit.

"You're close, aren't you, Princess? Going to come for me just like this."

Our foreheads are pressed together as I chase the orgasm that's lingering so close I can almost taste it. I press down harder against his hand, feeling his hard cock rub against me through his slacks as he continues to rub my inner walls.

The loud bar around us seems to fade and suddenly I really don't care who can see. We may get caught by his teammates, but none of that matters. The only thing that matters to me right now is the release that's about to consume me.

I'm overheated, overstimulated, but when Colton growls, "Come for me, baby, I want to walk out of here covered in your cum." I lose it.

Burying my face against his shoulder to muffle the scream I want to let loose as he works me through my orgasm. I faintly hear him say, "this is exactly what I was picturing while I watched you in the shower the other night."

As soon as the pleasure starts to subside, the fear sinks in. I'm scared to lift my head and see how many people are staring at us. I bet the entire place got silent and they all heard me.

I look up slowly, and I'm able to register the noises around us and that it hasn't lessened. It's still loud. I turn toward the bar where I see Colton's teammates are still enjoying themselves. The only person I don't see is the one who absolutely can't catch me in this guy's lap.

I jump off Colton and adjust my dress, wanting to take off the hoodie because it's way too hot. But I like that it's helping me hide.

"He left," Colton says easily while he adjusts himself before standing up.

"What?" I squeak out. I think the orgasm took my voice along with my rational thought.

"Captain Collee, he left. Didn't look in this direction. You're in the clear." He's standing now, and I'm just looking up at him struck stupid.

"Come on, Princess." He stretches out his hand and I take it too easily as he pulls me from my seat.

He yanks the hoodie off me, and I get the chills for absolutely no reason as he tosses it back on the seat of the booth we just desecrated. I want to ask what we are doing, but I'm too spaced out. Which is why I let Colton take hold of my hand, pulling me out of the bar and into his car.

It briefly crosses my mind how easily I'm going with him when I should probably put up some sort of a fight, but I don't. I just sink into the soft leather seats of his fancy car as he drives us away.

I can't believe I'm bringing Brynn to my house. I don't bring anyone here. I also can't believe she let me do that in public. Where her brother was. I was keeping an eye on everyone to make sure we wouldn't get caught. A couple of the guys looked over, but they couldn't tell it was Brynn since I covered her with that fucking hoodie. Her blonde hair hidden in the hood; her face buried in my neck.

The way she felt, how she sounded. *Fuck,* I need more. *She* needs more, I know it. Which is why I'm bringing her to my house where I plan to spend the rest of the night with my cock buried inside her.

My tongue too.

Maybe my fingers again.

This girl must have a magical fucking pussy because I need it again. And again and again.

Part of me is a little glad she didn't argue about coming with me, because if she did I don't think I would've been able to stop myself from shoving her against the side of my car and fucking her right there until she agreed.

We pull up to my house the only sounds in the car have been the music that was playing. Brynn just looked out the passenger window the entire drive. I want to know what she's thinking, but not enough to actually ask.

Once I park in my garage and get out, I meet Brynn at the passenger side, leading her inside with a hand on her lower back. She takes in my house, which is kind of surprising since I'm sure her brother has a nice place like this. I realize I don't know much about her past, but I'm sure she grew up with money. Most hockey families do, it's an expensive sport. My parents may not have given a shit about me, but they made sure to throw whatever money I needed at me to get me to shut up and go away.

I step up behind her, swiping her hair off her shoulder, onto the other side before leaning in to speak, "I want you to be a good little girl for me, go to my room, get naked, and wait for me kneeling on the floor."

She steels her spine and I prepare for a fight. "What if I don't?"

"Then I'll punish you. Decide which you want. To be treated like a good girl or a filthy slut."

Her breath hitches and I can't help but smirk. "I don't know where your room is."

"You'll figure it out. Better do it quickly." I give her ass a light smack that has her gasping and glaring at me.

But again, she listens.

She's so fucking pretty when she listens.

And when she doesn't.

Really, she's always pretty, but she can be a brat who hates me. Both sides turn me on, though, so I don't mind.

Giving her some time to follow my instructions or disobey them. I go into my kitchen and pour myself a glass of water because I'm going to be sober for tonight. I'm going to thoroughly enjoy everything I have planned for her. And how well she's going to take it all.

I chug the glass of water, slamming it onto the counter. I hope wherever she is in my house she can hear it and know that I'm coming for her. Taking my time as I walk toward my bedroom. Unbuttoning my shirt and dropping it onto the floor, unbuckling my belt and letting the buckle clank with each step so she can hear me approaching.

Stepping into my room, I'm not sure what I'm going to find. Which is why I'm pleasantly surprised to see Brynn stripped down to her lacy bra and matching panties, sitting on the edge of my bed, legs crossed and leaning back on her palms. The look she's giving me makes my cock twitch. She knows what she's doing.

I unbutton my pants. "This isn't what I asked for. I'll give you one more chance to drop to your knees and be in the position I told you to be in."

When she doesn't move a single inch, I know I'm going to have to work for her full submission. But I'm going to get it. I step forward so I'm standing right in front of her. "Take my dick out, Princess."

She looks up at me, defiance evident and again, doesn't move. I reach out, gripping her face, pushing onto her cheeks so her pouty lips part slightly. "Show me what a dirty girl you can be and take my cock out."

Keeping my grip on her face, our eyes locked as she reaches out slowly to push down my pants roughly. Then my boxers, she yanks on them so roughly I'm sure she's trying to prove a point, but the only point she's proving is what a little brat she can be.

"Now you're going to use our spit as you show me what a desperate slut you are for my cock and show me what your mouth can do when it's not talking back to me. Open."

I push on her cheeks harder to force her mouth open a little more. Leaning down so our mouths are almost touching, but not quite, I gather some saliva in my mouth before letting it fall into her open mouth. I stand up to my full height, letting go of her face.

"Suck," I command.

Her jaw is dropped slightly in surprise, but then she reaches out, taking my cock in her fist, pumping with a tight grip that has me hissing through my teeth.

"I said, suck, Princess."

Her eyes look up at me, our gazes locked as she takes me in between those puffy lips and as far back as she can.

"*Fuck*, that's such a good girl for me."

She hums and I feel the vibration as she pulls back to rub her tongue on the sensitive underside of my crown. She teases me with her tongue, and I tangle my hands in her soft hair, pulling at the scalp which makes her moan around me before taking me deep in her throat again, gagging slightly.

"Breathe, baby, you can do it."

She takes a deep breath through her nose before swallowing, constricting her throat around my cock. I groan, yanking her back with the grip I have on her hair and forcing her to look up at me.

"*Fuck*, I knew you'd have a talented mouth. You like sucking my cock? Am I going to find your hot cunt soaked for me after I fuck your face?"

She squeaks slightly, but squirms and I can tell she's trying to find some relief between her thighs.

"You like the sound of that? You want me to use you like the perfect pretty whore you are for me?"

"Yes," she says softly. I like it when she's feisty, and fighting with me. But I like this. I could get used to it.

"Tap my thigh if it gets to be too much," I instruct right before guiding her mouth back onto my thick erection that becomes enveloped in the warmth of her mouth.

She takes me even further and I guide her with the grip I have on her hair, and she just takes it. I pick up my pace. Her nails dig into my thighs and I know there's going to be little half moon imprints left by the time I'm done.

I give her a chance to adjust to my size, but it doesn't take long before I can't take it anymore and I'm thrusting into her mouth while she relaxes her jaw taking what I'm giving her. Drool runs down her chin, her eyes water as they look up at me. She's never looked better. And she doesn't tap my thighs.

It all feels too good, and she looks so dirty, all because of me which has me barreling toward release. I'd love nothing more than to shoot my load down her throat, make her open her mouth and show me while it drips out, then shove it back in just to make her swallow it down. But the first time I come tonight it's going to be while I'm buried inside her tight pussy.

I pull her off me, and she looks up, lips red and swollen, face a mess and I can't help myself from leaning down taking her mouth in a vicious kiss. Our tongues thrash against each other as I kick off my boxers all the way, and push Brynn back onto my bed. She wraps her arms around my back, scratching her nails down my spine as I settle my weight in between her thighs.

My cock rubs against the soaking fabric that's covering her. Reaching down, I rip at the scrap of lace until it tears off her body.

She gasps, putting distance between our mouths. "I liked those," she snaps.

"I'll buy you more." I try to take her mouth again, but she turns her head.

"Don't rip this bra too, I'll take it off."

I smirk down at her, my eyes dropping to the flimsy thing

covering her tits. Hooking a finger around the back I tug on it as the lace rips easily under my strength.

"I'll rip whatever I want off your body if it's in my way from getting to what I want. I'll buy you fifty of these things to replace them. I don't give a shit. But don't tell me what to do."

I attack her mouth once again before she can say anything and she bites at my lower lip in retaliation, which is cute. I back up slightly, gripping her hips and flipping her onto her stomach roughly before pressing my weight down onto her back. My dick rubs against her ass, and she gasps.

"Should I fuck your ass as punishment? You think you could take me there, Princess?"

"Not a chance." She shakes her head.

I slide down her body, spreading her legs for my view to see she's dripping. "Sucking my dick made you this wet? Or is this from the bar? Or are you just this desperate to take my cock inside you again?"

She squirms, and I hold her still with a hand on her lower back as I swipe my fingers through her slit with the other. Gathering her wetness on my fingers I bring it to my mouth, sucking loudly so she knows what I'm doing.

"Fuck you taste so sweet. Not sure how someone so bitchy can have such a perfect pussy."

She growls, and tries to buck up to get away, but I keep her in place. "Fuck you."

"In a minute. Let me eat first."

Diving forward, I latch my mouth onto her pussy from behind. She lurches forward moaning into the mattress as I lap at her wetness, tasting as much of her as I can. And it still doesn't feel like enough.

Running my tongue along her slit up further she squeals and tries to push away as I get closer to the other tight hole. I pull back slightly, landing a sharp smack onto her ass cheek. "Why are you interrupting my meal?"

She squirms slightly, but I hold her still.

"Because you were trying to go back there," her voice is soft and almost innocent, and it probably says something about me that it only makes me harder. I'm already starting to rut against the mattress.

I kneel back and with a grip on her hips, I flip her onto her back once again and she looks up at me with flushed skin, her nipples pink and hard, lips swollen and parted. Every inch of her is begging for my mouth and I wish I could taste every inch of her at once because a single spot isn't enough.

"Listen to me, I will put my tongue, fingers, and cock wherever I want when it comes to you and this perfect body of yours. And you will enjoy every single second of it. Your only complaint will be that you want more. Understand me, Princess?"

With a rough swallow, she nods right as her eyes drop to my rock-hard cock that is pointed straight toward her. She bites her bottom lip and I wrap my fist around myself, stroking slowly as I look at her.

"You wanting to be touched?"

She nods.

"Did you forget how to use your words?" I taunt.

She shakes her head.

"Tell me what you want then, Princess."

She hesitates, squirming around again and it's fun to see her so flustered like this. "I want your mouth on me."

"You going to interrupt me again?" I ask with another stroke with my fist.

She shakes her head.

"Words," I snap.

"No."

"Look at you, such a good girl. Now put your feet on the bed and spread your legs."

She puts her feet up with her legs parted. I grip underneath her knees and push back so she's folded in half, her pussy front and center for me to devour once again. And that's exactly what I do. I lick and suck, spearing her with my tongue then suck her clit into my mouth as she moans and grapples to find anything to hold onto. The sheets, my hair, my arms. I drive her out of her mind with my mouth.

This time when I push her further back, exposing her ass to me again, I dip lower, running my tongue over the tight hole there. I feel her tense, but she doesn't stop me this time.

She starts to relax and moaning at the new sensation, I take advantage of her pliancy, pressing a finger inside her tight cunt, curling and pumping while I eat her ass. She starts thrashing as she gets close. I feel her tightening. She's gripping the sheets so tightly they may pull off the edges, but I don't care. I want her to fuck up my room. Fuck up my entire house. It only proves she was here. Something about the thought of her leaving her mark on my place shocks the shit out of me, but I don't think about it too much because she's screaming out her release.

Her orgasm coats the stubble on my face, and it only makes me want to bury myself in her spasming pussy, face first, and make her do it again. As she comes down, she pushes me away whining about how sensitive she is.

I move up her body, hovering above her, making a show of licking her cum off my lips as I stare down at her.

"Aw, you can't handle anymore, Baby Collee?" I taunt.

She's breathing heavily, her eyes locked onto my mouth, suddenly her arms wrap around my shoulders yanking me down so our mouths crash together. It shocks me, but I catch up quickly as she laps at her release, tasting herself on my tongue which makes me borderline desperate to get inside her. This entire night has been foreplay and I'm worried the second I sink inside her I'm going to explode, but I need to. I need to feel her strangle my cock as she comes again.

It takes a huge effort to pull back from her, putting distance between us. We are both breathing heavily as I stand and walk over to my nightstand to grab a condom. Brynn watches the movement, her eyes never leaving my hand as I rip the wrapper with my teeth then roll the rubber over my length.

I climb back onto the bed, my back against the headboard. "Get up here, Princess. Ride my dick and show me what a slut you are for my cock."

She scrambles up the bed, straddling my hips and hovering over my length. I notice she's looking down between our bodies and I tilt her chin up so she's looking at me.

"I want to watch your face as you take every inch of me in this perfect cunt."

She bites her lip but does what I ask. Her eyes never leaving mine as she sinks down onto me. We moan together at the feeling. Once she's filled to the hilt it takes every ounce of self-control I have not to fuck up into her as roughly as possible. And also, not to come right this second.

Brynn wraps her arms around my neck as she adjusts to my size and when her hips start to rock slightly, she throws her head back and I just look at her. Her tits bouncing slightly from the movement, flawless skin shining with sweat as she rolls her hips against me chasing yet another orgasm.

"Fuck, you want it so bad, don't you? Such a slut for my cock, aren't you? Does it feel good?"

"Yes, so good, fuck me, please."

"Such a good fucking girl for me, baby." I grasp her hips and start to fuck up into her.

She gasps out a moan and tightens her hold on me as she meets me thrust for thrust with a roll of her hips to get the friction on her clit, I know she needs it.

"Colton, please, I need, *ugh.*" She's close again but can't quite get there.

I can't help the light chuckle I let out at her desperation.

"You wanting to come? Poor little thing can't get there without my help?"

"Fuck you, I just need...*please.*"

I tsk at her attitude, tossing her off my lap, onto her back on the bed and she squeals at the sudden movement, but I'm on her again almost instantly, thrusting into her so hard she cries out.

"You don't get what you want when you have an attitude with me, got it?" I ask, punctuating my point with a sharp slap of my hips.

"*Yes.*"

"Apologize and then maybe I'll give you what you want."

"I'm, *ugh*, I'm sorry, please Colton, please."

"You begging is fucking perfection, Princess."

I pull back to kneel between her spread thighs, keeping up a steady pace as I thrust into her, and I watch as I disappear inside. I gather spit into my mouth, and let it fall where we are connected, using the wetness from both of us to rub her clit.

As soon as my finger makes contact with the swollen bud she screams at the sensation.

"Yes, please Colton, oh my God!"

Angling my hips to hit the place inside that will make her see stars while continuing to rub her, it doesn't take long before she's squeezing me like a vice as she comes. Her moans and screams have some words woven in there, but I can't make them out. Especially because I'm focusing on keeping my own orgasm back until she's finished.

As soon as she goes limp from the strength and number of orgasms she's had I let loose, exploding inside her with a loud groan. I'm barely able to catch myself before I collapse on top of her.

Our heavy breathing fills the room and I anticipate her feisty side to come back any second, but I kind of want to lay with her a little before that happens.

And when I pull out, I quickly dispose of the condom in the attached bathroom, grab a warm washcloth, and find her exactly how I left her on my bed. She hardly reacts when I clean her up and when I climb back into bed and pull her body into mine, she doesn't even fight me as I wrap my arms around her, hugging her to my chest.

I think for a second she's already asleep, but then her hand lifts to rest on my chest and starts tracing the ink on my skin. Neither of us say anything, and I don't want to because I'm sure anything we say will turn hostile and I don't want that right now. For the moment I want to just enjoy this.

Pretend that maybe this could have been something real, that we actually like each other. But I know by the time morning comes it'll be reality again. She doesn't like me. I can't have her. That used to not bother me, I didn't want anyone. But I can't help this new feeling that's starting to appear. The feeling that's trying to convince me that it may not be the worst thing in the world if maybe she did like me. If maybe she did stick around for more than just sex.

I don't know what's wrong with me, but it stops me from doing anything to ruin this moment, I just fall into the feeling of her fingers dancing across my skin and act like maybe this could mean something. Even though I know it never could.

I don't know when I fell asleep, but when I woke up it was still dark, and I felt a warm body surrounding me. That's when I realized where I was and who I was with. As carefully as I could I got dressed and got out of his house as fast as possible. Called an Uber to take me back to my car and did the walk of shame into my apartment where I swear Ellie was judging me.

"I know I said just once, but I meant just twice," I tell her on my way to collapse on my own bed face first.

I pass out not long after my face hits my pillow, hating how cold I feel without his large muscular body wrapped around me.

I wake up to my phone ringing way too loudly. I'm not even hungover and yet I feel like my head is swimming. I search for the source of the noise and find it in my purse I dumped at the front door when I came home.

"Hello?" I answer immediately, clearing my throat because I sound terrible.

"You okay?" Brent's deep voice asks.

"Yeah? Why wouldn't I be?" I look down at myself as if I'm double checking. The only thing I see is rumpled clothes from sleeping in them. Or from them being tossed. And I'm out a pair of panties and a bra I really liked. Dammit, that reminder is enough to bring the entire night flooding back. And now is not the time for that.

"Because I tried to find you before I left last night but couldn't, so I've been trying to get ahold of you all night." He sounds like a scolding parent without raising his voice, only a "disappointed" tone.

Probably because I was getting fingered by your teammate just a few yards away from you and forgot I was even in public.

"Oh, yeah, I left pretty early, I was tired. I might be coming down with something."

"You do sound like shit."

"Wow. Thanks, bro. You sound like shit every day, but I don't feel the need to call you out on it all the time."

"You need anything?"

"An all-expenses paid trip to Bora Bora with a hot muscular masseuse on call the entire time."

"Hilarious," he responds, deadpan. "Well, drink some tea, eat some soup, and rest if you're getting sick because we can't have you around Evie even if it is Thanksgiving."

Shit, I forgot what day it is.

"Whatever you say," I roll my eyes at his bossiness. "I would never risk seeing her if I'm sick."

"Yeah, okay. Call me if you need anything, but we will see you later as long as you're feeling okay."

"I already told you I need–"

"Goodbye." He hangs up and I chuckle, but it burns because my throat is really dry.

After chugging two glasses of water, I dare look at my phone for any other notifications and am pleased not to see Colton's name on it at all. Maybe once wasn't enough, but twice was and I can finally be done with him.

The ache between my legs protests that thought slightly because my whore of a pussy would like to keep him, but my mind is pretty happy with the idea.

Mostly.

I shake away the thoughts and lingering fear of abandonment that is trying to claw its way out. Reminding myself this is what I want. Him to leave me alone.

Even though it is a holiday I can't help but look at my email, skimming for anything super urgent or important. My eyes land on an email from Kenneth's publicist. I'm a little surprised she's reaching out. The subject just reads:

POTENTIAL STORY RELEASING. CALL ME TO DISCUSS.

Hello Ms. Collee,
I wanted to reach out to inform you that there is a potential story coming
out that does not paint my client in the best light. We are trying to handle
it, but as it stands right now if the story leaks, we would like to come to
an agreement with Ms. Sparks that she would be willing to vouch for my
client's character as this story could be debilitating to his reputation and
career.

Please call me to discuss further. As previously stated, we are trying to
handle it before anything is released.
Thank you.

I send a simple email as a response because no matter what the story could be, the thought that Spencer would take Kenneth's side is laughable.

Ms. Reiner,
My client, Ms. Sparks, is not making any public statements at this time.
Nor is she doing any press. Also, knowing the history between our clients
I do not think it is reasonable to expect her to make any statement on his
behalf. As I'm not aware of the story you are referring to, but if it does
not directly involve my client, I respectfully ask that you leave her out
of it.
Thank you.

I have to erase the *"fuck you"* at the end which is directed more at Kenneth since I'm sure he put her up to this request anyway. It does make me wonder what the story is they're trying to get ahead of because it must be something good.

That's something I'm going to have to research a bit.

After a long, hot shower, food, and getting some underwear on.

———

FINALLY FEELING SOMEWHAT HUMAN AGAIN, I start to try and dig for information on what story could be coming out about Kenneth, utilizing all my sources to figure it out.

Seems like whatever it is they are working hard to keep it quiet, though, because I'm not able to find a single thing.

I do, however, start down a rabbit hole that is researching Colton because I realize how little I know about him and considering I've now slept with him twice I should learn something about the man other than how obnoxious he is and what his dick feels like inside me.

I'm able to find a lot of articles about him when he was younger, his hockey achievements. A shocking lack of scandals from once he started in the league. Mostly just his stats and the different women he's been seen with, but that's it.

Something does catch my eye further down and it's an obituary for a Josh Wheeler. I click on it, my screen is filled with a picture of a smiling boy who looks like a younger, happier version of Colton. They share the same light brown hair; this kid has freckles decorating his cheeks and is missing his top two front teeth as he smiles widely at the camera.

Their eyes are strikingly similar, the blue-silver that I've never seen on anyone before. My eyes catch on the dates that show he was only ten years old when he died. I read through the obituary which is where I learn this is Colton's brother. It doesn't give much information other than how much he will be missed and how much he lit up everyone's lives.

There's a pang in my chest as I think about this boy losing

his life so young, my immediate thought is that it had to be an accident. My heart hurts for his family, and then my own grief hits as I think of my own brother.

Mine dug his own grave in a way, but I can't help the lingering guilt I constantly feel when I think of Brandon. Of the things I should have done to help, even though Brent has told me there's nothing I could have done. I just feel like there should have been.

It didn't have to be like this.

I hardly notice I'm crying until a tear drops and hits the top of my hand just sitting on my keyboard.

Wiping my cheeks, I take a deep breath to compose myself once again. Ellie jumps up next to me, meowing as she pushes her head against my arm. I swear this cat knows things.

"I'm okay, El," I reassure her while petting her head.

My phone dings and I don't know why my immediate thought is that it may be Bryson or Bailey. Probably my subconscious is just hoping since now I have the pull to reach out to make sure they're okay after what I just learned about Colton's brother and the reminder of my own.

My shoulders drop when I see it's neither of them, but the man I was just researching.

> Colton: Was that enough time to let you freak out about what happened and not ignore me again?

> Brynn: It's a holiday, this number is out of service.

Colton: Almost forgot, but the only thing I'm thankful for today is how tightly your pussy strangles me. Especially when I tell you what a good little slut you are for me.

Brynn: It's a holiday, said pussy is also out of service.

Colton: Damn, I broke you? I'll come kiss it better.

Brynn: Go spend time with your family or something.

He doesn't reply right away, and I gnaw at my lip, worried that may have been too far, even for me especially with what I just learned. I don't know how close he is to his family, maybe it's like mine and strained. Maybe it's perfect, I didn't see any other obituary that could show his parents are dead, so I assume they aren't.

Colton: They don't live here. I could join yours. I'm sure mommy, daddy, and big bro would love to see me show up with you to the family dinner.

I let out a breath I didn't realize I was holding when he continues with his flirty banter. I've never cared about offending him or hurting his feelings, so I'm not sure why I suddenly do. Probably has something to do with my own issues that I'm shaking away again.

Brynn: No parents, just going to Brent's.

My thumbs hover over the screen as I think about what I'm about to type. I know I shouldn't, but something about what I recently learned has created this string connecting us in a way I didn't expect and didn't entirely want. But it's there and I can't ignore it.

> Brynn: You could join though if you want.

Colton: Uh, to your brother's house? That he shares with his girlfriend who he shares with two other guys?

> Brynn: Never mind.

Colton: I'll pick you up at three.

> Brynn: Two conditions.

> Brynn: No being a dick to everyone. They are your teammates, act like it.

> Brynn: Nothing has happened or is happening between us. I invited you because I feel bad.

Not a total lie.

Colton: One condition of my own, then.

Colton: You come back to my place and don't sneak out this time.

> Brynn: Only if my conditions are met. If not, then you take me home and delete my number.

Colton: Ha ha. I'll see you soon, Baby Collee.

One way or another I'm going to regret this.

WHEELER

24

I'm going to be on my best behavior. Mostly just to piss Brynn off more. I know me just being there will piss off Captain Collee and the rest of the guys. I don't even need to do anything, just being there will be enough. I wouldn't be surprised if McQuaid took the opportunity to try and clock me the second he sees me step foot into their house.

I promised Brynn I would be nice, and I plan on it. She may see how nice I can be when I sneak her into a bathroom and eat her pussy as an appetizer. Or dessert. Or both.

I show up to her apartment five minutes before three. I assumed this wasn't some fancy Thanksgiving, so I threw on jeans and a hoodie over a t-shirt. When she opens the door, I have to clench my fists to stop myself from yanking her body into mine. She has some sweater dress thing on, fishnets covering her legs, and boots up to her knees. Her blonde hair falls in waves around her shoulders, and I want to fuck it up.

Well, I'm going to, but not in the way I want to right now.

"You look hot as fuck, Princess," I tell her.

She rolls her eyes. "Thanks."

She locks her door and as we get into the elevator I'm tempted to push her up against a wall and kiss her, but hold back. We exit her building and I lead her over to my bike. She pauses, staring at the motorcycle as I swing my leg over it, straddling the seat, pulling my helmet on, and reaching out to offer hers.

"No way." She shakes her head.

"What's the problem?"

"You're going to kill us."

"I've been driving a bike since I turned eighteen and haven't killed anyone yet. Have a little trust in me."

"You haven't?" She scrunches her nose and the look she gives me makes it seem like she has more she wants to ask but doesn't.

I shake my head. "Nope. Everyone who has ridden me has survived."

"You mean with you."

I shrug. "Sure, however you want to take it. Get over here."

She hesitates, but takes the helmet from me, pulling it on her head. I reach out to adjust the straps to fit it to her.

"Hug me with your thighs as tight as you do when I'm fucking you, and wrap your arms around my middle," I instruct.

I hear her scoff.

"And lean with me when we turn," I say.

"Anything else?" she sasses.

"Yeah, go ahead and give me more attitude, just call me daddy when you do."

I cut off whatever smart remark she starts to make when I start up the motorcycle and rev it a couple times. She climbs on behind me, wrapping her body around mine and my dick immediately takes notice, but I force the distraction away as I pull out of her complex and take off toward her brother's house.

When we arrive, there are several cars parked inside the gated driveway Brynn had to let us in with a code.

"Who all is here?" I ask, taking off my helmet after parking.

"Probably Vince's family, Spencer and Jared. I don't think Audrey and Charlie are here though, she talked about going to his family's and that we will see them tomorrow for something called pie party."

"The fuck is pie party?"

"What it sounds like. A party. With pie. It's tradition the day after Thanksgiving according to Chandler."

I want to say how weird these people are, but I hold back because I'm trying to be good tonight like I told her I would be. Though, I think it's going to be harder than I thought.

I'm about to walk into a house where the three guys share a fucking girlfriend for fucks sake. And she just had a baby. Doesn't get much weirder than that.

But at least the one with glasses that wants to rip my balls off isn't going to be here. I'm pretty sure that's Audrey, I can't keep track of everyone. That's a lot of effort when I don't give a shit about any of them.

Except maybe Brynn.

A little tiny bit.

Like the bit that is her pussy.

And mouth.

But that's it.

We walk up to the front door, and I expect her to ring the doorbell or knock, but she just walks right in. I follow closely behind her.

"I'm here," Brynn calls out to the large house.

We follow the voices further into the space, walking into a large open kitchen and dining area. The second we step into view of the small crowd of people, and they look up to see us, the talking stops.

"The fuck you doing here?" McQuaid is the first to break the silence.

I bite back my smirk. "Brynn invited me." I drape my arm around her shoulders. The move makes her stiffen.

"As a friend," she quickly spits out. "Not even. Acquaintance really. I felt bad for him. A pity invite."

"You two talk?" Captain Collee steps forward, eyes locked on where my arm is innocently touching his sister's shoulders.

Baby Collee says, "no," the same time I say, "yes."

"She just felt bad that I was going to be alone today and invited me to join, not a big deal," I tell him.

Brynn moves herself out of my hold and beelines toward Chandler who's holding a baby in her arms. I watch as Brynn takes the baby into her arms, and it gives me a weird thought of how it may feel to see her hold my child like that. But I shake that shit away. I don't even want kids, so I have no idea why the thought even occurs to me.

Conversations start to pick up around us, Spencer starts talking to Brynn and Chandler while Vince and Jared go back to their conversation and who I can assume is Vince's sister and her husband join them. McQuaid just glares at me while taking a sip of a brown liquid. I start to walk forward, but I'm stopped with a hand on my shoulder.

"I don't know what the fuck you think you're doing but knock it off. Be pissed at us, at the coaches, the organization, the whole fucking NHL if you want. But don't you dare try to take it out on my sister. She's not a toy and you know nothing about her."

I meet his threatening gaze. "I know more than you think. And she's not a toy, but she is an adult."

"After tonight, leave her the fuck alone, Wheeler, I mean it. She doesn't deserve to be a part of whatever game you're trying to play." He's keeping his voice low, so the conversation is just between us, not alerting anyone else around.

"There's no game, *Captain*, maybe I just like her and like I said, she's an adult. You may be able to control most of the team, and your weird little family, but you can't control everyone. Not her and especially not me."

"If you hurt her, I will kill you," he threatens, and I do my best not to smile.

"I'd like to see you fucking try," I practically growl before pushing out of his grasp and walking toward the rest of the guests, but right up to only one.

Brynn passed the baby to Spencer, so I come up behind her, wrapping an arm around her chest, pulling her body back into mine. I feel how she started to melt against me, but then freezes. I bring my mouth to her ear so only she can hear what I say. "Your brother just threatened to kill me if I hurt you, but what if he learned you liked to be spanked when I'm buried deep inside your cunt while you're begging for more?"

Her breath hitches and she looks around, probably making sure no one else heard, but then pushes my arm off her. I chuckle, standing up straight and the first person I see has their sights set on me is fucking McQuaid. The look he gives me almost seems like he heard what I said.

I know he didn't, but I remember what he said to me when we were stuck in the penalty box together where he already guessed something may be going on with me and Brynn. I may have just confirmed his suspicions, but I don't care.

I'd fuck her right here on the table in front of everyone if it wouldn't result in my dick getting chopped off by at least five people. But for some reason I do have this incessant need for it to be known she's mine.

Not forever, and not for real.

But at least for now, she's as mine as she ever can be.

Throughout the extremely awkward dinner I get looks that vary from questioning to threatening. Mostly from Chandler's boyfriends. Even Dumont, who tends to keep his distance from me, has sent a death glare in my direction every once in a while.

The only people that don't seem to care much about me is Dumont's sister, her husband, and their two daughters that they're busy wrangling.

"So, Colton, how are you liking Denver?" Spencer asks, attempting to break the obvious tension around the table.

"It's cold and I miss L.A., don't you?" It takes everything in me not to go off on how much I hate it here.

She looks up at her boyfriend, Jared, and smiles. They look at each other like no one else is here and it makes me want to gag. "No, I prefer it here."

"Cool," I mumble, looking down at my plate stacked with food.

The meal goes on semi uneventfully other than I'm bored out of my mind and getting annoyed with the looks I keep getting. And the lack of looks I'm getting from the woman I came here with.

I try to put my hand on her thigh, but she's quick to push me off. Which only pisses me off, so I bring my hand back, gripping her thigh and leaning down to her ear.

"Push me away again and I'll put my hand underneath that dress you're wearing and rip these sexy fucking fishnets to touch you in front of everyone again. Right here at this table. So, if that's what you want, then keep ignoring me and I'll make you come before dessert."

Brynn's eyes snap over to mine, and her breathing is rough, which is how I know my words are affecting her. She opens her mouth to say something, but another voice beats her to it. This one much deeper and across the table.

"What the fuck are you talking about over there?" Collee snaps and all eyes land on him. The look of shock evident for everyone since I don't think anyone has seen him lose his shit before.

A sly smile spreads across my face at the outburst. I go to answer, but Brynn stops me with a tight grip on my leg, digging her nails in so hard I might have marks, even through my jeans.

"Nothing, Colton is just getting a little tired and is going to take off early." Her eyes swing to mine. "Right?"

"Sure, I'll take Baby Collee home since she's getting tired as well."

"No," Captain Collee isn't yelling, but his voice is so deep and demanding he may as well be. And I fucking love that I'm getting under his skin. "I'll take her home."

"It's okay, I really don't mind." Brynn squeezes my leg even tighter as a signal to get me to shut up. "I'd hate for you to leave your family when I'm more than capable of it."

"Brynn is my family," he says darkly, glaring at me.

"Brent, it's fine. Colton can take me home, just drop it," Brynn announces, waving her hand between us.

"See, it's all good, Cap." I wink at him and his fists clench, but I watch as he tries to retain his composure and it makes me want to laugh.

"Anyway, pie party tomorrow," Chandler says, trying to diffuse the tense air of the large room. But it feels like the damage is done.

Though, I wasn't a dick, I just offered to take her home. Which means she has no choice but to come home with me.

A fter dinner is finished, I help with some of the dishes before being shooed away and into the waiting arms of my captor for the night.

Okay, I didn't go into his arms and I'm technically going willingly, but still.

We head out to his motorcycle, putting our helmets on to leave. "You know, by my standards you were a bit of a dick, so I don't think my condition was met."

"How was I a dick, Princess?" he asks, leaning back against the bike, folding his arms across his broad chest. I won't lie, he looks extremely hot like this, but I'll never tell him that.

"You argued with my brother," I say weakly because if I'm being honest, he really wasn't that much of a dick to anyone. He kept quiet and tried to tease me, but that was about it.

"He started it, I was just talking to you," he shrugs, turning and straddling the bike. "Hop on, we can argue at my house. You can get naked and try to distract me, so I'll let you win."

I roll my eyes, getting on behind him, barely having time to wrap myself tightly to him before taking off.

I'll never admit it, and I'll deny it if anyone ever asks, but I really like being on Colton's bike. The way the wind feels as he speeds down the street. How warm I feel with my body pressed up against his.

The part I'll *really never* admit, is how the vibration from the bike, combined with the way I'm hugging him, is turning me on more than it should. At one point I find myself shifting slightly, either to get more friction, or move away from Colton. But because my entire life is me being at war with myself, I'm not actually sure, which.

At one point we are at a stoplight, and he reaches back, wrapping his hands behind my knees, yanking me forward so I'm plastered to him completely. He lifts up the face shield on his helmet, turning back toward me, "If you don't stop moving around back there, I'm going to bend you over this bike when we get back, and spank you until you're screaming so loud my neighbors call the cops."

His words only make me squirm more, again unsure if it's in discomfort or because I can feel the wetness in my panties. Fuck this guy, seriously. I tighten my arms around him again as the light turns green. It's taking everything in me to continue to hold onto all the reasons I don't like this man. Other than how much of a dick he can be, he knows what he's doing when it comes to my body. Including all the right words to make it react to him.

Though, I never promised him anything sexual tonight. That wasn't a part of the deal, so as long as I can hang onto my self-control for dear life, I may be having some fun torturing him.

We get to his house, and I waste no time putting some distance between us as I get the helmet off and adjust my dress. Colton isn't far behind, taking his own helmet off and shaking out his hair. The second his eyes lock on mine he's closing the distance between us, gripping me by the back of my neck and moving to press our mouths together.

I stop him with a hand over his mouth, not breaking our eye contact. "I'm thirsty," I say simply, doing everything in my power to hide the fact that my heart is pounding.

His grip on me loosens, so I slide my hand down off his face, tracing a teasing finger down his chest before taking it away completely.

The look he gives me isn't mad or disappointed, but that same cocky smirk he always has, and I feel like he knows what I'm up to. "Then let's get you something to drink, Princess."

He leads me inside and I give myself a mental pep talk that I will get through the night without sleeping with him. No part of him will get to touch any part of me. Not tonight. I can control myself. I don't need to fill the loneliness void I have with him. Even if it feels good at the time.

And kind of afterwards.

He's never hurt me or anything.

Maybe he's not that bad and I could just enjoy this.

No. Fuck, Brynn, stop it. This is how I've continued to get myself into these situations.

Tonight is going to be different.

Which is what I keep reminding myself as Colton leads me into his kitchen, gesturing for me to sit on one of the barstools as he starts to make some drinks.

"I just want water," I say flatly after he's already mixed the drinks.

He chuckles, gulping down one of the drinks in one swallow. "Water it is."

He gets me a large glass full of ice water I ignore, standing up to look around his house. I hear his bark of laughter behind me as I walk into the living room taking in the décor that was clearly done by a professional because there's not a single personal touch here.

I wonder if he has any pictures of his family anywhere, anything to remember his brother by. But I won't ask. Especially because I don't have anything to remember my brother by. Sometimes I wish I did, but there's really nothing that I could have since we didn't have very many personal memories together.

Making my way through the large space, I look at the artwork, one piece in particular catches my eye and try to decipher what the seemingly random color splotches could symbolize. This is why I could never be a part of the art world because it all just looks like random paint splatters to me. It's not exactly colorful, the background a tannish brown color while splotches of black and white decorate a majority of it with random pink spots on it.

I feel the second he steps up behind me, the woodsy smell mixed with the whiskey he just drank hits my nose right before his fingers gently move my hair from my shoulder, and he grazes his lips against the sensitive skin of my neck.

"What do you think this painting is supposed to be of?" I ask, making an extreme effort to sound unaffected by him.

He huffs out a breath that I thought would be annoyed, but it's more of another laugh. "Paint," he answers simply, sliding a hand over my collarbone and starting to move down my arm.

"But like what does it symbolize?"

"Hm," he stops his caress, stepping up behind me so I can feel the heat of him, but we aren't touching. When I glance behind me, I see him looking at the picture and he actually seems to be thinking about it. I'm kind of curious what bullshit he's going to spew. "I think it's about pain."

My head snaps back to look forward at the painting again, trying to see what he is because maybe he's actually taking this seriously. Especially when he continues.

"The black I think is the pain, and the white is happiness because it looks like they're battling. Then the pink is coming in and that's healing." He sounds so serious as he speaks, I'm unsure what to say.

I go with humor, turning back toward him, smacking his chest lightly. "You're drunk."

He looks down to me, and I catch the flash in his eyes, what

I think is the pain he sees. The pain that mirrors mine. But it's gone in a second as he slips easily back into the obnoxious man I know. "Not drunk. I am hungry, though. But not for food."

I roll my eyes, stepping away from him, brushing off the seemingly one good moment we had just then. "I want to go to bed."

"Damn right, Baby Collee." He steps up to me, but I stop him with a hand on his chest.

"To sleep. I said I would stay the night and not sneak out. I never said I would have sex with you."

"Yeah, okay, let's go to bed." His tone makes it sound like he doesn't believe me.

I don't really believe me either.

Of course, I was so sure I wouldn't end up coming over here that I didn't bring a change of clothes. Colton must notice my dilemma because as soon as we step into his room, he's grabbing clothes from his closet and tossing them onto the bed.

"Those are for you, Princess. Unless you'd rather sleep naked, which I would not be against."

I snatch the clothes and lock myself into the bathroom to change. His t-shirt falling to my mid-thigh, which feels nice considering I'm pretty tall for a woman, it's rare for me. I forgo putting on the boxers he offered since the shirt is long enough to cover my underwear.

Colton is already on his bed, reclined with an arm stretched behind his head showing off his muscular bicep. He's shirtless so I see all the toned muscles on him along with all the tattoos. I clench my thighs together at the sight but will my traitorous vagina to calm herself because she's not getting touched by this man tonight.

"I don't want these," I say, throwing his boxers at his face.

He pulls them off revealing his smile. "Oh, my dick can be inside you, but wearing my underwear is too much for you?"

I grumble, climbing into his bed, remembering that the stupid thing is softer than a magical cloud. Making sure to stay as close to the edge as possible so there's no way I could accidentally touch him.

Or accidentally find myself falling on his dick in my sleep.

Basically, I don't trust myself. And I know he won't tell me no or push me away. Colton may be a jerk, but he would never actually force me to do something I don't want to. He may be pushy, but at the end of the day I've wanted everything we've done. However, he will jump at the chance any time I give him the green light.

"Night," I mumble, pulling the blankets up to my neck and face away from him.

He just laughs at me. "I'm not tired."

"I am. Night."

"Want to watch a movie?"

I'm slightly taken aback from his offer. I was sure he was

going to offer something involving our clothes coming all the way off, not that. Looking over my shoulder at him skeptically.

"What kind of movie?" I ask because I'm particular when it comes to what I watch, listen to, and read. I'm easily bored, and it needs to catch and hold my attention.

He presses a button on a remote that has a piece of the wall opening to reveal a large TV. I roll my eyes at how fancy it is but decide against getting into a verbal sparring match with him for now. Instead, I sit up, letting the blanket fall onto my lap as Colton starts scrolling through movie options.

I pointed out a new romantic comedy that came out that I was actually interested in. "That one," I tell him.

"Good choice." He clicks on it, and I look over to see if he's joking, but it doesn't seem like it. "Want any popcorn or anything?"

I shake my head as I lean back against the headboard and pat my stomach. "No way, I'm still stuffed from all the Thanksgiving food."

He does the same, running his hand along his stupidly sculpted abs. "Yeah, me too, I'll have to go extra hard in the gym tomorrow to make up for it."

"Oh whatever," I mumble, sinking down slightly, folding my arms across my chest and focusing on the screen where the movie is starting to play.

"Come over here, Princess." Colton gestures in his direction.

I shake my head. "No way, this isn't going to turn into Netflix and chill. I'm going to stay comfortably on my side."

"This isn't Netflix, so I didn't think that at all. I just wanted to lay with you." He almost sounds sincere.

I try to read his expression, but he always looks like he's up to something and yet I give in anyway. Because I'm a pathetic excuse for a woman.

Okay, that's not true, but part of me is touch deprived, which has been the case my whole life, and sometimes it's nice to be pressed against a large warm body. That's it, it doesn't matter who that body is attached to in this case.

Which is why I scoot over an inch, but it's not enough for him, he wraps his arms around my waist and pulls me so I'm flush against him. His giant arm wraps around my shoulders as he sinks us down slightly. Eventually, I feel myself relaxing against him and it feels...good.

Too good because I don't even notice as my eyelids start to get heavy, and I end up drifting off before the movie is even over.

I rouse slightly when Colton pulls the blankets up, but the last thing I remember is being pulled tighter against a wall of muscle, lips touching my hair and I think I hear him say, "Sweet dreams, Princess." But I'm already asleep.

Chapter Twenty-Nine

WHEELER

24

The first thing I notice when I start to wake up is that my arms are wrapped around a woman. The second, is that her floral shampoo scent hits my nose and I just bury my face deeper into her blonde locks to get more of it.

She stayed this time.

We didn't fuck and I could tell that was her plan. For once in my life, I didn't even mind. Though, right now my dick has also woken up and is on another page. I'm hard as a rock and if she was awake, I know she could feel it against her ass.

As if she can hear my thoughts, she wiggles slightly which rubs up against me. I have to bite back a groan from the sensation. I lean forward, burying my face in the crook of her shoulder. She lets out a little moan while swiveling her hips again.

"Baby Collee?" I whisper.

"Mm," she murmurs.

"You awake?" I push her hair away so I can run my lips along her exposed skin.

She makes a noise like she's saying no, but the way she presses herself against me and rubs harder contradicts that.

"If you're awake, and you don't want me to start our morning by fucking you into this mattress, then you might want to stop rubbing your tight ass against my dick."

I hear the little moan she lets out, but she tries to hide it by turning her face into the pillow. I press harder against her so she can really feel how hard I am for her.

"What'll it be? Are you wet for me already? Should I enjoy your pussy for breakfast first?" I say while darting my tongue out to lick a line up her neck before biting her lobe lightly.

She turns on her back to look up at me, her hair is fanned out against the pillow, eyes squinted as she adjusts to waking up. She has a crease on her cheek from the pillowcase. But fuck she's as beautiful as ever.

I've always thought she was hot, obviously, but it was fucking with her I really enjoyed. Right now, though, I don't even want that, I just want her to tell me to make her feel good. She still hasn't said anything, so I lean down to press my lips against hers.

I'm barely a breath away when she says, "I need to shower." Her tone is harsh, and it has me pulling back to look at her, confused.

She presses her palms against my chest to push me off, and I let her, but unable to wipe the look from my face. "What's your deal?" I ask.

"I don't have one," she responds, stretching her arms up before getting out of the bed.

I get up to follow her. "You sure as shit seem like it. What just happened?"

"Nothing, I just need to shower then you need to take me home. I stayed the night like you wanted." She goes into the bathroom, turning on my shower. I can't even think about how comfortable she seems because I'm irritated at her blowing me off.

"You wake up rubbing against my cock and suddenly you hate me again?"

"I wasn't even awake. I didn't know what I was doing. Get out, I'm going to shower."

I lean back against the sink, folding my arms across my chest to show her I'm not going anywhere. Her eyes sweep over me for a moment before she shrugs and pulls my t-shirt off her body, and my mouth goes dry at the sight of her almost naked. She pushes off her panties a moment later and I have to clench my fists.

"What is with this fucking attitude?" I snap, annoyed with her blow off.

"I don't have one, but you asking that is going to make it worse." She steps inside the large rainfall shower.

I consider how this may backfire, but I don't care, I'm fucking annoyed with how she's acting like we didn't actually have a decent time yesterday and now she's being a brat to me again. In a single movement, I push off my boxer briefs and step into the shower.

She turns toward me, shocked, "What are you–"

I spin her around, pressing her against the wall, she lets out a yelp as the cold tile presses against her bare skin.

"You do have an attitude and I don't know why, but I think you need it fucked out of you." I press my front against her back completely so she can feel my erection against her ass.

"I don't need anything from you. Get out," she says weakly.

I thrust my hips against her, and she whimpers, but tries to smother it. "I think you need a couple orgasms so I can have nice Brynn back. I liked her." My fingertips graze her bare stomach, moving lower to the apex of her thighs.

"You get what you get," she breathes, but I feel how she adjusts her stance, slightly spreading her legs for me.

"And so will you. You're going to take what you get and you're going to thank me for it." I swipe a finger through her pussy lips and find the wetness there that isn't from the shower. *I fucking knew it.*

"I'm not going to thank–"

I pull my hand back and use it to swat a sharp smack onto her ass that has her gasping.

"You're going to thank me, Princess," I grit out, rubbing the area I just hit.

"You can't just—"

I spank her again and she moans.

"Can't what, Princess? You want to keep going? We could make this a full-on punishment if you want."

"I won't thank you," she says through her teeth.

I bring my hand back to her front to graze over her clit, which has her knees buckling. "You will," I say directly against her ear, ghosting my fingers over her most sensitive area. "Now, ask me to touch you. Nicely."

Her head turns toward me, and it makes me want to kiss her, but she doesn't get that while she's acting like a brat.

"Give me your worst, Wheeler."

Challenge fucking accepted.

I grab the handheld sprayer from the wall and turn it on, bringing it between Brynn's body and the wall. I spread her before aiming the water to hit her clit. The second it makes contact she moans, and I have to make sure she stays standing on her unsteady legs.

"That feel good?" I ask her.

She nods, and I take it away, making her let out a frustrated noise.

"Words, Princess. When I'm making you feel good you tell me."

"Technically it wasn't you making me feel good, it was the shower head," she sasses.

I drop said shower head, then press her completely against the wall with my large body, tangle one hand in her hair, and yank her head back so she's looking up at me.

"Talk back to me again and I won't make you come at all, is that what you want?"

She sinks her teeth into her bottom lip, and I can tell she wants to say something else but is taking my threat seriously. As she should. I raise an eyebrow, daring her to say it.

"If you don't, then I'll just do it myself. I don't need you," she seethes.

The smile that I let free is so sinister she has to know she just fucked up. She's going to learn how badly.

I pull her away from the wall and walk us over to the built-in seat in the large shower, pressing between her shoulder blades so she has no choice, but to lean forward and catch herself with her hands or face plant into the stone.

"You think you don't need me to make you feel good? You think you can do it better than me? You don't picture me telling you what a perfect little slut you are for my cock? Or how it feels when I'm inside of you? I know you do, which means every time you come it's because of me." I punctuate the last word with a sharp smack on her ass that has her gasping right before I shove two fingers into her drenched pussy.

She lurches forward and cries out but pushes herself back

harder on my hand as I curl my fingers to find the sensitive spot on her inner walls.

"Tell me, Princess. Admit you need me to make your cunt come harder than it ever has."

She shakes her head. "I don't think about you at all," she moans. I bring my other hand around to pinch her clit which has her screaming.

"My good little Princess wants to be a naughty little whore today, don't you?"

My words only make her moan louder as she grinds against my hand harder, doing her best to chase her orgasm. She clenches on my fingers, and I feel how close she's getting, so I pull them out and spank her ass once again.

She yelps and growls at the same time. She tries to turn around, but I don't let her, keeping a grip on her hip and grabbing a fistful of her hair.

"Colton," she whines.

Groaning, I rub myself against her bright red ass. "I fucking love it when you say my name, Princess. The same name I'm sure you're screaming when you touch your pussy thinking about me while saying you don't need me."

"Please," she cries.

"Aw, you want something, baby? You need something from me?" I tease.

"Fuck me," she pushes back against me.

I chuckle, letting go of my grip on her hair so I can fist myself, running the head of my dick through her slit, coating myself in her wetness. When I rub against her clit she tries to rub harder, but I pull back, rubbing myself up higher, up to her ass. When the head of my cock presses against her tight hole she freezes.

"Should I fuck your ass for the way you're talking to me? Leave your pussy needy and dripping for me?"

She squeaks out a little noise but doesn't tell me no. Interesting.

I shake my head, going back to run myself against the length of her slit again. "Nah, not today. I'd rather get inside your tight cunt again. That what you want?"

She nods furiously, trying to push back on me.

"Such a greedy slut for me, aren't you, Princess? For someone who doesn't need me, sure seems like you're pretty desperate for my cock."

"Colton, please."

"Such a good whore to beg for me."

I position the tip at her entrance, watching as I slowly start to push in, the way her pussy swallows me when she cries out, "Wait." I pause even though it's making my head spin not being able to slam into her.

"Condom," she breathes.

"I'm clean, but I'll pull out," I tell her. Needing to feel her bare, especially since I'm only an inch in and dying for the whole thing.

She nods. "I'm on birth control but pull out."

"I will see my cum dripping from your pussy one of these days, but today I'll settle for it marking your skin," I say right before slamming my hips forward so she's full of me.

Her body lurches forward as she screams, and I don't let up even a little. I set a punishing pace with my thrusts and have her struggling to keep up. I feel myself getting too close to coming, so I quickly pull out, maneuver her to sit on the bench, drop to my knees, and latch my mouth onto her pussy.

She cries out at the initial contact as her hands fly up to grip my hair, pulling hard to hold my face against her.

"You taste so fucking good, Princess, how did you ever expect to keep this pussy from me when it cries like this for me."

I flick my tongue against her clit quickly and I feel how her release starts to build, and that's when I pull away, sitting back on my haunches, looking up at her while dramatically licking my lips.

She lunges forward to crash our mouths together, licking her taste off my mouth and I groan against her lips as our tongues tangle together. This kiss is messy, chaotic, and fucking perfect. Without breaking apart, I spread her thighs, and push inside her once again. The feeling of her bare pussy squeezing me has my vision tunneling.

"Still think you don't need me?" I ask through gritted teeth as my release is inevitable, no matter how much I try to hold it off a little longer.

Brynn's hands latch onto my shoulders, nails digging into my skin as I pound into her. "I just...*ah, fuck* Colton, I, please."

"Please what? Brats don't get to come." I'm not able to hold back any longer, pulling out of her and fisting my cock, pumping it furiously for only a couple seconds before shooting ropes of cum on her soft skin, marking her body. My mind is completely fixated on one thing and that's how perfect she looks like this. A little pissed, a lot turned on, covered in my cum.

Most of all she looks like mine.

C olton washes my body with a gentleness I didn't think he could possess.

Except, I'm annoyed because he followed through on his threat and didn't let me come. My clit is throbbing. I feel so empty, and the repeated orgasm denial has me weak. I want to bitch at him more. Complain about how he used me, but I don't feel used with the way he washes me.

His rough hands lather me in soap before he takes the shower head, rinsing me off. When I think for a second, he may press it to my clit again as he gets close, he doesn't. I huff out a frustrated breath and all he does is smirk.

He washes my hair, working the shampoo on my scalp, rinsing it out then applying conditioner, running it through my strands.

We step out of the shower, immediately I'm wrapped in a warm towel. Sending a surprised look up to Colton, I don't even need to say anything when he shrugs. "Heated towel rack."

I roll my eyes at the pretentiousness. Of course it's nice, but unnecessary when there are people starving out in the world. My annoyance with him not letting me come is replaced with the distaste I always have for him.

Though, for some reason part of me doesn't want to feel like that. Which is the whole reason I was pushing him away as soon as I woke up.

I enjoyed waking up and having him right there. I liked how it felt. So, I had to remind myself who he is again and that we don't like anything to do with him.

Even if I ended up enjoying what we did. Everything except the fact that I am uncomfortably desperate for an orgasm that he refused to give me.

I look at my clothes, regretting not bringing something else, but I pull on the sweater dress and forgo the fishnets. Once I'm dressed Colton grips my hips, turning me to face him, sliding a hand to the back of my neck, forcing me to look up at him.

"If I didn't have to be on the team plane today, I would keep you here with me, bringing you to the edge over and over until you couldn't take it anymore," he tells me seriously.

"How sweet," I say sarcastically.

He drops his forehead to mine. "If you're a good girl and don't finish what I started then when I get back, I'll make you come so many times you pass out from all the pleasure."

"You'd never know if I did it or not," I retort.

"Oh, I'll know. Up to you, Baby Collee." He drops a quick kiss to my lips. He pushes his tongue in, to tangle with mine, but pulls away almost right away. "Let's get you home."

Despite my protesting to taking his motorcycle, I end up on the back of it once again as he drives me back to my apartment. I wanted the distance of a car between us because I'm not liking how jumbled my mind is when it comes to him, and I need to get it back on straight.

Luckily, with him leaving for a week I'll get the distance I need. I won't talk to him, won't think about him. I'll distract myself with my friends, my niece, maybe with my siblings if any of them would fucking talk to me.

I have enough on my plate to deal with, I won't think about Colton Wheeler for a single second.

"You really don't need to walk me to my door, I'll survive," I try to tell him as he's already following me off his bike.

"I want to," is all he says.

Once we are at my front door, I unlock it and try to rush inside. He grabs my arm, stopping me, turning me so he can press me against the wall next to the door before he kisses the life out of me. His mouth moves against mine. His tongue licks against mine desperately. When we break apart, both panting I don't even know what to say.

"Talk to you soon, Princess," are his parting words before walking back to the elevator.

I rush inside, locking the door behind me before pressing my back against it and breathing heavily.

Ellie looks up at me from where she's perched on the couch.

"Please don't judge me, I can't take it," I tell her. I swear, she rolls her eyes at me before dropping her head to rest on her paws.

I want to scream, but that may not go over well with my neighbors. Instead, I know I need to do something to distract myself and all the thoughts flying around in my brain. Christmas will be here soon, which means I have presents to buy.

Shopping is going to be my solution. Anything to avoid thinking about Colton for the foreseeable future.

———

WAY too much money spent later I have several large shipments on the way from my online spending spree. Evie is going to get spoiled to a point I'm sure Chandler is going to tell me to return most of it. She'll probably say the same for the things I got for her as well.

I hope I didn't get Audrey things she already has. Even if I did then, she has two.

Spencer is the hardest person to shop for because she has everything she could ever want or need. Doesn't matter because I'm always able to surprise her.

I got Brent, Bryson, and Bailey each a few things. Bryson might come visit, but I know Bailey won't. Which is okay because Brent has a whole storage closet full of presents he got her and Brandon. He would get presents for everyone every year just hoping we would all be together.

He's never told me that, but I found them when snooping through his house one day. We've never talked about it. And likely never will.

After much debate I even got something for Colton, which was only because I saw it and couldn't help myself. Not because I'm still thinking about him. I just enjoy giving presents to people. I think it's part of the result from not having anything growing up. I like to spoil those around me now that I'm able to.

Ellie of course is getting an extravagant Christmas as well because there's no way I could forget about her.

I flop back on my couch looking at the ceiling in the aftermath of my online shopping spree and wish that it made me feel better, but it didn't. As soon as my mind isn't distracted, I'm back to thinking about him. And the neediness he left me with by not letting me finish. I could take care of it myself and he'd never know.

Sliding my hand down my chest, I run my fingers across my nipples attempting to tease myself before sliding lower, under the waistband of my panties. Grazing my clit I suck in a sharp breath. Closing my eyes I try to picture someone else touching me. Of course, the only face that comes to the forefront of my mind is that of a big ass hockey player with light brown hair and blue eyes.

"Naughty little slut touching yourself when I told you not to," he says in my fantasy, making me rub my clit harder like he's here watching me.

I feel the tingling of an orgasm starting, but it feels just out of reach. I slide a finger inside myself and rub harder.

"Tell me you need me, Princess. You need me to make your cunt feel good."

I refuse for that to be true as I keep rubbing, pumping my finger but it's not enough. I press another one in and bring my other hand up to play with a nipple as I work myself. The release is dancing right there, I can see it, but as I feel like I'm getting closer it moves further away. It's right there.

"Admit you need me," his voice growls.

I scream out in frustration, removing my hands from my body at the realization I can't fucking do it. It's like my body won't let me. It has to be him and that pisses me off even more.

My phone rings and I look over expecting it to be him like he knew what I was trying to do, how it failed, and how he expects to punish me for it. But when I see it's Bryson it's like a bucket of cold water was poured over me as I answer.

"Hey, everything okay?" I ask because it's so rare he actually calls me.

"Yeah, just realized I, uh, never called you back before."

"Oh, yeah, it's okay. We missed you for Thanksgiving yesterday." I pick at a piece of lint on my couch cushion.

"Yeah," he sighs. "Sorry, I was with Emma's family," he sounds nervous telling me this.

I perk up. "Who's Emma?"

"My girlfriend."

"You never said you were seeing someone," I scold.

"Do we all need to update each other when we are dating?"

"I mean, no, I guess not. Just didn't know."

"Sorry, she's great, you'd like her."

"Are you going to bring her to visit for Christmas?" I ask hopefully.

"Oh, I don't know if we will make it out there."

I deflate. "But you haven't even met your niece yet."

"I know, I'll try, okay?"

"Yeah, okay." I know he can hear the doubt in my voice.

"Are you okay?"

I sigh, gnawing on my bottom lip debating if I should say something to him about Colton. He's my older brother too, and maybe he would talk some sense into the situation since he doesn't know him, but he knows Brent.

"I'm actually seeing someone too." I cringe because I don't think that's what this is, but I'm not going into more detail.

"Yeah? Who is he?"

"He, uh, hah, well get this," I hesitate, "he's one of Brent's teammates."

Bryson is quiet on the other end of the phone, and I want to take it back. Tell him I was kidding or something.

"Does Brent know?" he finally asks, and his voice was so low he actually sounded like our oldest brother for a second.

"Not exactly."

I don't know what I expected, but the last thing was for him to laugh. Yet, that's exactly what happens and not just a little laugh. No, like hysterical, gut clenching laughter. "What I wouldn't give to see how that goes over when you tell him."

"If it gets you to come here then maybe I will," I grumble.

His laughter finally subsides. "Seriously, though, Brent is going to lose his shit."

I roll my eyes. "Yeah, okay, thanks for that. It's nothing serious so he doesn't need to know."

"Whatever you say, sis."

"Have you heard from Bailey?" I ask as a change of subject.

"Just a text once in a while. I doubt she will be around for Christmas either."

I sigh. "I know."

"Hey, I'll try to come visit, okay?"

"Okay."

We say goodbye after a couple more minutes of general

check in and I'm glad he called me, but part of me still feels extra lonely not even knowing my brother was dating someone. Add in the fact that he hasn't come to meet Evie yet.

I'm hit with a memory that I suppressed like most of my childhood.

"Do you think it'll always be like this?" I ask Bailey one night as we lay in our shared twin bed.

Brent and Brandon got into it again, but Brandon seemed different. He was talking weird, and he's lost a lot of weight. He looks like one of those skeleton Halloween decorations.

"No, I think it'll get better when we are all grown-ups," Bailey replies softly.

Brent told us he has to go away because he got a hockey contract. I don't know what that means since he plays hockey here, I don't know why he has to go away to do that. But he said he will be making money doing it. A lot of money. And will take care of us.

Bryson will help take care of us like Brent has. Which is why he and Brandon had another fight.

Bailey and I tried to hide, but they were so loud, and our trailer is so small, we can't go far.

"When we are grown-ups can we all be together? I don't want everyone to leave like Brent is." My eyes start to fill with tears thinking of our oldest brother having to go away.

"We will. The Collee's will always stick together, we all help take care of each other," Bailey says firmly.

I nod, wiping my eyes.

At that moment I believed her. Now, we're adults and I've realized what a fucking lie it was. Of course, at the time I was only eleven and Bailey was thirteen so we didn't know any better.

Yet, now, the Collee's are the furthest thing from together and at the end of the day all I want is something I've never really had.

A family.

My family.

We board the plane to head out to our first stop on this weeklong road trip. I'm refusing to think about the fact that one of the stops we have is in Calgary. My mom might try to get me to see her if she bothers to look at the schedule.

Though she probably doesn't even know I've been traded to another team and thinks I still play in California. I do have one thing to do during that stop. The one thing I do every time we have a stop in Calgary. It can be hard when we have a quick turn-around, but I'll always figure out a way to make sure it happens.

I go see my brother.

After I'm settled in my seat on the team plane, I close my eyes and listen to the music blasting in my ears. No one will try to talk to me, but then I think about Brynn. I glance around briefly to make sure her brother isn't breathing down my neck before pulling out my phone.

> Colton: You better be following directions like the good girl I know you want to be.

Baby Collee: You'll never know either way.

> Colton: Oh, I'll know. I hope when I come back in a week it'll be to reward you, not punish you again.

Baby Collee: Guess we will see.

"What're you grinning about?" A voice says next to me, and I look up to see Colver looking at me from across the aisle.

"Nothing," I mumble as I go to start my music again because I didn't even notice it stopped playing.

After starting it up again, I lock my phone and raise my head to find Colver still looking at me. I take an earbud out, "What?"

"Just curious about something."

I swear all these guys are so chatty on the team plane it's like a fucking gossip session on here half the time when I'm just trying to tune them all out.

"What are you curious about?" I ask with a sigh, so he knows how annoyed I am.

"Are you still friends with Richardson?" Referring to Kenneth Richardson from my old team and I just scoff.

"No, I was never friends with him, he's a prick."

He nods. "Yeah, I don't know what Spencer ever saw in him."

"Same," I agree because it's true. Spencer was always way too good for him, and I think he knew that which is why he used her the way he did. I've heard rumors about shit he would do on the road, but never paid attention to him to know if it was true.

"I know you don't like being on this team, but at least you don't have to deal with him anymore."

"Just another group of assholes," I gesture toward McQuaid in particular.

"He's not that bad if you get to know him."

"I'll pass, thanks Colver." I put my headphones back in because I'm done with social hour.

Though, being friendly with Brynn's best friend's boyfriend may come in handy. I'll have to keep that in mind, but for now he doesn't seem to completely hate me and that may be good enough.

———

WE MANAGE A WIN AGAINST VANCOUVER, and then head to our next stop, Calgary. I was surprised when I went to plug my phone in at the hotel last night that it lit up with a text.

Baby Collee: Congrats on the win.

Colton: Thanks, Princess. What do I get?

Baby Collee: That text and a virtual high five.

Colton: How about you tell me if you figured out you need me yet?

Baby Collee: You'll figure it out when you get back.

Colton: Can't wait.

Now, we're landing close to my hometown, and I look out at the scenery as the plane hits the ground. The bus takes us to the hotel, and I stare out the window the whole time as the memories come back like they always do when I'm here. The good, the bad, and the worse.

At the hotel, we all go up to our rooms and I'm quick to change and leave because we're heading out right after the game tomorrow afternoon, so this is the only chance I have. I get a ride-share to come pick me up and take me to the cemetery a town over. Pulling my hood up over my head as I walk the familiar path to my brother.

His headstone is simple.

> Joshua Wheeler
> Son and brother
> Forever loved

I threw a fit about it at the time. That didn't encompass who he was as a person. He was only ten when he died, but those ten years were so full and that's all they could come up with. Of course, it wasn't up to me, and my parents did what they wanted anyway.

Sitting down in front of the grave, I wipe away the dirt and grime that is covering the stone.

"Hey bro," I say, resting my arms on my bent knees. "Sorry I can't come see you that often, you know how I used to play in L.A.? Well, I got traded to Denver, our biggest rivals. It's been rough, but I'm sure you would love to give me shit."

I chuckle remembering the dumb little fights we would get into.

"I miss you every day, you know?"

The inevitable tears start to well in my eyes when I really think about how much I miss him. There's not a day that goes by where I don't think about him.

"I met a girl. You'd like her. I bet you and her would gang up on me and she'd probably like you more than me anyway." I smile, but it only makes the sadness worse knowing Brynn will never get the chance to meet him.

I can picture it so vividly, though. The way they would have exchanged embarrassing stories about me and probably plotted some pranks to play on me together. I can almost imagine the conversation I would've had with Josh about her.

"Pretty sure you've met my dream woman," he'd tell me.

"Back off and get in line, this one is mine."

"She likes me better; you're too mean for her."

I'd laugh. "She likes me mean."

"Fuck, man, I wish you were still here." The tears come down and I can't stop them. I just want him to say something. Anything. Just give me one more minute with him. To hug him, say goodbye.

Doesn't matter how long he's been gone I always wish we had more time. Time I'll never get back. Which is when I have to remember the last thing he said to me and it's when I pull myself together enough to say goodbye. His last words to me play back like he's saying them in real time.

"Live for me."

The same words I have tattooed on my chest over my heart.

"Bye, Josh. Love ya."

By the time I get back to the hotel I'm emotionally exhausted. All I can do is collapse on the bed and go to sleep. The weirdest part, though, is at this moment when I usually want to be alone, I'm wishing a certain blonde woman was here with me. Because all I want right now is to have her wrapped in my arms and that's the image I have as I fall asleep.

I have yet to hear back from Kenneth's publicist so I'm hoping whatever they're trying to deal with has been snuffed out. Or at least they have decided to keep Spencer out of whatever it is. Either way is fine with me. I have enough going on myself I don't need to deal with anything involving that asshole.

Speaking of assholes, Colton is coming back today, and I'm conflicted.

On one hand, the distance from him is nice because it helps me not feel like I'm going insane because when he's nearby I seem to lose all rational thought. On the other hand, I have yet to get myself off without him and aside from that, I kind of miss him.

Ew, who am I?

Colton sent me a text before their plane took off earlier and I'm pacing thinking if I should pull a disappearing act on him or just go with the flow. I feel like my hard to get game has been thrown out the window at this point and wonder what would happen if I gave in and stopped fighting. Maybe it would take away the fun for him and he would finally leave me alone.

Which I may not want anymore.

Sighing, I look back at the texts he sent and decide I'm going to try going along with it. Just this once and if it backfires then I'll have proved that everyone eventually leaves.

> Colton: Get ready for a ride.

> Colton: On my bike, get your mind out of the gutter, Baby Collee.

The weather is cold, so I dress in jeans and a hoodie over my long sleeve t-shirt before plopping onto my couch. Ellie hops up next to me, settling in her spot on the cushion next to mine.

"Are you going to be nice to him again?" I ask. She settles with her head on her paws, and I take that as a yes. I hope we both don't regret it.

It isn't much longer before there's a knock on my front door. I take a steady breath before opening it to reveal the tall, broad, tattooed hockey player whose life mission is to bother me to the point of insanity.

At least it used to be.

"Hey Princess," he greets with a wide smile as he steps forward, taking my face in his hands and pressing a hard kiss to my lips before I'm even able to say anything else. The kiss effectively steals my breath away, but also ends too soon. "If I tell you I missed you, will you admit you did too?"

"I'm willingly going with you, let's not push your luck," I retort.

He chuckles, "Get your pretty ass on the back of my bike." He taps said ass as I walk back to grab my phone and keys.

We get outside and I let him put the helmet on me, adjusting it for me before putting on his own. I get on the motorcycle after him, plastering my body against his, wrapping my arms tightly around him. He starts the machine and the loud engine and vibration underneath us has me tightening my hold before he takes off.

I'm unfamiliar with the roads we're on, but I hardly focus on the surroundings. I'm mostly focused on the way I'm holding onto Colton. How my legs are hugging his hips, how the spot between them is pressed against him as the bike vibrates. If I wasn't already so pent up from the last time we were together and still not getting any relief I may be able to control myself.

But that's not the case, which is why I find myself slightly rubbing against him just to get some steady friction. We end up at a stoplight on a deserted street. Colton lifts up his visor and turns to look at me over his shoulder.

"You keep rubbing your pussy on me, we aren't going to get to where we're going," he threatens.

Leaning into him even more. "You going to fuck me in the middle of this intersection instead?"

"Don't tempt me, Princess. I'll do it."

The light turns green, and Colton waits an extra beat before taking off once again. We continue on the mountain roads. I'm unsure where we're going and for once not even worrying about it.

We slow down and he parks in a dirt lot, but there's no one else around as we get off the bike. When I take in our surroundings all I see is frost covered trees.

"What is this place?" I ask.

"A place to be alone." He shakes out his hair after taking off the helmet.

"Because either of our places isn't 'alone' enough for you?" I joke.

"You caught me, I wanted an excuse to have you pressed against me."

I let out a small grin, walking toward him until our chests are almost touching. "And now what are you going to do about it?"

"You're going to tell me one thing first."

"What?" I narrow my eyes, wondering if this is going to ignite another fight.

"Did you come while I was gone?" He smirks like he already knows the answer.

"If I did?"

"Then you'll be punished again." He leans closer, his lips grazing my ear, "But this time it would be for lying to me."

"How would you know I'm lying?"

"Because, Princess, I can feel how needy you are from here. You're needy for something only I can give you and we both know it."

My thighs press together at the reminder that he's right. He's so right, but I don't want to admit it. I refuse to admit it. I can't admit it.

"Answer me. Did. You. Come?" He crowds me against the side of his bike. I love that I can look up at him since it's so rare for me but at six-foot-five I have to crane my neck to meet his stormy eyes. And once I do, I forget about fighting this. Just this once.

"No. I tried, but I...I couldn't," I practically whisper the last word.

He's on me less than a second later. One hand tangled in my hair, the other wrapping around me as his mouth attacks mine in a vicious kiss. It's like he's making up for the last week as he kisses the life out of me. His tongue invades my mouth, teeth nipping at my bottom lip. There's no sweetness between us. This is pure primal lust and need.

Which is why I can't help the way my hands slide up his shirt, feeling the hard muscles underneath. I run my nails along his abs, and he growls against my lips before biting them so hard I'm yelping which only makes him plunge his tongue in deeper, kissing me even more thoroughly than before which I didn't think was possible.

Colton pulls his lips away from mine, but his grip on my waist tightens like he's struggling to hold onto his control. And there's something about that which makes me want to jump him even more.

"You couldn't make yourself come? Not even when you thought about me?"

I shake my head.

"Not even when you thought of the way it feels when I'm eating your delicious pussy? The way she's always so desperate for me?"

I take in a quick breath, and clench my thighs even tighter, needing some sort of friction as I shake my head again.

"Not even when you thought about how it feels when my cock is inside you? When I'm fucking you so hard and all you want is more."

I bite back a quiet moan. I can't even respond anymore; I just need him to touch me.

"None of that was enough to get you off? You need me to help you, Princess?"

I nod. "Please, Colton."

"*Fuck,* I love the way my name sounds coming from your mouth. Let's see how loud you can scream it."

His mouth is on mine again, and he's not stopping, but I don't want him to. Ever. His hand moves from my hair to collar my throat and I'm melting in his arms. His grip on my waist tight as he holds me against his body where I feel the hard erection press against my stomach.

I want more.

I *need* more.

Reaching down between us, I undo his belt and unbutton his pants eagerly. He chuckles against my lips.

"So eager for me, Princess. Need me to make your pussy feel better? So desperate for me to make you come."

"*Please*," I reach into his pants to grip him tightly in my fist.

He only allows me a single stroke before pulling my hand out, grabbing my hips, turning me roughly, and shoving me down against the motorcycle. He covers my body with his, so I can feel him against my ass.

He speaks as he reaches around, unbuttoning my jeans, "Told you, I'd bend you over my bike. Now I'm going to fuck you like this to remind you and your cunt why you couldn't come without me."

Colton shoves my pants and underwear down just below my ass, pulling back to look. "Already dripping for me. You and your pretty pussy have been missing me."

I muffle my whimper with my arm, but I know he heard it anyway when he chuckles.

"Don't worry, baby, I'll be taking care of both of you. I know you want to be a good girl for me this time."

I try to shift my legs slightly, but they're trapped by the fabric around them. It doesn't matter anyway because Colton is back to touching me, sliding his hand up the back of my thigh, up to my ass and I almost collapse over the semi-innocent, barely there touch.

"Colton," I whine when he continues trailing his fingers along my skin, but never touching me in any spot that I want him to.

"Yeah, Princess?" I hear the smirk in his voice, but I'm at a point I don't even care anymore. I want the depraved things only he can give me. I want it all.

"Please fuck me."

He groans, leaning over me again, "I knew you could submit so beautifully for me."

Without wasting anymore time, he brings his hand around, running a finger along my slit. I want to spread my legs wider but can't. Then he shoves a thick finger inside me, and I cry out from how good it feels. Mine didn't even come close to how it feels when it's him and I'm already about to combust from just this. Since I can't move my legs apart it's a tight fit and I don't care, I just start to grind against his hand, chasing the orgasm I've attempted to give myself.

"So desperate, so fucking needy all for me. Your pussy is soaked, I'm going to make you come on my hand, then I'm going to taste how much you've missed me before you get my cock. How does that sound?"

I nod. "Yes, please, I just need ah–" I can't finish my sentence because he curls his finger, rubbing against my G-spot and I see stars. This time my knees really do buckle, but he uses his other hand to hold me up.

"I know what you need."

And he does. He *really* does.

Which is only proven more when his palm rubs against my clit while rubbing my inner walls and I'm detonating in only a few seconds. The orgasm hits me so hard I couldn't hold back my scream if I wanted to. I'm pretty sure I black out for a second at the power of the release.

I think I hear Colton praise, "That's my girl," but I really can't be sure because I swear, I lose the ability to see and hear for a second as my body comes down.

Before I'm even fully aware again I'm being turned around, lifted, and laid down on the bike seat. I'm barely able to lift my head in time to watch Colton rip my pants all the way off, drop to his knees, throwing my legs over his shoulders, and burying his face between them.

My head falls back on a loud moan the second his mouth is on me. I'm overstimulated, but also wanting more. Already feeling myself building toward another orgasm the moment his tongue flicks against my clit. I squeeze my thighs against his head, and he groans against me, licking a long languid trail up my pussy before looking up at me.

"Keep squeezing my head, Princess, the next time I have you in my bed you're going to sit on my face so I can drown from how much I make your pussy flood for me."

Diving back down, he sucks my clit into his mouth, and I cry out again. One of his hands slides up my body, under my shirt, squeezing a breast, he roughly pulls the cup of my bra away to tug at my nipple at the same time his tongue dips lower, fucking me with it.

It has taken effectively no time at all to be close to yet another orgasm and I want to be embarrassed by that because it's just proving him right even more, but I can't fight it. Everything feels too good, and I might actually lose it if he were to stop.

"Give it to me," he says against me, moving back to my clit, flicking his tongue against it rapidly. When he presses two fingers inside, I lose it, crying out another orgasm. There's an unfamiliar flooding feeling and when I'm able to I look down at Colton worried about what just happened.

His chin is actually dripping and the smile on his face has me confused and mortified at the same time.

"Wha–" I start to question, but he rises up, standing over me.

"You squirted, Princess and that was the prettiest thing I've ever seen. Open."

I don't have it in me to question anything anymore. So, I do what he says, opening my mouth slightly, but he grips my chin, opening my mouth wider, his thumb pulling my bottom lip down. He lets the mix of his spit and my cum fall into my mouth, landing right on the tattoo I keep hidden.

"Now, that's a good girl for me." His thumb rubs along the two words inked there.

Flicking my tongue out, I lick his finger, tasting the tang from my cum mixed with him. He pushes it in further into my mouth, closing my lips around him and sucking. I graze my teeth lightly across his skin and it has him pulling out of my mouth quickly replacing it with his lips on mine roughly.

He kisses me like he needs me more than air and I take it all greedily. Wrapping my legs around his waist I attempt to push his pants off with my feet, quickly becoming frustrated when it's taking too long.

Colton is clearly impatient at this point too because he works them down enough to free his dick from the confines, lines up with me and shoves forward, fully seating himself in a single thrust. I scream at the quick intrusion, clenching down on him as I try to adjust.

"There she fucking is," he practically growls.

I melt against the bike seat where I'm still lying, my head falling off the edge because I can't hold it up any longer. Suddenly, I'm being lifted up into his arms. I wrap my legs around his waist and my arms around his neck.

With an impressive show of strength, he holds me up completely while pulling back, then thrusting forward again. I can't help but meet his thrusts, grinding as best I can from this angle.

"Bounce on my cock, Princess, you can do it. Take what you need from me." He grips my thighs tightly, guiding me to do what he's demanding.

It's a little hard at first, but then he groans, and it lights a fire inside me that has me doubling down as I move harder and faster against him. He continues to fuck up into me while I bounce and grind. My moans increase as I feel another orgasm starting, but then he lifts me off him, and bends me over the bike again.

There's no more teasing or taking anything slow. This is pure primal need as he slams into me again, this angle hitting everything I need perfectly. When his hand comes down slapping against my ass I push back harder.

"That's it, you're doing so good. Give me one more."

He rubs the area he just hit, then slides his fingers to where we're joined, collecting the wetness I'm dripping with before moving up to my ass, and pressing a finger to the tight hole, not pushing in just adding pressure. I moan and push back, silently giving him permission.

The second the tip of his finger pushes inside I lose it. Coming so hard I lose my balance. Colton pushes his body against mine, keeping me up as his thrusts increase as he chases his own release.

"Ask for my cum, Princess. Ask nicely for me to fill this pussy up."

I'm so drunk on orgasms and the perfect way he's filling me now just makes me want more and to never stop. Which is why I say words I never thought I'd say to Colton Wheeler.

"Come inside me, Colton, I want to feel you leaking out of my pussy."

That does it for him.

He comes with a loud groan, and I feel his cock swell right before he goes off, completely filling me.

We are both sated and breathless. I wait for the regret to kick in, the urge to push him away. But it doesn't happen. Not even when he pulls out, swiping his fingers up my thigh where his cum is dripping out of me. Not even when he uses those same fingers to push it back inside me.

"This is the prettiest thing I've ever seen. You did so good for me." He presses a kiss to the side of my head.

With a gentleness I didn't know he possessed, he helps me get my pants back on. I'm not sure what to say, and once we're both dressed, I expect him to rush to get us out of here and take me home.

Instead, he pulls my body against his, and kisses me. This time isn't rough or rushed, it's soft and almost...sweet. His tongue teases my lips and I let him in. He kisses me tenderly like I'm something precious to be savored.

When we pull apart, the look in his stormy eyes is something I don't think I've ever seen before. I don't know what it means, and I refuse to read too much into it.

"Let's go to my house," he says, brushing his thumb against my cheek.

All I can do is nod.

As we drive back to his place I can't help but wonder what's happening. I don't hate it, but I do know that it's scaring me. I've been comfortable with my dislike for this man, but right now that's not what I'm feeling.

Not even close.

Chapter Thirty-Three

WHEELER

24

I'm sure Brynn would rather I take her home, but I need her in my bed tonight. I've been away from her for a week, and I want her around longer. Which is new for me. I've never felt that way about a woman before. Ever. Usually once we're done, I can't get out of there fast enough.

Not Brynn.

She also nodded, and I may have fucked the thoughts from her head, but she agreed and that's all I needed.

I fucking missed her while I was gone. I hated how that felt, but being around her again feels so good it makes me not want to be apart. But I know I have to. My schedule is crazy during the season, and I still don't think she even likes me. So, I'm taking what I can get.

The drive back is quiet between us. I would think she's sleeping, but her hold on me remains tight so I know she's awake. At one point we stop at a stoplight, and I can't help but reach back to squeeze one of her thighs, running my hand along it as well. I keep my hand on her until I need it to turn.

I just want to keep touching her.

Once we get to my house, I park in the garage, removing both our helmets. I scoop her up with one hand around her back and the other under her knees. She wraps an arm around my neck to hold on.

"I can walk you know," she snipes as I walk us inside.

"I think you could, but I probably fucked the ability out of you."

She rolls her eyes, but I catch the small smile she lets out before turning her head away. I bring her directly into my en suite bathroom, setting her on the vanity so I can fill up the bathtub for her.

"I didn't bring a change of clothes again," she says once I've felt the water is warm enough for her.

"Good, you can wear more of mine. Arms up."

"Colton," she scolds with a sigh.

"Baby Collee, let's not fight. You're tired and if you argue with me it only makes me hard for you which means I'll have to fuck you again and I was going to let you go to sleep. Up."

This time she listens, lifting her arms so I can remove her shirt, then her bra. I bring my knuckles to my mouth, biting at the view. "I may have to fuck you again anyway," I tell her as her rosy nipples peak, practically begging for my tongue and teeth on them.

My eyes flick up to hers and I see the exhaustion there, so I hold back my own need to make sure I take care of her.

Another first for me.

I guide her off the counter, she holds onto my shoulders as I gently pull off her jeans and underwear. The beast inside me that's dying for her again is close to losing it when I feel how wet her panties are with the mixture of our cum. Knowing she still has mine inside her makes me want to fill her again. It's taking every bit of restraint I have not to right now.

She's naked, and I help her into the large tub. After she's settled, she leans her head back and closes her eyes, sighing at the feeling of the hot water.

"I'm going to get you some clothes." I press a kiss to her temple, and she sighs, sinking lower into the water.

I bring back a t-shirt and a pair of my boxers I'm hoping she will wear this time since her panties are essentially fucked. She hasn't moved so I take it upon myself to clean her. I take a wash-cloth, getting it wet and putting soap on it as I wash her body gently. She lets me do it, which is how I know she's extremely tired.

When I bring the washcloth between her thighs she sucks in a sharp breath, before relaxing further as I clean there. It makes me want to touch her like this, someday, but not today. Once I'm done, I unplug the tub and bring over a warm towel, holding it open for her. She stands and I wrap her in it immediately, lifting her and setting her onto the cool floor that I wish was also heated.

I dry her off thoroughly before putting my clothes on her. She doesn't fight me on any of it. After she's dressed, I pick her up again to carry her the short distance to my bed, laying her down, then pulling up the blankets.

She looks up at me, watching as I take off my shirt and pants, climbing in my side next to her. Wrapping my arm around her waist I pull her against me.

"I know you're tired, but I have been dying to know the story behind your tattoo." I can't help but bring it up.

She breathes out a light laugh, tucking her face into the pillow. I think she's not going to answer me, but then surprises me when she does. "I mean I think it's pretty obvious to you my...preferences in the bedroom. And I don't know I thought it would be a fun little secret to have for just me and whoever discovers it."

I tense at the thought of anyone else discovering that *little secret* she has. I don't want any other guy to experience what I do with her. None of them could give her what she needs like I can. I don't like that anyone has discovered it before me.

She clearly feels my reaction because she chuckles, rubbing my arm banded around her waist with her soft fingers.

"Calm down over there. We both know you have had quite the past and I'm not jealous or weird about it," her tired voice teases.

Part of me wishes she would get jealous about my past, that

would show that maybe she cares even a tiny bit. The reminder hits me that she still doesn't like me. And that only makes me feel like I do. That my feelings have shifted in a way I would have never guessed. I feel her soften in my arms, her breathing evening out so I know she's asleep.

I lay awake with the terrifying realization that I may be falling in love with the woman in my arms. I don't just like her, we've moved past that and are flying headfirst into dangerous foreign territory for me.

If only there was a chance she could ever love me back.

———

MY ALARM WAKES me from a dead sleep, and I turn it off quickly, so it doesn't wake up Brynn. She stirs slightly but ends up snuggling closer into my hold. I wrap my arms around her, tightly, not wanting to have to leave and go to practice.

Women never come to my house because I never want them to stay. Brynn is the first woman who has been in my bed, and I don't ever want her to leave it. Which is why when I finally have to get up or be late, I'm careful to remove my hold from her as I get out of bed.

Even as I pull on my sweatpants, hoodie, and tennis shoes I keep my eyes on her as she stays passed out in my bed. *Mine.*

I'm dragging my feet, but when I can't wait any longer, I grab my gym bag, leave a quick note for her on the counter before heading out the door.

At the practice arena I barely have enough time to change into my gear before the time we're expected to be on the ice. I may do what I can to piss off the guys on the team, but pissing off the coaches for being late to practice is not the way to go. Plus, I could get penalized by the organization and that's the last thing I need right now.

My skates hit the ice with less than a minute to spare and everyone is already starting their warmups. I do the same, keeping to myself as I always do.

There's a moment when I look up and see Collee looking at me. Part of me wants to ask what his deal is and make it known that I left his sister in my clothes in my bed before coming here. But I don't. Because for the first time since any of this started, I don't actually want to fuck this thing up with her.

These feelings are fucking weird.

I break my gaze away from his and get back to stretching.

We start on drills and I'm standing behind Dumont as we wait to run the drill when he turns toward me, "You good?"

I raise an eyebrow at him. "You care?"

"No, just thought it's weird you haven't tried to piss anyone off today, thought maybe you're sick or something."

I scoff, "Not sick."

He looks at me for a second longer like he can see what I'm hiding and who I'm hiding but then it's his turn to run the drill. That breaks the weird little stare off we had going on for a second. I skate forward when it's my turn and race through the drill.

Afterwards, I skate to the bench to grab some water and Collee skates up next to me. "Wheeler," he says, curtly.

"Collee," I do the same.

"You talked to my sister lately?" he asks.

It takes effort to suppress my smirk, the fact that he's actually asking me this. Especially here, it seems so out of character for him, and I can't help that the little part of me that still enjoys pissing him off is happy about that.

Yeah, Cap, she was just screaming my name last night and I left her in my bed this morning. Hoping for round two after I'm done here.

Instead of saying that I just shrug. "I don't really share my personal business with people."

I know my response pisses him off even more, but I skate back out onto the ice to continue with practice. I do my best to keep my focus on hockey for the remainder of practice, but it's impossible to forget what's waiting for me when it's all over.

Chapter Thirty-Four

BRYNN

I wake up alone in Colton's bed. It's so unbelievably comfortable I don't want to leave the softness of the mattress, the pillows, the blankets. Add in the fact that I can still smell him, and it makes my insides feel warm.

Throwing an arm over my eyes, I groan not liking my body's reaction. Forcing myself to leave the comfy cloud, I decide to take advantage of being alone here to do something extremely important. Snoop through his stuff.

Since I'm not sure how much time I have until he gets back, I start in the bedroom, quickly glancing in the night-stand and dresser drawers. The nightstand has a box of condoms which is to be expected. Though, despite what I said last night, I can't help the jealous thoughts of who else has been in here. In his bed. Maybe he's left them like this to snoop too.

I shake the weirdly jealous thoughts away and continue my searching. I make a pit stop in the kitchen to get a drink of water, which is when I see the note he left me.

BABY COLLEE, I HAD TO GO TO PRACTICE. I'LL BE BACK SOON WITH COFFEE.

NO NEED TO RUN AWAY, I'LL TAKE YOU HOME.

XX

COLTON

Glancing at the clock, I'm not sure exactly what time his practice is or for how long, but I assume I don't have a ton more time before he comes back. I find myself peeking into rooms to see if any of them may have something interesting. Which is how I ended up finding an extra bedroom that had a pile of boxes in it.

When I open the first one, I see a variety of sports memorabilia. Mostly hockey, but there's a stack of baseball cards and a deflated basketball. The next box has pictures. I instantly recognize Colton, he's younger and he's with the boy from the obituary I found. Josh.

They're both smiling in every single photo I find. Josh is on Colton's back; another one he's pretending to choke him and Colton is making a dramatic face. Another is them both asleep on a couch with the tops of their heads touching. Another is both of them in hockey gear. Josh is several inches shorter than Colton, but they have matching eyes and beaming smiles as they lean on their respective sticks.

I go to pick up another stack when a deep voice behind me makes me jump, dropping the pictures instantly.

"What are you doing?" Colton questions.

I stand up instantly, even though he already caught me. "I was just looking."

His eyes move from me to the box. "Find what you were looking for?" His voice is sharp.

"I don't know what I was looking for," I answer honestly, looking down at my feet. "What happened to him?" I dare to ask.

He doesn't say anything right away and I finally lift my gaze up to his. I expect to see him angry, but I don't. He looks...hurt. I open my mouth to tell him I lost my brother too, but can't make the words come out, so my mouth closes again.

"You ready to go home?" he asks, and my shoulders that I didn't even realize were hiked up, deflate.

I thought maybe he would share something with me. Share a part of himself with me that could show that he's a human under his tough exterior. A human with feelings and that those feelings could maybe be shared with another person. But he doesn't. He shuts down just like I do, which is why I can't even be upset about it.

The only thing I can say is, "Yeah."

He doesn't follow me when I go back to his bedroom to change back into my clothes. Though part of me wants to keep his t-shirt on, I reluctantly change back into my own sweater. When I walk out to find Colton, I see him staring at the painting in his living room again. I don't think he notices me yet, so I just take a second to look at him.

His light brown hair is slicked back and slightly damp from the shower he clearly took after practice. I can see the bulge of his muscles underneath his hoodie as his arms are crossed across his chest. The sweatpants he's wearing hug his thick thighs. While his body is mouthwatering as always, I'm drawn to his eyes staring at the splattered colors. His silver eyes look conflicted while lost in thought.

I shift on my feet, and a floorboard creaks, making myself known. He looks over at me, but the look on his face doesn't change.

"You ready?" His tone is flat.

"Yeah."

We go to his garage and I'm a little surprised he still wants to take his motorcycle; I figure he would want some distance from me with the way he's acting. Even after he helps put my helmet on and we're on the bike I try not to be plastered against him, but he grabs the backs of my knees and pulls me forward so I'm as close to him as possible.

When I wrap my arms around his middle, I rest my helmet against his back and try not to think about how disappointed I would be if this was the last time I got to feel him.

We get to my apartment sooner than I would like but I pretend like I'm okay like I always do. I'm standing when I hand my helmet to him, and he has taken his off as well and takes mine.

"See ya around I guess," I say when the silence between us has gotten awkward.

I turn to walk away, but I'm stopped with a warm hand on my wrist. He doesn't say anything, just pulls me back toward him.

Giving him an expectant look because he's giving me mixed signals right now, I realize I should probably apologize, and I start to do just that when he finally speaks.

"I'm not mad at you."

"You seem like it," I retort, automatically regretting it. I don't mean to be bitchy with him. I'm the one who messed up here.

He just shakes his head. "I'm not, I just," he sighs, "I don't talk about him. With anyone."

I can't help it; I close the small distance between us so I'm standing right in front of him as he still straddles the bike. Lifting my hand, I brush my fingers through his hair softly.

"Maybe you should," I tell him. Fully realizing the giant hypocrite I'm being right now. "It could help."

"If I don't talk about him, then sometimes I can pretend he's still here." His deep voice sounds so vulnerable, and it makes my heart crack for this giant man in front of me.

"I understand. I really do," I agree. I never forget that Brandon is gone, but if I don't think about things too deeply, or talk about them I can pretend my family isn't so broken.

He brings his hand up to the back of my neck, pulling me down the couple inches to meet his mouth in a gentle kiss. Just a simple pressing of lips. His tongue teases mine slightly when I open for him, but everything about this kiss is delicate. Even his grip on the back of my neck isn't rough, but more comforting.

"Come to my game tomorrow." It's not a question, but I nod anyway.

With another kiss I'm tempted to invite him inside, but I know that's not a good idea. Clearly, we are both in weird head-spaces now and I'm still not supposed to want him. We break apart and he gives my neck one final squeeze before letting me go. I instantly miss the warmth, and only grow colder each step I take away from him and I don't even think it has anything to do with the weather.

"I'll see you tomorrow, Princess. I want to see you in a jersey, preferably mine," he calls after me and the side of my mouth kicks up in a smile, noticing his teasing is back.

"You'll get what you get, Wheeler. You'll be lucky if I even show up," I sass.

He smiles, pulling his helmet over his head and kicking the bike into gear. I turn to walk into my building when I hear him rev the engine and then take off. Finally feeling like I can catch my breath.

One thing is for sure, there's no way I can show up tomorrow wearing his jersey. We both know it, but I do have an idea that might make it fun to mess with him a little bit.

———

"BRYNN!" Audrey greets as I step into the friends and family suite at the Dragon's game. She's wearing one of Charlie's jerseys like a dress with black boots that reach over her knees.

"You look amazing," I tell her. I wish I had the confidence to pull off what she's wearing. Since I'm on the taller side even an oversized jersey would be way too short on me. Which is why I have leggings under the Collee jersey I'm wearing, paired with black ankle boots.

She spins, making the jersey rise a little bit, but not enough to reveal anything. "Thank you, so do you. I'm sure Brent *loves* you wearing his number."

I roll my eyes. "He couldn't give a shit. He used to bring me to every game and even then, wouldn't make me wear a jersey."

"And what does Colton think?" She gives me a knowing look.

My eyes widen at her. "He shouldn't care."

She looks me up and down with a smirk, "He'll care."

"You're crazy. No alcohol for you tonight, you're already on something."

She laughs. "Just high on orgasms, my friend. Always just high on orgasms."

I bite the corner of my mouth on a laugh, turning to hide the blush because I'm not going to admit I know how that feels. She would never judge, because Audrey is the least judgmental person I know, but I still can't bring myself to tell her.

"But seriously, I'm drinking. Do you want anything?"

"I'll take a seltzer, but I'll come with."

After we grab our drinks, Audrey convinces me to go down to the ice level with her for warmups. I'm reluctant because I have seen hockey players stretch more than I ever should in a single lifetime, but she guilts me by bringing up that Chandler isn't here to do it with her because Evie is struggling with sleep, and she was actually asleep when she would've had to leave for the arena and wasn't going to mess with that.

Which is why I'm standing here as the players skate out of the tunnel. Audrey cheers next to me, especially when she sees Charlie. After the guys skate around for a minute, and shoot some pucks toward the net, Charlie skates by where we're standing, taps on the glass with his stick, and winks at his girlfriend.

My eye catches on another player who is currently across the ice, on his knees, stretching out his groin. His gaze is locked on mine as he does the warmup exercises.

"Your boy is showing what he's going to do to you later," Audrey jokes.

I snort out a laugh, breaking the intense eye contact with Colton. "He wishes."

"I bet he does," she says, bumping my shoulder.

After warmups are over, we head back up to the suite. I'm still nursing my drink, but Audrey gets another one on the way up. We're joined by a few other WAGs who have always been decently nice to me, but I think it's because I'm a family member, not a WAG, so they don't hold the same judgements I know fall on Chandler and Audrey.

I'll always stick up for them, even though I know Audrey can more than handle anything thrown her way.

The game starts and I can already tell this one is going to be intense with the way both teams are going at each other from the second the puck drops.

Throughout the first period each team draws multiple penalties, but it's the second period when things start to heat up. Vince gets checked face first into the boards so hard he falls, and Matt is on the other player within a second, but the whistle blows and they're pulled apart before anything else can happen.

My eyes find Colton, unsure of how he would react to the scrum because he's always down for a fight, but I don't know if he would actually defend any of his teammates. He's standing, leaning on the boards like he's ready to jump out onto the ice.

The player who checked Vince gets a boarding penalty and the Dragons start their power play and try to use the one-man advantage to score the first goal.

I notice a certain player keeps messing with Colton, enough to be annoying, but not enough to draw another penalty. I'm impressed as Colton focuses on the puck and doesn't give in to the antagonizing.

That is until that player gets the puck on a breakaway and all the energy is on chasing after him to stop him from getting into the Dragons zone. Colton tries to regain possession of the puck, swinging his stick, doing his best not to draw a tripping penalty. He doesn't get it before the player reaches Colver, and instead of trying to shoot from a normal distance, he keeps going way too fast, then trying to shoot when he's too close, hitting Colver with his stick moments before crashing into him.

The arena erupts in anger for the outrageous move by the opponent. The anger quickly turns to cheers as Colton has grabbed the player by his jersey, yanked him up, and is pounding his fist into his face repeatedly.

The rest of the team joins in, causing an all-out line brawl. Colton and the other player are the center of it all, and despite the efforts from the refs he's not letting up. They're both on the ice, helmets knocked off, blood contrasting the white. I find myself biting at my thumb, worried for the source of the blood, but from the look of everything I don't think it's from the man I know.

The brawl is put to a stop, and I watch as Colton and the player are separated and sent to their respective tunnels. Other players are sent to the penalty box, but it's clear those two have been ejected.

"Well shit, your boy is in trouble," Audrey says.

"He's a dumbass." I shake my head.

"You going to go check on him?"

My eyes swing to hers. "What? No, that's not allowed."

Audrey rolls her lips between her teeth. "Hasn't stopped Chandler...or me."

"What do you mean?"

"Just saying there was a game a couple years ago, Brent got hit pretty bad, Chandler went to check on him and–"

"Ew. Stop, too much info. Not needed."

Audrey laughs. "Just go, maybe he'll take his left-over aggression out on your body."

"If I get caught, I'm telling them my name is Audrey Hudson."

"Do it," she challenges, nudging me toward the elevator.

With a sigh, I go, knowing this is probably a dumb idea, yet I can't deny the idea of doing something so forbidden is pretty hot.

Fucking dumbass, thought he could get away with that dirty shit and now we are both out for the remainder of the game. I might get a suspension, but I don't give a shit. He deserved it, doesn't matter what team I'm playing on, you don't touch the fucking goalie.

He's lucky his stick wasn't a few inches higher because that would've hit Colver in the neck at the right angle. I'm fuming as I rip off my jersey and start taking off my gear while I wait for the game to end.

"Was it worth it?" A familiar feminine voice asks from behind me. I can't help the smile that pulls at my lips at knowing she came down here.

I turn around and my eyes catch on the Dragon logo across her chest on the jersey she's wearing.

"Turn around, Princess," I instruct, needing to know if she's wearing my name on her back.

Brynn folds her arms across her chest, looking annoyed already. "You sure you want to see whose jersey I'm wearing?"

"Better be mine."

Slowly, she turns around revealing the name and number on her back that aren't mine. Instead, I'm staring at "Collee 52" across her back.

"Hm," I hum, removing my shoulder pads so I'm shirtless as she turns back toward me.

"Disappointed?" she sasses.

Pushing off my pants so I'm just in compression shorts as I sit on the bench. "Get over here."

"I need to get back."

"Get your ass over here, Baby Collee."

Brynn walks closer, and I don't miss the way her eyes track over my chest as she steps up in front of me. I wrap my hands around the backs of her thighs, pulling her down so she straddles my hips, her hands resting on my bare shoulders.

I rub my hands up the sides of her thighs, pushing the jersey up slightly. "The only reason I'm not going to rip this off your body is because it's your last name. But if it was any other name this would be on the floor, and you would be forced to walk out of here in just your bra or with my name on your back."

"How generous." she rolls her eyes, and I'm already so pent up from the fight I feel the need to correct the attitude she's giving me right now.

Pulling her tighter against me, rubbing her pussy against my cock that's already wanting to break free of its confines, I say, "I may not do that, but I'm going to fuck you in this jersey. Because if you're not wearing my name you sure as shit are going to scream it."

"We're going to get caught." She tries to push away from me.

"I don't give a shit. My teammates can walk in and see me fucking you. That way they can know you're *mine*."

I see the alarm on her face and the retort on her tongue, unsure if it's because I actually called the guys my teammates for once, or because I said she's mine. I don't give her a chance to say anything else before slamming my mouth onto hers, silencing any questions, comments, or fucking attitude.

My hand slides up to her throat, using my grip to angle her head exactly how I want as I kiss her thoroughly. I want to take my time with her, but she's not wrong and we're going to get caught. There were ten minutes left in the period when I got ejected so we have less than that now. And I refuse to let her leave without feeling her sweet cunt.

Reaching my other hand into her waistband I'm immediately met with wetness as soon as my fingers graze her center.

"Fuck, Princess, you're so wet for me. You're going to take me so well while I fill up this pussy."

"Better do it quick," she pants, grinding against my hand, already using me to chase her pleasure. I want her to do the same thing on my dick.

"Pants off, you're going to ride me," I say, pushing her off my lap so I can push mine down as well.

She wastes no time, pushing the tight leggings off before climbing back onto my lap. With a grip on her hips, I hold her above my erection, and don't let her drop down.

Brynn whimpers, trying to fight my hold, but I don't let her.

"Colton, *please*," she begs, and my eyes practically roll to the back of my head at the sound of her begging. It breaks the last bit of my control as I guide her hips down, her heat wrapping around me, and I can't help the groan that comes from the back of my throat.

"Fuck baby, do you know how good you feel?" My fingers dig into her hips hard enough I'm sure I'm going to leave bruises, but it just makes her start to move. "Use me to make yourself come; I want to feel your tight pussy strangle my cock."

"*Yes*," she cries, throwing her head back, as her hips start to work harder. Bouncing on my lap and grinding against me every time she drops down.

I move one hand up to the back of her head, fisting her blonde hair, pulling it back so she's arching as she continues to ride me. Moving my thumb to her clit, I rub tight circles the way I know drives her crazy.

"Come for me, Princess."

I pull on her hair a little more and she moans at the bite of pain, along with the way I'm toying with her clit as she chases her orgasm. I feel her getting close with the way her walls start to grip me. I continue to rub her as she starts to buck against me, losing her rhythm right before I feel her tighten as her plea-sure consumes her.

It takes everything in me not to blow, but as soon as she comes down, I stand, holding her against me, setting her on her feet, and guide her to bend over, then end up on all fours on the small bench. I kneel behind her, slamming into her heat.

She cries out, and I bring my hand around to her mouth, muffling her sounds as I snap my hips hard against her. I'm staring right at her back that has the glaring name and number right at me. I grip the jersey in my free hand, bunching it up, using it as leverage to fuck her harder.

I can feel her moans and cries against my hand, but she continues to push back against me with each thrust and I'm fucking possessed with the need to claim her. There's nothing I want more than for everyone in the fucking arena to know she's mine. Including her brother.

Which is why I start to fuck her even harder, hitting her as deep as possible with each thrust.

"Come for me again, I need you gripping my cock so tight while I fill you with my cum."

I think she moans my name against my hand, but I can't tell.

"Do you want that? Want me to fill up your needy cunt?"

She nods against my hand, and that does it. I slap a hand on her ass, causing her to moan and clench against me. I'm so close I'm not going to be able to hold back much longer. Letting go of my grip on her jersey, I reach around to rub her again and she detonates seconds later. I'm not able to hold back any longer, leaning over her back as my own release consumes me.

I don't even try to stop my own groans as I come deep inside her. The way she's tightened around me, I couldn't pull out even if I tried.

Once I come down, I pull out slowly, seeing my cum start to drip out of her, and I can't help, but push it back in. If this is our secret, and no one else can know she's mine, I'm going to make sure at least she knows it.

I want to leave with her. I want to make sure she's okay, but the buzzer goes off signaling the end of the period and it pulls Brynn out of the sex induced haze she was in, and into a panic. Which is obvious with the way her wide eyes swing up to me.

Grabbing her pants, I hand them to her. "Hide in the shower, no one is going back there during intermission."

I lightly push her in that direction, adjusting my pants back to cover my deflating dick right as the first of the guys enter the locker room. I'm met with a glare from McQuaid, disappointed looks from Mann and Dumont. Captain Collee is who I try to avoid because I just fucked his sister in his jersey while she's now hiding only a few feet away full of my cum.

Yeah, I don't need him looking at me right now.

Of course I get reamed by Coach for being ejected, but luckily the intermission goes quickly, and everyone is heading back out onto the ice.

I feel like I'm in the clear, but Collee is the last to leave and before he steps out, he turns toward me. "You may think I'm an idiot, but I know more than you think. Consider that before you try anything else with my sister."

I don't know what to say because there's not a chance he knows she's hiding in here. He has to be talking about something else, but either way I have nothing to say right now. This isn't the time to tell him what's going on, and it really isn't the time to try and voice my feelings because if I was ever going to do that, I would need to tell her first. And I have no idea where to even begin.

After he leaves, I go to the showers to get Brynn who is dressed, which is slightly disappointing.

"What do you think that means?" she asks, panic evident in her eyes.

I cup her face, brushing my thumbs across her cheeks as I take her in. Something about the way her bright green eyes are looking up at me, and the way she slightly melts into my touch, has me falling even deeper in this moment.

"I don't know, but everything will be fine," I try to reassure.

The look she gives me seems like she doesn't believe me, but I lean down, pressing my lips against hers lightly. When I pull back I just look at her, and don't miss the way she looks back up at me.

For the first time it seems like I might not be alone in my feelings. But I know that neither of us are going to say anything about it.

"Go back, Princess, I'm sure your friend is worried about you."

She chuckles. "I'm not sure worried is what she's feeling."

I press another chaste kiss to her lips before sending her out with a pat on her ass. She glances back once before walking out of my eyesight.

Fuck me, I'm so fucking gone for that woman.

The season has become intense for the Dragons now that they are in the thick of it, leading up to the holiday season. After the new year it's going to be even crazier with the build up to the playoffs. I know this is when I know not to bother Brent as much, but I know Chandler is going to need more help with Evie.

Help I'm going to be more than happy to give because I need the distraction. Ever since Colton fucked me in the locker room my head has been a mess when it comes to my emotions.

Over the last couple weeks since that happened, we've seen each other a handful of times and I've done my best to make sure it was purely sex. No sleep overs. No talking about anything outside of what we are doing. Only physical.

The last time I saw him was right before the team was going to their last away game before Christmas and as I was getting dressed, I was tempted to ask what he was doing for the holiday. I knew that could easily lead to him joining my Christmas and we don't need a repeat of Thanksgiving.

I really don't need any other reason to fuel the emotions toward him.

Now, it's Christmas morning and I spent last night wrapping all the presents I got for everyone, mostly Evie, and am shoving them all into my car to head over to my brother's house. I almost tried calling Bailey, but then didn't want to start the day off on a negative note when she inevitably doesn't answer. Though, I know I'm going to end up trying later. Bryson too, since he did decide to go to his girlfriend's instead of coming here.

Jared and Spencer went back to their hometown in New York. Charlie and Audrey are at his parents so it's going to just be me with my brother's family. I shake away the pang of disappointment that I'm not showing up with someone who I'm sharing my life with. That my whole family won't be there. I wish things were different, but I slam my trunk shut, letting the sound pull me back to reality and am determined to enjoy this day.

My phone goes off after I climb into my car. For a moment I think it might be one of my siblings, but when I look down and see Colton's name, I can't deny the mix of disappointment and excitement hearing from him. Instead of acknowledging the text, I turn my phone on "do not disturb" and toss it into my purse, vowing to ignore it for the rest of the day.

Once I get to my brother's house, I do my best to bring all the gifts in with one trip. I'm struggling to balance it all and have to use my foot to knock on the front door. I'm pretty sure it's all going to come crashing down when I hear it open and a male voice says, "Whoa, let me help you out there."

Vince takes some of the packages from me which lightens

the load significantly and I don't feel like my arms are about to give out.

"Hi!" I call out in greeting to the house.

"Aunty Brynn," Chandler's cheerful voice calls back.

I find her sitting in the living room with Evie dressed in festive Christmas footies lying on her chest. Vince and I drop off the presents under the large tree in the corner of the room.

"Those better not all be for Evie," Chandler scolds.

I place my hand on my chest, feigning a gasp, "Of course not. What kind of an aunt do you think I am? One that is going to spoil that little precious bean rotten?"

Chandler is quiet for a few seconds, narrowing her eyes. "Yes."

Smiling wide, I respond, "You're right, but there's presents here for everyone, not just her."

Brent walks into the room with a large cup of coffee he hands to Chandler. She looks up at him and I see the love written all over her face the second her eyes meet him. The pang in my chest increases at the sight. I see my brother give her the same love filled look and it's a look I've only ever seen him give Chandler. He never brought girls around when we were younger. I'm sure he had girlfriends, but I never met any of them until her.

Because I'm needing to break some of the tension in my own chest, I do what I do best, which is joke to lighten the mood. "That's enough, break up the love fest and let's open some presents. Brent," he looks over to me, "I expect to find something fancy and expensive from you."

He comes around to sit next to Chandler on the couch. "Speaking of spoiled," he retorts.

I smirk until I realize he's referring to me, "Wait, what? I am not."

"Are you kidding me?" he scoffs.

"I'm not," I insist again.

He just looks toward the large pile of gifts I brought with me like that makes his point.

"How does that prove anything? I'm a *giving* person."

"Okay the two of you, it's Christmas, no arguing is rule number one." Chandler attempts to mediate.

"Bunny making rules? What are the other ones?" Matt chimes in, entering the room and taking a seat in the open spot on the other side of Chandler.

"Rule number two is that you get to deal with all dirty diapers today." She smiles sweetly at Matt who frowns.

"Yeah, I was hoping for rules that are more fun. Maybe a little sexier." He wraps an arm around her shoulders.

She smacks his chest lightly with the back of her hand. "Rule three is not to make Brynn uncomfortable."

I raise my hands, shaking my head. "I only get uncomfortable when my brother starts to talk. Or move. Or breathe."

"You have never been good at following the rules, must be the whole *spoiled* thing," Brent says with a glare in my direction.

"That's not arguing, right, Chan?"

She shakes her head. "Vince, help," she calls out.

Vince comes running back into the room like there's an emergency. As soon as his eyes lock onto Chandler and Evie his posture softens seeing that there's not an emergency.

"Why did you call for help?" he asks, concerned.

"I need a buffer." She smiles at Vince which makes him immediately relax even more. I can see the way he actually melts for her.

That damn pang is back. I rub my hand against my chest trying to make the feeling go away.

"Why am I not enough of a buffer?" Matt asks, offended.

"You're the cause of most of the problems, you can't be a buffer," Vince rolls his eyes.

"It wasn't even me this time, it's those two," Matt says as he gestures between Brent and me.

"Present time!" I announce because clearly they will keep going. I may not want to know much of anything that goes on in this house, but I will admit I am curious how those two both live here and don't kill each other.

I'm sure Brent has to step in quite a bit, just like he did with Brandon when we were younger.

Chandler and I open the presents with Evie, while she mostly sleeps through it all, only waking up and looking at the toys that make noises. I got her lots of things that she can't use for a couple months, but I don't care. At least she will have them when she gets older.

The day goes on and I can't help but start to feel like an outsider to the family they have started. Obviously, Chandler does what she can to include me, but it doesn't matter because seeing how they all are together makes me see how I truly don't have a place within their close knit group.

I'm sitting on the couch after dinner, watching Vince and Chandler play with Evie while Matt watches with a small smile on his face. Brent was cleaning up the kitchen, but then I feel him sit next to me.

"Are you okay?" he asks.

I do my best to relax my posture because I realize how stiff I've been sitting.

"Yeah, I'm fine. Why?"

He shrugs. "You just looked a little zoned out."

"I'm just tired, I should probably head out."

"You going to see Wheeler today?" he asks suddenly, taking me aback.

"No. Why would I see him?" I try to act like that's completely ridiculous, but the way my heart sped up at the sound of Colton's name.

"You saw him on Thanksgiving."

I sigh. "I get you're looking out for me, but I've told you before nothing is happening with him. Nothing will happen with him. We can't stand each other, and it was a one-day pity truce." The lie tastes bitter on my tongue. The more I say the worse the lies feel.

"If he ever tries anything you know you can tell me, right?"

"Oh my God, yes *Dad*. I get it, you don't have to look out for me anymore. I'm twenty-five and am able to handle the big bad world."

"I know you can," he agrees softly.

I leave not long after that, saying goodbye to everyone, giving Evie the most attention before heading out. The second I close my car door; the pain of the loneliness I know I'm going home to hits me. Which is why I pull out my phone for the first time all day and read the text Colton sent this morning.

> Colton: I know how badly you miss me. So, if you need to see me today, just say the word and I'm there.

I can hear the cocky tone he would have as I read it, and it makes me scoff. I don't want to admit he's right and I don't want to use him to cure the loneliness again. It's something I've been doing and part of me knows it's not healthy. There's only one way this ends and it's with me hurting.

Turning up Spencer's latest album, it doesn't matter how many times I've heard it, her songs resonate with me which is why I sing along to them the entire way home.

By the time I park at my apartment complex I'm still determined to not reply to Colton. I keep that commitment as I walk inside. Even still as I greet and feed Ellie. I continue to stay strong as I change into t-shirt and boy shorts.

But when I drop onto my couch, and the silence surrounds me, I give in.

> Brynn: Come over.

Colton: Demanding. I like it. Already on my way, Princess.

And just knowing he's going to be here has me feeling slightly better. Which makes me even more worried about how this is going to blow up in my face.

A s soon as I open the front door, I grab Colton's hoodie in my fist, yanking him toward me, crashing our mouths together. All because I don't want to talk, I just want to feel.

He goes willingly, thoroughly kissing me like he needs this as much as I do. When I start to rip off his clothes, he grabs my hands stopping me.

"Are you okay?" he asks, while I'm trying to break out of his hold.

"Yes, just fuck me."

"So, you want to be my good little slut tonight, Baby Collee, is that it?" His hold on my wrists tightens slightly.

"Yes," I breathe.

He takes my wrists in one hand and uses his other to pull my bottom lip down to reveal the tattoo there to him. "You're going to be a good girl for me then, and live up to this tattoo?"

To prove that I'm going to do exactly that, I drop down to my knees, while he keeps his grip on my wrists, so they are being held above my head. And I want it like this. I want him to use me. I want to show him I can be a good girl for him. I want him to take every thought away that isn't him and the pleasure between us.

Instead of trying to get my hands free, I look up at him and drop my mouth open, sticking my tongue out, silently asking for what I want.

"Oh, you're ready to be my fucktoy tonight, aren't you, Princess? Want me to use your mouth first?"

Keeping my jaw dropped and eyes locked on him I nod.

He works his belt and jeans enough to push them down so he's able to free his erection that springs up right in front of my open mouth. I can't help but swipe my tongue up the head, tasting the drop of precum that's already there for me.

"Fuck, Princess," he groans, grabbing the base of his shaft and guiding the head into my waiting mouth. "Close your lips and suck."

I do exactly that, bobbing my head as I do, taking him further into my throat each time to get used to his size yet again. It doesn't matter how many times I have him or in what way, I don't think my body will ever be used to his massive dick. Yet, I crave the slight bite of pain every time.

"Your mouth is so fucking good, baby, you suck my cock like

it's the best thing you've ever tasted, and I never want you to fucking stop."

I don't ever want to stop either.

I push him further into my throat, trying to tell him without words that I want more. He's holding my hands up by his chest, and I grip the fabric of his sweatshirt he's still wearing as some leverage. There's something even more erotic about this entire interaction with both of us still basically fully clothed.

"You want me to fuck your filthy mouth, Princess? Use you like the whore you are for me?"

I moan around him as I nod because that's exactly what I want. Use me. Take it all. Take everything.

"Slap my chest twice if it becomes too much, got it?" he says seriously.

I tap my hand once in confirmation. And that's when he lets his control go.

His hand not holding my wrists fists the hair on the back of my head, shoving me down so I'm forced to take him in further than I have been. I gag around him, but don't want him to let up.

"Breathe through your nose," he instructs through gritted teeth.

I do what he says, making my throat relax slightly so I'm able to take more of him. He pulls on my hair so only the tip remains in my mouth, before he pushes me back down again, this time I don't gag as he fills my throat. I swallow around him, and he lets out a loud groan above me. I can't help but smile.

He pulls me back slightly before holding my head while his hips thrust forward and all I can do is take it. Just like I've been wanting. He continues thrusting his hips forward, pushing himself into my throat while tears well in my eyes, and spit falls all around him and I've never felt so used and loving every single second of it.

"You're turning into such a mess for me, Princess. Such a pretty little mess, but you love it, don't you? Love being my perfect slut."

My eyes roll back at his words, my underwear are so drenched from everything that I know there will be no saving them. I want to touch myself, but I also don't want him to let go of my hands because I like being completely at his mercy like this.

His movements start to become erratic, and I can tell he's close, I don't want him to stop, despite my jaw burning and my arms going numb from being upright I never want him to stop. Yet, he pulls himself from my mouth and I make a noise I don't recognize in protest. Especially when he drops my wrists, my arms feeling like dead weight. I don't have time to think about that though because he's holding my mouth open with a thumb on my bottom lip, pulling it down. His other hand pumping his dick roughly until his cum shoots out onto my tattoo.

His moans make me feel even more powerful as his orgasm takes over. It makes me feel like I could come the second he touches me from how turned on I am.

When his pleasure subsides, my mouth is still being held open and I taste him on my tongue. He opens his eyes, looking at me, while I know I really am a mess, the look he gives me makes me feel like the most beautiful sight he's ever seen. His thumb runs over my lip where the black ink marks my skin, smearing his cum along it.

"Yeah, now that's my good girl," he growls.

Not a good girl. *My. Mine.*

And how in this moment I wish I really was his.

Instead of dwelling on how that single sentence is making me feel, I shift my legs trying to get some friction between my thighs to help the ache that's there.

"You need some help? You did so good for me, you want me to touch you?" Colton asks.

I nod with a small whimper.

"Aw, you need me to make you feel good?" he coos, reaching down to lift me up and taking me into his arms. My limbs feel weak as I wrap my legs around his waist as he walks the short distance to my bed, dropping me down onto it.

He doesn't waste any time shedding his clothes, revealing his toned frame that has my mouth watering all over again. My jaw may be sore, and I'm covered in tears, drool, and cum, yet I want to lick every inch of his toned frame. When his cock is free, I don't even think it ever fully went down because it already looks hard once again.

"You're looking at me like you want my dick in your mouth again." He smirks.

"Maybe I do." I smile.

"You will, but I need to taste your pussy and make you come at least twice before you get my cock again."

"What if I beg?" I taunt as he pulls off my t-shirt.

"I do love when you beg, but it's not going to work this time. I'm going to make you feel so good before I fuck you." He rips off my panties, seeing how wet they are, and his lips pull up. "Sucking my dick made you this wet, Baby Collee?"

I nod, closing my thighs, but he pushes them open roughly.

My instincts are to sass back, but I can't bring myself to do it because his head is dipping down, tongue running up my entire slit roughly. I throw my head back on a moan, and I already feel ready to combust.

My fingers grip his hair, yanking to hold his face right where I want him. Groaning, he follows my silent direction and keeps his mouth on my clit, flicking his tongue against the bundle and the noises he lets out sends a vibration through me that has me practically screaming.

"Please Colton, fuck," I cry. "Don't stop."

He hums again against me, and then pushes a finger inside and the orgasm crashes over me. It's almost violent in the way I can't stop shaking and screaming from the force of the release.

"Fuck, baby, do you know how good you taste? I'll never get enough of you," he says, lapping up my release, the tip of his tongue grazing my overly sensitive clit.

"Show me," I plead.

Colton looks up at me, and I won't ever get enough of seeing his lips glisten with my wetness while he looks at me from between my legs. I open my mouth to signal what I mean, but he understands instantly. Moving up my body, dragging his tongue along the skin of my stomach, over one breast, licking my peaked nipple, then the other one before holding himself up over me.

I stick my tongue out for him.

"Goddamn, look at you. Such a dirty slut for me wanting to taste yourself from my tongue."

I nod, tilting my chin up slightly.

He drops down, running his tongue up the side of my neck, to my chin, licking mine before pushing it into my mouth. He kisses me like he never wants to stop. Our tongues tangle as he devours my mouth, the taste of both of us on his tongue. I suck it into my mouth, wanting to be completely consumed by him at this moment and lose myself in all the feelings he can give me.

Suddenly, two of his fingers press into me once again and I gasp into his mouth at the invasion. He doesn't stop his fierce kisses. I grab the wrist of his hand that's pumping and rubbing my sensitive pussy.

"Fuck, wait," I cry.

"No. You're going to give me another one, then you're going to take my cock like the good little slut you wanted to be. You wanted me to use you so that's what I'm doing. I get to do whatever I want and you're going to fucking take it."

"I can't, too sensitive," I plead.

"You can and you will. Give it to me, Princess."

His mouth is on mine again as his hand works me closer to another release. This one is almost painful as it builds.

His fingers curl, rubbing my inner walls and my legs start to shake as the pressure builds. The mix of pain and pleasure that I crave, but fear at the same time.

"Look at you, shaking for me. Soak my fucking hand, baby, show me how ready you are for my cock to fill you up."

With another rough shove of his fingers, I'm exploding around him once again. Crying out against his lips that are swallowing every sound.

"Fuck yes," he praises as I come back down.

Without wasting any more time, he kneels between my spread legs that have fallen open from exhaustion and lines up with my entrance.

"Think you can take me?" he teases.

"Do I have a choice?" I reply breathlessly.

"Nope."

He pushes forward, burying himself to the hilt. I moan at the feeling, it doesn't hurt because I'm so wet from the two previous orgasms, but the feeling of being so full is overwhelming.

"*Fuck*. Your mouth may be heaven, but your cunt is going to send me to Hell, and I'll gladly take any punishment that comes with it."

I have no words to respond because he sets a punishing pace as he fucks me into the mattress and all I can do is take it, gripping the sheets in my fists for something to hold onto. It's amazing how quickly it feels like I can come again, despite just having two earth shattering orgasms back-to-back. There's something about the way he takes me that makes my body respond in the best and worst ways.

Best because I feel so wanted, so needed, so beautiful and perfect to someone.

Worst because it can't be him. It can never be Colton Wheeler.

Yet, at this moment nothing else matters except him and me.

"Come on, your pleasure is mine and you're going to give me what's mine."

"Oh *fuck*," I cry.

"Let it go, Princess, you can do it," he encourages, his thumb reaching down to rub my overstimulated clit, the same moment he pulls my hips up and angles his slightly to hit a magical spot within me.

A spot that has me falling apart so hard I swear I black out as the orgasm consumes me. I hear him groan as his hips pick up speed while his hands gripping my hips tighten so hard I'm sure there will be bruises, but I'm so lost in pleasure that it barely registers. It's when I feel his movements stutter and his noises become louder, I know he's coming as well.

Catching himself on his elbows above me as I register the sensation of him releasing himself inside me, and that only makes the aftershocks of my own release heighten as he fills me. I wrap my legs tighter around his hips wanting to keep him there.

We're both limp, and he rolls off me, starting to get off the bed, but I stop him with a hand on his wrist. He looks back at me with a questioning look.

"Stay," I say. I know I've had him leave every single time we've done this the last couple weeks, but something has shifted tonight, and I can't name it, but all I know is that I don't want him to leave.

His lips quirk in a small smile. "I was just going to get stuff to clean you up, Princess. I wasn't going to let you kick me out this time no matter what."

"Oh." I drop my hold on him in embarrassment.

He comes back with a damp washcloth, and carefully cleans between my legs before tossing it aside, pulling back the sheets and laying down as he pulls my body against his. The way his arm wraps around my middle as I feel his warm body against my back, I can't help but melt against him.

As I'm drifting off, I recognize how things have shifted between us and there's no denying it anymore, no matter how much I want to. I thought I couldn't stand him, and fought against that changing, but I can't do that anymore. I'm falling for Colton fucking Wheeler.

I wake up in the same place I fell asleep, which is wrapped around Brynn's naked body. Burying my nose into her hair I take in everything about her. How she feels pressed against me, how she smells like her shampoo with the mix of sex and me. I can't help but rub my already hard dick against her ass. She makes a soft noise, and I'm not sure if she's awake or not, but she moves herself against me in response.

"You awake, Princess?" I ask quietly against her hair.

"Mm," she hums, circling her ass again.

"You may want to answer me, because if you keep rubbing your ass against me, I'll think you want me to fuck it."

That gets her attention, she rolls onto her back, her exposed breasts tempt me to suck on her peaked nipples. But the way she's looking at me makes me want to just be with her, and stare. We've been fucking for weeks, and I'll never get sick of it, but this is one of the only times I've gotten to just look at her. Unguarded. Glowing and so fucking beautiful.

"What?" She shifts slightly as if she's uncomfortable.

"Just looking at you," I tell her honestly, which only makes her narrow her eyes in suspicion.

"Why?"

"Because you're beautiful."

Her jaw drops slightly before she takes her bottom lip between her teeth. I can't help but continue the honesty with her, taking it even further because for the first time in my life I'm wanting more with someone. I'm wanting more with *her*.

Brushing my fingers along her cheek, pushing her hair behind her ear then moving further to the back of her head, gripping her soft strands before dipping my mouth down to hers. I brush a gentle kiss to her lips.

"You remember that picture you found in my house?" I whisper.

Nodding, she places her hand on my chest, "Yes, but you don't have to talk about it. It's fine."

I take her hand in my own. "I want to."

She swallows roughly, and I give her hand a squeeze. "But I need you to have some clothes on because you're too fucking tempting lying next to me with your sweet pussy so close."

Chuckling, she rolls her eyes and moves to get off the bed. I watch her bare back as she stretches her arms up and continue to watch as she gets up and goes to her dresser to grab clothes. I can't help but think about how my cum is still inside her and how I want nothing more than to fill her up again.

But this is more important. She needs to know everything if there's any chance of this becoming more than just sex. I want her to know me. Then, maybe she'll let me know more of her as well.

She's in an oversized hoodie, some cotton shorts, and fuzzy socks as she curls up on her living room couch. I threw on my t-shirt and boxers to join her. I can see her nerves written all over her face, and I'm not sure if it's because she's afraid of how I'll react considering what happened when I found her looking at the picture of Josh and me. I never react well when people learn about him. I'm protective of him, even now, and I never know how to talk about him.

Brynn wraps her arms around her legs that are up by her chest, and she waits for me to talk.

I sigh. "Josh is my younger brother," my mouth already feels dry, "he died when he was ten."

She hugs her legs tighter, and I already see the pain on her face. "What happened?" her voice cracks.

Running my hand through my hair as I prepare to tell a story I have never told anyone before.

"He was born with a heart defect that required him to have surgery right after he was born. It was a success at the time and growing up he got to have a normal life. We would play hockey, though my parents didn't like it because it was too dangerous for him according to them. I was four years older, and never played too rough, but I also never let him win." I smile at the memories of us playing together.

"When he was nine, it got worse. He needed a transplant and was put on the list and would always say he would get his new heart. We talked about all the things we could do with his new heart. Even as he grew weaker, he was so determined to get that heart." I shake my head. "He didn't get one. His heart grew weaker until it just couldn't handle it anymore and he had to let go."

Brynn's eyes are filled with tears that match my own. I want to pull her into my arms and hold her, but I need to finish first.

"He told me to live for him. Those were the last words he said to me, and it's something I promised I would do. That's why I have the words tattooed over my heart, a constant reminder of that promise."

Tears fell down her cheeks, and I pulled her into my lap because mine are about to do the same and I want her as close as possible to me. She doesn't fight it, instead, she wraps her arms around my neck as she melts into me, and she cries against my shoulder.

I don't fight my own tears as they fall like I usually do, because right now my main concern is comforting her.

"I'm sorry," she whispers.

"No need for you to be sorry," I tell her.

She pulls back, wiping her eyes as she looks at me. The green irises seem so much brighter from her tears, and I can't help but wipe the wet remnants of her grief for me from under her eyes.

"I lost my brother too," she whispers so softly, almost like she doesn't want me to hear her.

"What?"

"Three years ago. My older brother."

"I thought it was just Brent and you?"

She shakes her head. "No. We have two other brothers and a sister. Well, I guess we had two other brothers. Bryson, Brandon, and Bailey."

"Why do you all have B names?"

That makes her chuckle lightly, "Not sure, my parents were always drunk or high so I'm sure it had something to do with that."

Her statement surprises me. I figured the Collees came from privilege like a lot of us have. My parents may have neglected me after Josh was gone, too lost in their own grief it's like they forgot I even existed. But there's no denying I had access to anything and everything I wanted and needed.

"What happened?" I ask, brushing her hair behind her shoulder, gripping the back of her neck and rubbing gently.

"Brandon always struggled with things. Brent practically raised us because he's the oldest, but those two were only two years apart and never got along. I don't know when Brandon turned to drugs exactly, but I know he never turned back." She's crying again and I wipe the tears streaming down her face because I want to just take all her pain away.

"I tried to help, I wanted to help so badly. I wanted Brent to help. I know he did what he could, but I just wish there was something that could have saved him."

Her sobs start and I pull her closer, burying her head in my shoulder, just holding her as she cries. I may have wanted there to be more for Josh, the anger I had about him not getting a heart in time has consumed me before, but at the end of the day I know there was nothing we could do. I can't imagine how she feels thinking maybe her brother could have been helped.

"Addiction is a disease, baby, an awful disease and there's nothing you could have done if he wasn't going to put in the work," I try to soothe her.

"I know, I just," she takes a shaky breath, burying her head tighter against me. "I want a real family."

Her words are like a dagger to my chest. I lost my family the day I lost my brother, and there have been times I wished for the same thing, but I can tell it's not in the same way as Brynn. I don't think she's ever had the family she wants.

"You do. You have your siblings. You have Chandler and your friends. That counts as family."

She shakes her head. "No. I don't have my siblings. I have Brent, yeah, but Bryson barely talks to me, he is so focused on his own life, acting like he's having fun partying and doing things I don't even want to know about. Bailey doesn't talk to any of us anymore. She used to, but it became less and less and now I feel like she's doing everything she can to distance herself from all of us to forget we even exist. I know I have my friends, but it's not the same. I," she sighs. "I don't want to be so broken."

"You're not broken. You could never be broken," I tell her seriously.

My words only make her cry harder, and all I can do is hold her.

When her crying slows, I hear her soft voice speak almost too quiet for me to hear, "You're not who I thought you were."

I don't have it in me to tell her, that's not true. I'm exactly who she thought I was, but because of her that's changing because now I want to be a man who actually deserves her. The *only* man that deserves her.

I t's New Year's Eve and my brother is hosting a party at his house for the whole team and their significant others for the holiday. I tried to tell him I didn't fall into either category, but he said I'm family and that counts.

I haven't seen Colton since he left after our emotional conversation the day after Christmas. We've texted, but he's been busy with hockey and for the first time I didn't want the distance from him. Something changed that morning and I know there's no going back.

Yesterday while we were texting, I asked about the New Year's party.

> Brynn: Did Brent invite you to the party tomorrow?

> Colton: Unfortunately, last I checked I'm on the team, so yeah, he did.

> Brynn: You can knock off the act, I know you don't mind your new team now.

Colton: I better see you there. I need to taste you again. And my cock misses you.

Brynn: Just your cock?

Colton: I guess the rest of me may miss you too.

I smiled at our exchange, though I didn't know what to say back. I miss him too, but my fear holds me back from telling him. I feel like once I say something that shows how I'm really feeling about him everything is going to explode in my face.

I get to the house early because I want to see Evie and make sure Chandler doesn't need any help beforehand. She has all three of the guys put to work setting things up while she cares for their child. Audrey is directing all the guys like a drill sergeant and I'm pretty sure her boyfriend is just drooling over her instead of whatever he's supposed to be doing.

Spencer said she was coming with Jared and I'm excited to spend some time with her, but I can't deny that I also want to sneak off with Colton at some point.

"Matt, what the fuck do you think you're doing?" Audrey snaps just as I walk into the living room.

"Moving the table where you told me to," Matt replies, his tone extremely annoyed.

"No, I told you to put it over there." She points to a corner. "That's the other direction. You get hit in the head with the puck lately?"

"Mann not fucking you good enough? Because you're being a real b–"

"Finish that sentence McQuaid I fucking dare you," Charlie chimes in, wrapping an arm around Audrey's shoulders.

"Don't be mad because you don't know how to listen," Vince says to Matt, shaking his head.

"Okay fuck all of you." Matt points around the room.

"Just put the table where she told you to, it's not that fucking hard." Vince rolls his eyes before resuming setting up the kitchen island.

"Who put you in charge anyway?" Matt grumbles, picking up the table once again.

"I did because I know she will put your ass in place when you need it," Brent says, coming down the stairs.

"Of course you fucking did," Matt mutters.

"Hey shorty," Brent greets me while I hold back my laugh from the exchange I just witnessed.

"It's like wrangling cats here, isn't it?" I tease.

"Speaking of, how's yours? Have you added any more cats to your collection because I think crazy cat lady would suit you." Brent smirks and I smack his arm.

"You're a dick, I have one cat. You should get a pet, might be good for you. Might I suggest something gross and slimy, so you have something in common with it?"

"Maybe I will. I'll make sure to get the biggest snake I can find, and you can be in charge of pet sitting for me."

I'm glad he seems to be in a good mood today, something I feel like I haven't seen from him recently and it lightens something in my chest. It's the same lightness I saw in Colton when I told him about everything and he told me about his brother. I would have never guessed we had something so huge and morbid in common.

"If you trusted me with such a creature, you would not come back to it alive." I shiver.

"You would kill it?"

"Absolutely not. I would leave the door open and let it make its own decision. Or you'd come back to a house full of different wild animals. Guess we'll find out."

Brent wraps his arm around my head, pulling me in for a hug. I want to tell him I miss him, and I've missed this between us, but I can't because I'm going to cry, and I refuse to do that right now.

"You going to help too, Collee, or are you just going to stand around?" Matt calls out.

Brent drops his arm and faces his teammate. "Not sure who you think you're talking to, but who was the one who was up with Evie all night while everyone else slept?"

"Uh, Bunny?" Matt responds, dumbly.

"No, dipshit. I wanted her to get some sleep," Brent retorts.

"Speaking of, I'm going to escape this lovers quarrel and go see my two favorite people in this house." I raise my hands up and walk toward the stairs.

I find Chandler carefully backing out of a bedroom, closing the door softly and raising a finger to her lips signaling me to be quiet. She gestures for us to move away from the door.

"I just got her to sleep," she whispers once we are a few feet from the door.

"But I wanted to snuggle her," I complain.

"I'm sure she will wake up in the next thirty minutes and you can have all the snuggles."

"Deal, I'll probably need to come up here and hide most of the night anyway." I shake my head.

"Why?"

I give her a look, and she just laughs.

"Don't think too much about me, but you may want to go downstairs before Audrey kills all your boyfriends," I divert.

"I'm sure they deserve it." She waves me off.

We get downstairs at the exact same time Audrey yells, "Matt if you don't stop moving those fucking glasses, I'm going to shove one of them up your ass!"

"Oh boy," Chandler sighs.

"Stop telling me what to do, they are my cups," Matt yells back.

"Do I need to separate you two?" Chandler interrupts.

"Yes."

"No."

They both answer at the same time.

"Hi baby, how did she do?" Vince comes up, wraps his arms around Chandler and kisses her.

"Good for now, but I'm sure these loud mouths will end up waking her up." Chandler sighs.

"Brent, get your tall ass over here and help grab that for me," Audrey calls out.

"See," Chandler chuckles.

"Anything I can do to help?" I interrupt.

"You can just hang out and be pretty." Chandler smiles.

I shake my head, and Vince gives her another kiss before going back to help the rest of the group and the damn pang in my chest is back seeing them. Seeing everyone, even with the arguing it's lighthearted and doesn't make me want to run away and panic but makes me love this giant group even more.

Yet, I still feel like an outsider. The way Vince came up to Chandler, the softness he has toward her. The way that Charlie helps Audrey and loves her through her annoyance with everyone. Brent doing what he did when we were growing up and is really the one in charge but doesn't need to scream and yell to make it known. Then there's Matt, he may piss everyone off, but I can still see the love everyone has for him.

Everyone has their place here. Everyone except me.

"Heard there's a party," someone announces from the front of the house.

My head snaps up at the voice because it's one I recognize instantly, and it makes me both excited and nervous hearing him here. In this house.

"You're early," Audrey accuses.

"So?" Colton shrugs.

"So, is there a particular *reason?*" She narrows her eyes.

"Wheeler, didn't expect you yet," Brent comments.

"Yeah, figured it would be boring here without me so you're welcome." He turns toward me and sends a wink in my direction that I'm hoping no one else caught.

Luckily, Spencer and Jared walk in not much later and I breathe a sigh of relief that I can try and keep some distance from him by using my best friend as a buffer. I don't care if I have to physically hang onto her, I'm going to do it.

It doesn't take long before more of the team and their families are showing up. Noise fills the large house and Chandler was right about Evie waking up soon, when she does. I volunteer to go get her.

"Hi pretty girl," I greet as I enter her room.

She coos as I pick her up and I smile at her tiny face as she lets out a big yawn.

"How sweet," Colton's voice says from behind me.

I turn around. "Don't think you're supposed to be up here."

"No one will even notice. I wanted a second alone with you."

"We aren't alone." I lift my arm slightly.

"She wouldn't tell on me."

"She might, she has three dads, poor girl has no chance of hiding anything from them."

He looks down at my sweet niece in my arms and the look that crosses his face seems to soften.

"Do you want kids?" He asks.

I look down at her as I think about how to answer. I've wanted a family for as long as I can remember, but that hasn't necessarily included kids of my own.

"I don't know," I say softly. I may want to foster or adopt to help kids have a safe space unlike I did growing up. "Do you?"

Colton reaches out, running his knuckle along my cheek. "I want whatever you want."

My jaw drops at the simple words that have so much more

meaning behind them. A meaning that I'm not going to think too much about because I'm sure he's just saying it. He's just trying to ruffle my feathers again.

"You should go back downstairs," I tell him, looking back down at Evie.

His hand slides to the back of my neck, gripping me, forcing me to look up at him again. The sincerity written on his face is something new, and scary.

"I will, but only if you promise to spend midnight with me."

"I promise."

He smiles, giving my neck one final squeeze before letting go and leaving me alone with Evie. Looking down at her again, her eyes are open looking up at me, so sweet and innocent.

"God help anyone who tries to date you one day, baby girl."

T he whole night I'm aware of where Brynn is while
keeping my distance. I don't talk much to anyone, but
I'm aware of the looks I'm getting from Collee and
McQuaid. Dumont, Colver and Mann are the only ones that
don't seem to have an issue with me at this moment.

It's a lot with practically the whole team and their wives and
girlfriends here, but it'll only make it easier to sneak off with
Brynn later.

She's been spending most of the night with Spencer, Audrey,
and Chandler, and keeping her distance from me. It's now ten
minutes to midnight and that's about to change because she
made a promise and I know she'll keep her promise.

I finish the last of my one and only beer as my eyes lock on
her again. She throws her head back laughing at something that
was said and I watch the length of her throat, and even though
she's across the room I can hear her over all the noise. It's like
every part of my body is aware of every part of hers and as I

stand here staring at her it hits me harder than any hit I've taken on the ice.

I'm so fucking in love with Brynn Collee.

"It's almost midnight," someone announces, and everyone migrates toward the large TV where the countdown is about to start.

My eyes don't leave Brynn as she starts searching for me. The second she sees me I nod my head to the side, signaling her to join me in another area of the house.

I make my way down a hallway where the lights are off, and I lean against the wall as I hear the announcement of the last minute before the new year.

Her silhouette appears and she walks closer. Once she's within arm's reach I grab her around the waist, pulling her against me.

"Have you been having a good night, Princess?"

"Yeah, it's been fun. What about you?"

"Yes, I've liked watching you be so happy."

Thirty seconds.

"You've just been watching me? Creepy," she jokes.

"Not creepy, I just like looking at pretty things."

"Gee thanks," she scoffs. "That's all I am, a pretty thing?"

I chuckle. "No, but if I told you everything else you were to me, you'd run away."

Ten seconds.

"Why don't you try?" she breathes.

"Maybe next year. I have something else I need to do first."

I turn us around so her back is against the wall, my body hiding hers as I slide my hand up to her throat, resting it there, using my thumb to angle her chin up. It's so dark, but I can still see her face. So fucking beautiful, her green eyes shining with something as they look up at me and the desperation to tell her my feelings is overwhelming, but instead I hear the countdown hit zero and crash my mouth onto her, showing her everything I'm feeling with my lips on hers.

She gives it back just as she always does, opening her mouth for my tongue to dip in and explore. This kiss is slow, deep and meaningful. Her fists grip my shirt, pulling me to press against her completely. There's no space between us and I want more like I always do with her. I want to take her into one of these rooms and fuck her, not caring who's here, who could catch us. I just want her.

I want her today, tomorrow, the next day, next year. I fucking want her. And I kiss her like I'm telling her that.

"Oh shit, I'm sorry," a voice sounds from the opening of the hallway.

We break apart quickly, Brynn buries her face in my chest with a gasp, trying to hide.

"Wheeler, what are you–" Dumont starts, and I just look at him, waiting for him to make a scene about who I'm with.

"You going to run and tell?" I snap while Brynn tenses against me.

Dumont shakes his head, looking behind him, probably to see if anyone else is nearby. "No, I saw this coming, and if you're okay with Collee killing you if he finds out that's on you."

"He shouldn't want to kill me if being together is something we both want," I argue.

Brynn tenses even more against me. I may be speaking for her, and she doesn't deny it, because I know deep down she does want me. We may have been playing games around it for a while, but we're past that now. So beyond past that.

Dumont raises his hands up. "You don't have to convince me."

For a brief moment I wonder if he would be helpful whenever we do have to tell Captain Collee, but I know that won't be tonight and I can already feel Brynn freaking out just like I knew she would.

Dumont walks away and I look down at her once again. "Please don't run, Baby Collee."

She shakes her head. "I'm not running."

———

WE MANAGE to both leave the party separately and without anyone noticing, I left first so she could say goodbye to everyone. I know she won't be far behind me, so when I get home, I change into some black sweatpants and leave my shirt off. When I'm in my closet I come up with a little plan to have some extra fun with her.

She said she wouldn't run, but I want to make extra sure she won't.

She knocks on the front door a half an hour later and that's another thing I plan to change. So, when I open it, I immediately hold my hand out, "Give me your keys."

"Why?"

I raise an eyebrow just waiting for her.

"I told you I'm not running."

I just gesture with my hand for the keys. With an eye roll she slaps her keys into my palm and walks past me. I shut the door behind her, then slide a key to my house onto her keychain before bringing it back to her.

"I believe you." I hand her keys back to a very confused Brynn.

"What did you do?" she asks, looking at them.

"I added something."

"That reminds me," she digs in her jacket pocket, producing a small gift box, handing it to me. I furrow my brows at it.

"What's that?"

"Your Christmas present. Just open it."

When I do I see the pink crown keychain inside and the side of my mouth pulls up in a smile at the item, but don't say anything, I just look up at her where she's shifting on her feet.

"It's just something stupid because you call me Princess," she shrugs, then looks back down at her own keys and sees the unfamiliar key and looks up with wide eyes. "I hope this isn't to your house and is to something else."

"It's to my house, Princess. I'm not asking you to move in so don't worry. I wanted you to have it so when I'm on the road and tell you that I want you here, naked when I come home, you will be."

She raises her chin up. "What makes you think I'll actually do that for you?"

Closing the distance between us, I grip the hair in the back of her head, forcing her to keep her eyes on me.

"Listen to me, when I tell you I want you waiting for me when I get home, then that's where you'll be. If I tell you I want you in my bed you'll be there. If I want you spread out on my dining table, you'll be there. I know you want this as badly as I do." Her breath hitches.

"And what about if I want to find you in certain positions," she retorts, weakly.

I smirk. "If that's what you want, I'd do it. But I know you'd rather be my good girl." I pull her bottom lip down, to prove my point. If she wanted to find me on my knees for her, I would do it in a fucking heartbeat.

"What if I use your key to break in and steal all your stuff," she sasses.

"Do it, baby. Do whatever you want, but I would give you anything you wanted, no need to steal it."

"What if I just come in here and destroy your house?"

"Sounds like you want to be punished."

She takes her bottom lip between her teeth. "Why me, Colton?"

"Why you what?"

"Why do you want me?" She's asked this before, and my answer was different. Now, there's so many reasons.

Because you're the only person that has made me feel something. Because I have never wanted anyone as much as I want you. Because you make me happy. Because you get me. Because I love you.

I don't say any of that. Instead, I say, "Because you're everything."

She lifts up on her toes and crushes her lips to mine. I wrap my arms around her, lifting her up, her legs instantly wrapping around my waist.

"I need you, Colton, please," she pleads against my lips.

"I know, baby. You have me."

She kisses me deeply as I carry her up to my room. I grip her ass tightly as she rubs herself against my cock that's already hard for her and has been all night just waiting until I could have her in my bed.

There's no part of her that's holding back right now as her tongue plunges into my mouth. I can feel how desperate she is, but there's more there. It's like she's desperate for more than just sex and if I haven't made it clear to her yet, I want to give her everything.

We get to my room, and I toss her onto the bed. She yelps when I grab her ankles and pull her to the edge. I pick up the tie I set here earlier and slide it through my hands, looking down at her flushed face. She's already squirming, trying to rub her thighs together, but can't since I'm standing between them.

"Wrists, Princess," I command, and she brings them together in front of her, easily.

I tie the fabric around her wrists, making sure it's not too tight because I don't want to leave those kinds of marks on her. If I leave any, I want them to come from my mouth. Or maybe my hand on her ass.

She watches as I bind her hands. "I didn't take you for someone who wears a pink tie."

"I've never worn this one, but it made me think of you." I finish the last knot.

"Why's that?"

I push her hands up above her head, leaning over so my face hovers above hers. "Three reasons. This pink is the exact same shade your ass turns when you take your spankings like a naughty little brat. It's also the same shade your skin flushes when you come for me like a good girl."

She gulps. "What's the third?"

"The painting."

She looks at me confused, but I don't want to explain right now, she'll understand later. Right now, I need to taste her. Sliding down her body, I work her pants off quickly, my patience is nonexistent at this point, and I need her.

Without wasting any more time and without any teasing, I throw her legs over my shoulders and dive into her sweet cunt, licking a long line up her entire slit. She lets out a low moan, her bound hands dropping to my head. I lift up, pushing them back above her head.

"Keep them there, or I'm going to have to tie them to the bed.'"

I dive back down to her sweetness, spreading her lips with my thumbs, zeroing in on her clit and sucking the hard nub into my mouth. She bucks her hips, rubbing herself against my mouth as I eat her. Humming against her as she cries out at the vibration.

Running my hand down to her entrance I push a finger inside her tight heat. "You're officially my first meal of the new year. I don't think I've ever had anything so sweet. You going to give me your first orgasm of the year, Princess?"

She nods. "Yes, please make me come, I'm so close. I need it, Colton. I need you."

"Damn fucking right you do. You need me to make your cunt feel good," I growl before diving back in, devouring her like I'll never stop. And fuck if I don't want to. Part of me wants to bring her to the edge over and over so this never has to stop. The other part of me wants to continue to make her come until she physically can't take it anymore.

Wrapping my arms around her thighs, I make sure she's not going anywhere. Especially as her orgasm starts to build, hips bucking up against me as she cries out, "More."

And what my girl wants, my girl gets. Which is why I latch onto her clit, flicking my tongue in the rhythm she craves. I continue to pump my finger as she starts to soak my hand, and when I push another finger at her back entrance, without pushing in she goes off.

Her orgasm has her trying to kick me away, to slide up the bed and get away, but I won't let her. I hold her down with a hand on her lower stomach as I continue to work her through her release.

"Too much, I can't, no more," she complains, but I don't let up.

"Aw, you wanted more, but you can't handle it?" I pull my finger from her pussy, and lick her orgasm off them, needing more of her taste.

"I just need a second," she breathes.

I chuckle, "No."

Diving back in, I don't let her get a break as I work to bring her to another orgasm. She's screaming, bucking, and squeezing my head between her thighs, but she doesn't move her hands from where they're resting above her head.

"Such a good fucking girl for me," I groan against her.

I reach down to palm my dick because it's painfully hard and I can't wait to fuck her, but not yet. She must notice because I hear her taunt, "Aw, you need your cock touched? Now who's needy."

I bite the inside of her thigh and she screeches.

"Want to give me more attitude? I won't leave this spot for the rest of the fucking night, but you won't get to come again. I'll bring you to the edge all night, baby, don't tempt me."

"You wouldn't," she challenges.

I rise up, looking at her with a raised eyebrow.

"You want to test that?"

She sucks her bottom lip into her mouth and doesn't say anything.

"Go ahead, say one more thing and see what happens."

I see her think about it, then shake her head slowly.

"Are you going to let me finish my meal then?" I ask.

She nods.

"Then are you going to let me fuck this perfect little pussy?"

She nods again.

"Yeah, that's what I thought."

As soon I have my face between her thighs again, I fuck her with my tongue while rubbing her clit with my thumb, lapping up all her wetness that's dripping out of her and I greedily lick every sweet drop I can.

"You're making such a mess on my bed, Princess. How about you show me how well you can soak the whole fucking thing."

I work her harder, the wet noises filling the room mixing with my groans and her cries as I push two fingers inside her while she grips them tightly before a gush floods my hand as she comes for me.

"Fuck, that's so pretty," I groan, cleaning up the mess she made with my tongue.

"Colton, please," she gasps.

"Please, what? I need your words."

"Please fuck me. I want your cock."

I climb up her body, my lips ghosting over hers. "It's yours. Take it."

She brings her bound hands down and I smirk at her silent request.

"You don't need your hands to take what you want, Princess."

Her lips quirk to the side before she pushes at my chest and I go easily, laying on my back as she throws her leg over me. She rests her bare, hot, soaked pussy on my chest while bracing her hands on me. She rocks slightly, rubbing herself against my abs and I grab her thighs.

"Tell me something, Princess." I run my rough hands against her soft thighs, pushing her shirt up her hips.

"Hm?" she hums.

"Tell me you're mine."

She stops moving, darting her eyes to mine in fear, which makes me hold her harder.

I repeat, "Tell me you're mine, for real. I don't want anyone else, and I don't care what happens with your brother. I fucking want you and I know you want me."

She stares at me, and when she opens her mouth it's not what I was expecting. "Untie my hands."

My shoulders drop slightly. This is it. The fun is over, and I ruined it by pushing too hard. I'm not going to force her to stay and I'm not going to pretend this is all I want from her anymore. So, I do what she asks. Gently, I take her wrists in my hands and undo the tie around them.

Once she's free I expect her to jump up, get her pants on, walk out, and not look back.

That's not what happens. As soon as she's free, her hands grab my face, and she kisses me. I hesitate for a moment, wondering if this is a goodbye kiss, but when she opens for my tongue and lets me deepen it, nipping at my bottom lip, I realize that it's the opposite.

Wrapping my arm around her back, I sit up, holding her against me as our lips move against each other. I feel her through my sweatpants, my cock screaming at me to fuck her right now, but just holding and kissing her, knowing she's mine feels better than anything else could. Even an orgasm. Which is how I know I'm way too gone for her.

She rests her forehead against mine, and whispers two words almost too quietly for me to hear, "I'm yours."

I crush our mouths together again in a frenzy, flipping us over again so I'm hovering over her. I need to feel every inch of her. I need to fuck her as mine. I need to feel her as mine.

My Princess.

My Brynn.

My fucking everything.

I pull off her shirt, my lips immediately latching onto a nipple, sucking it into my mouth as she moans, pushing her hands through my hair. Her nails scratch at my scalp as I take a long hard pull on her nipple before releasing it and moving to the other one to do the same.

Brynn pulls harder on my hair, so I'm forced to look at her. "Please stop teasing me, I need you."

"So nice to me tonight saying please and using your words."

She lets out a small whimper with her nod.

I flip our positions again so she's on her back and I stand so I can easily shed my pants. As soon as my cock is free of its confines, I can't help but run my hand along my length. As I do, Brynn watches the movement, running her tongue along her lower lip.

"You told me to fuck you, but you didn't say where."

"Anywhere." She rubs her thighs together.

"So, I could fuck your mouth if I wanted?"

She nods.

"And your needy little pussy?"

"Mhm."

"What about your perfect ass?"

That one makes her hesitate before she responds, "I've never...I don't know...you're so big."

I can't help but smirk. "I know, baby. You can say no. Everything we do is for you."

Her knees part and fall to the side. "I'm yours. I trust you to take care of me."

Fuck me, if I didn't already love this girl, that would have done it.

"That's my girl, get over here and get me nice and wet for you then. Make it sloppy."

She grins, quickly crawling over to the edge of the bed, fisting me, looking up through her eyelashes as she lets her saliva pool in her mouth then lets it fall onto me. I have to stop my eyes from rolling back, and she doesn't waste any more time before her mouth is on me, taking me as deep as she can.

She gags around me, and I run my hand through her hair. "Breathe through it, baby, you're doing so good."

Brynn relaxes under my touch and words, pulling back before trying again, relaxing her throat to take me further. When she hollows her cheeks and sucks, I almost lose it, my grip tightens on her hair. "Fuck, that's too good."

She hums at the praise, doubling down her efforts, bobbing her head, teasing the underside with her tongue and when she brings a hand to my balls, tugging slightly, I have to pull her off and crash our lips together. It's messy from her drool as I devour her swollen lips. It's dirty and chaotic. Just like us.

I need to get inside her, she was going to make me come and it's going to be a fucking miracle if I hold off much longer, but I have to. Pushing her back, I move her body so she's on her stomach and like the perfect girl she is for me, she moves to her knees and arches her back.

With a grip on her hips, I angle against her entrance and push inside, our moans mingle as I fill her completely. Solidifying how mine she is. I grab her arms, banding them behind her, using the leverage to pull her against me with each thrust.

"You take my cock like it was made for you, Princess," I groan.

"Feels so good, Colton, *ah*," she tries to scream into the mattress, but I keep her lifted with my grip so I can hear it.

"Are you close again? You going to come all over my dick and show me what a needy slut I have below me?"

"Yes, harder," she cries.

And because I'll give her anything she wants, I do what she says, fucking her harder, our skin slapping together with each punishing thrust. I feel her tighten around me as she gets closer. I can read her body and I know how to send her over the edge, I drop my grip on her arms, leaning over to rub her clit in tight circles.

She squeezes me tighter than a fucking vice as she comes again, and I somehow manage to hold my own release back. When I pull out of her, I groan at the sight of my soaked dick, I swipe some of it onto my finger, rubbing against her ass and she jolts as I press the tip of my finger inside.

"This okay? Tell me to stop if it's too much, understand?" I tell her seriously.

"I told you, I trust you," she breathes, and I feel her relax, so I'm able to push my finger in past the first ring of muscle.

"Such a good fucking girl."

Even though she soaked me, I'm not going to risk hurting her, so removing my hand I go to my nightstand to get the small bottle of lube and coat my dick with it. I climb back on the bed, shifting Brynn up so I have plenty of room to kneel behind her as I drip the liquid onto her backside, rubbing it between her cheeks and working the same finger inside her once again, easier this time.

I join a second finger, working to prep her, but thrusting them and spreading them slightly. Her soft whimpers turn into moans, and she starts to back up onto my hand.

"Does my greedy slut want my cock in her ass? You're pushing it against me like you're dying to be filled by me."

"Yes," she sighs. Her willingness, her fucking trust, means more to me than anything.

"You think you're ready?" I ask, working a third finger in.

Nodding, she says, "Yes, please, I want to feel you."

Fuck I love this woman. Removing my fingers, I coat more lube on myself just to make sure. When I press the tip to her tight hole she tenses again.

"You're going to have to let me in, baby." I run my hand up her back to try and help her relax.

She does, letting me sink in just an inch and my vision blurs at the tightness. I don't even know if I'm going to push all the way in before coming with how tight she is. Her knuckles are white from her grip on the sheets.

"Are you okay? I need to know you can handle it," I check in. She may like to be degraded, but I would rather chop my dick off than hurt her.

She turns her head to the side, her hair is a tangled mess around her. "Keep going."

I push in a little further and she whimpers into the bed but relaxes again and I'm able to push in more.

"That's it, fuck, you're doing so good. You love this, don't you? Such a good. Fucking. Girl." I push in further, and before I get the chance to compose myself, she pushes back all the way so I'm fully seated in her ass.

Our moans fill my bedroom and I grab her hair, turning her head so I can lean down to seal our mouths together, needing the connection to her.

She gives me exactly what I need with her mouth opening against mine, tongue sweeping against mine as I thrust slowly against her.

"Colton," she moans against my lips.

"Yeah, Princess?"

She looks like she's going to say something else, but instead says, "More."

I need to see her better than this. I need her flushed cheeks, swollen lips, and dazed eyes. Pulling out carefully she makes a noise of protest, but I flip her onto her back, settling between her legs, and push back into her ass. She arches her back at the new angle adjusting once again. Her nails dig into my shoulders and her legs wrap around my thighs, push-ing me.

I pick up the pace of my thrusts slightly, but make sure I'm not hurting her. When her moans start to get louder, I reach between us to rub her sensitive clit once again, and when I can tell she's almost there, I push a finger inside her soaked pussy which sends her over the edge instantly.

Not able to hold back anymore, I follow behind with a loud groan, shooting ropes of cum that seem to go on forever. I barely catch myself from crushing her with my weight as I come down from the release.

When our eyes lock onto each other, I see my feelings reflected in her green irises. Neither of us say anything, we don't have to.

Even when I take her limp body into my bathroom, and we get in the shower together we both remain silent. I make sure to wash her thoroughly, taking care of every inch of her body before we get out, dry off, and climb back into my bed, not bothering to put any clothes on.

She doesn't fight my hold on her as I press our bodies together. The silence isn't awkward between us, it's full of everything neither of us will dare say, but it's okay. Because enough was said tonight. She's mine and nothing can change that, I won't let it.

B efore I even open my eyes, I feel how sore my body is. A delicious, perfect soreness that brings back the memories from last night that play like a movie across my eyelids. Safe to say this new year is off to a pretty amazing start.

I turn over and frown when I'm met with an empty bed. My guard goes up instantly. I should've known better that all that "mine" talk was just in the moment. I don't know why I thought he may have meant it at all.

Getting out of bed, I slip on one of his t-shirts because it's right there and I'm in desperate need of some water. Then, I'll go home and pretend like last night was the same as every other time with him.

As I walk toward the kitchen my eyes catch on the weird painting again and I remember how he mentioned it last night. My eyes catch on the pink splotches and my face flushes. He compared me to that.

Suddenly, I feel his warmth behind me and have to stop myself from melting against him.

"What are you doing, Princess? You were supposed to stay in bed while I brought you breakfast," he says.

I can't help myself; I turn around and joke, "You don't have to try so hard."

He chuckles. "Don't care, I want to." He nods his head at the painting. "Do you get it yet?"

I turn back toward it, and he wraps his arms around my middle as I shake my head. "No, I think you just like pink."

Colton nips the place where my neck meets my shoulder.

"See how the pink color looks like it's taking over the white and black?" He points out.

I guess I kind of see that, so I nod.

"Remember, how I told you I thought the pink was healing?" he asks.

I remember what he said about what the painting represented. At the time I thought he was just talking out of his ass, but the longer I look at it I can see what he was trying to say.

"You're the pink for me, Brynn," he says softly.

I turn around toward him again, my eyes wide. "What?"

He cups my face with both hands. "I've never felt like this with anyone. You make me happy and that's not something I've felt in a long fucking time. You get me in ways no one else gets me. You bite back when I deserve it, you surrender to me when we both need it. I've been a shit for a long time, I know it, but you make me want to be better. You've healed the broken parts inside of me."

My jaw is dropped because I can't believe Colton fucking Wheeler is saying these things to me. I have no idea what to say. I can't admit that he's also healed something inside of me that's been broken for as long as I can remember. That he gives me exactly what I need, even when he's pissing me off, I need that push. But I can't make the words come out, so I just stare at him with my mouth gaping in shock.

"Come on, I have breakfast, but you're eating it in my bed," he says, breaking me out of my trance. Turning me back toward his bedroom with a grip on my waist, he leans down to my ear and whispers, "Then I'm going to eat my breakfast."

He swats my ass with a light smack that has me lurching forward to take the first step back to the bedroom.

Despite him saying I'm the one who healed him, I think I broke him. In the best way, but I don't know why my mind won't let me just accept this. It's like there's a roadblock in the way warning that it's too good to be true. I may have given him every piece of myself physically, but there's a tiny shred of my heart I'm not able to part with because I know once he has it, I'll never recover.

But when he comes into his room, joining me on the bed with a tray full of eggs, bacon, toast, and fruit I push the worry away for now.

When he pushes our empty dishes away and drops his face between my legs I forget everything else completely.

————

THE ONLY REASON I was able to leave Colton's bed the day after New Year's is because he had practice in the morning and a game that night. A game I had to promise to be at or he threatened to not go to practice to make sure I stay in his bed.

"That is stupid, you'll get in trouble and I'm not worth that," I told him with a giggle.

"You're worth everything, Princess," he replied before kissing me senseless.

Now I'm home, and Ellie shoots me a look that says she's not happy.

"I'm sorry, but you have an automatic feeder and water fountain," I tell her.

She meows, hopping down from her cat tree and walking away. I sigh because I'm getting the silent treatment from my cat, after spending way too much time getting railed by a man I thought I hated. What a turn of events.

After a long hot shower, I settle into checking on work. Now that the holidays are over it's back to being serious and I need to check anything I may have missed. I also know I'm about to be met with an overload of requests on Spencer's status since we told the label to check in next year and they take that a bit too seriously sometimes.

Like, hello, it's two days into the new year, do you have an album for us yet?

No, no she doesn't, and no one is going to rush her.

When I log onto my email, a subject line in all capitals catches my eye and it's not just from the label. My stomach drops as I read what it says.

STATEMENT REQUESTED AFTER KENNETH RICHARDSON ABUSE SCANDAL.

Abuse scandal? This is going to be bad.

I click on the email, quickly skimming it to make sure no one is saying he abused Spencer. If that fucker ever put hands on her, I would be at his door with several large pissed off men as my backup to kill him.

What I gather is that several women have spoken out about Kenneth's treatment toward them. Forcing himself on them, fear for their life when they tried to leave, and he hurt them for it.

This is bad. *Bad* bad.

My eyes catch on the last part that has my heart bottoming out. "Sources have also said Kenneth is not the only player on the Spartans that has treated them this way. There are reports that him and another teammate were involved. The sources would not name the other teammate at this time."

My mind immediately goes to Colton. Sure, he hasn't been on that team in a little while, but he was and there's no time-frame given in this email. Even if he wasn't involved, maybe he knew about it. It's no secret he wasn't a great guy before. In fact, that's fairly new.

I was waiting for the other shoe to drop, and it just might have.

I immediately call Spencer, but as her phone rings I know this isn't going to be a conversation to have over the phone.

"Hello?" she answers.

"Hey, can I come over, we have a situation." I try to keep the panic out of my voice to not scare her, but this is terrible.

As my best friend, she can read me like a book. "Um yeah, everything okay?"

"It will be," I sigh before hanging up.

I scratch behind Ellie's ears. "I'm sorry to leave you again, but this is an emergency."

She purrs, rubbing her head against my hand and I know she understands. I don't care if that makes me seem crazy, clearly I've lost my mind on all fronts and me thinking my cat understands me is the least of my problems.

I make it to Spencer's house in record time, knocking as calmly as I can. Spencer opens it with a concerned look on her face.

"Is Jared still at practice?" I ask, walking past her inside.

"Yeah, but probably not for much longer, why what's going on?"

I sit down on the couch, pulling out my laptop. "Would you rather I tell you or would you rather read it?" I ask because I know she can change how she wants to learn things.

"I'll read it," she states easily.

I hand her my open laptop with the email ready and sit back, watching as her eyes roam over the screen. Her jaw drops and I bite at my thumb nail as I wait for what she's going to say. It looks like she reads the entire email, unlike me who just skimmed it.

When she's done, she sets the computer carefully on the coffee table. "Spence," I start gently. "Please tell me, did Kenneth ever hurt you?"

She sighs, then shakes her head. "No. He never physically hurt me. But I can't say this is entirely surprising either."

I don't know how she's being so calm right now. "What do you mean?"

"He's always been an asshole, emotionally abusive for sure. He never liked being told no or not having his way, but I think part of him was scared of me. I intimidated him, which is why he never hurt me this way. But I'm not surprised," she explains.

Seeing her so calm about this makes me get into full on publicist mode. "We need to get ahead of this. Obviously, they want you to make a statement defending him, but clearly that's not what we're going to do. I'm sorry, though Spence, we can't stay quiet about it either because then they can spin the story with you in it however they want."

She nods. "I understand. I'm behind whatever you want to do."

"Okay, we're going to post a statement on your social media, I'm not giving any tabloid the exclusive or chance to spin it a certain way." I immediately pulled up a Word document to start drafting her statement.

"Who do you think the other teammate is they're talking about?" she questions.

I shake my head. "Not sure."

She's quiet for a moment, the only sound is my fingers tapping at the keys before she speaks up again. "Do you think it's Colton?"

My heart stops when she wonders that too. I stop typing to look up at her. "Do you?"

She seems to think, but then purses her lips, "No. I don't actually."

"What makes you so sure?"

"I know he's been an asshole, but frankly, I saw how he was with you on New Year's Eve. His eyes never left you. Men like Kenneth aren't capable of that kind of...emotion."

"What kind is that?"

"Love."

I scoff. "He doesn't love me, Spence. He loves sleeping with me."

She chuckles, "That may be true, but that man loves you. And he seems softer than he has been. Kenneth was never like that, never could be. Even with me I'm sure he was faking everything and looking back it was so obvious. So no, Brynn, I don't think it was Colton."

I sigh in relief, but there's still a lingering worry in the back of my mind. "But what if he knew about it? Two of the guys may have been involved, but there's nothing to say that more of the team didn't know about it."

"I guess you'll just have to ask him," she tells me.

I wave her off, pushing away my own problems like I always do to focus on something else. "Let's finish your statement, send it to your lawyer before posting it and keep you out of this drama as best we can."

Spencer agrees easily and we get to work. Though, I can't stop the worries racing through my mind that everything has been too good to be true. The more I think about it the more the walls around my heart harden once again.

I'm riding a high I've never experienced in my fucking life. I'm happy. I had a beautiful woman in my bed this morning. The woman of my dreams that I didn't even think existed. I have a lightness to me that I don't think I've ever felt, and it was clear during practice that I'm not skating with the weight of the world on my shoulders.

I feel like Coach and my teammates could see it. *Yeah, my teammates.* Fucking crazy, but just feeling this way has made me accept more than just my feelings but accept being a part of this team.

After practice, we're all in the locker room, some guys are hitting the gym for an extra work out, but some of us are just heading home. I think about surprising Brynn at her apartment because I already miss her.

"Good practice today, Wheeler," Mann says to me as he walks by.

"Thanks, Mann, you too." I see the shock on his face, and Dumont's who overheard me, but he doesn't say anything else.

I continue to get changed, and as I'm slipping my hoodie over my head, I hear Jones from across the locker room, "Did you guys see this?"

A few mumbles sound from around the room, but I ignore them because I'm just trying to leave and I'm sure it has nothing to do with me. Until my name becomes involved and I perk up.

"Wheeler, do you know anything about this?" Colver asks.

"About what?" I'm being handed a cell phone with a news article pulled up and I read about the accusations against Richardson.

I never liked that guy, but I was rarely around him outside of the rink and definitely never cared to know what happened behind closed doors. This is fucked up though, and I hope that asshole gets what he deserves for pulling shit like this.

The end of the article states how Spencer, his ex, was asked for a comment, but has not made one at this time.

It makes me want to get to Brynn even more because I'm sure this entire situation has her freaking out and I want to be the one to help. I want to be the one to hold her. The one to be with her as she navigates this and the one that can make sure she relaxes. I'll do whatever needs to be done for her.

I show up to her apartment, and I notice her car isn't in the parking lot. Sending her a text, part of me wonders if she's at my house.

> Colton: Came to your apartment to see you, but you're avoiding me again. Thought you might actually like me now, Baby Collee.

I can't help but tease her, though part of me is nervous for her response. Especially as the seconds turn into minutes and I don't get anything back.

After ten minutes with nothing from her, I actually start to get nervous. I'm about to send her another text when I see her car pull into the parking lot. She gets out and still doesn't notice me.

"Brynn," I call out, and she turns quickly to face me. I can see the stress written all over her, but when her eyes lock onto me her shoulders visibly drop. I rush over, gathering her into my arms because I need to feel her.

She doesn't fight my hold, instead, her arms wrap around me tightly as her body melts into mine. I kiss the top of her head and say, "Let's go inside."

She nods and lets me lead her into her building. I refuse to let go of her as we take the elevator up to her apartment. I feel like a part of me needs to constantly be touching her and I'm not sure who needs it more.

Once we step inside Ellie hops down from her spot on the couch to greet us, though she bypasses Brynn to rub her side against my leg.

"Your pussy really likes me," I tease.

Brynn just rolls her eyes, but when she doesn't say anything back, I know there's something really wrong. I turn her toward me, pushing some of her golden hair behind her ear, tracing my hand along her skin. "Talk to me," I encourage.

She takes a deep breath. "What do you know?"

"Just what some of the guys showed me at practice. Some article about that shithead Richardson. He didn't hurt Spencer, did he?"

She shakes her head. "Not like that, no." I can see her hesitate. "Did you know?"

My brows furrow. "Did I know what? About Richardson? Fuck no."

She looks up at me and I see her walls back up again. The ones I could've sworn we've worked to break down, but she's looking at me like she used to. Like she doesn't trust me. "You didn't know anything? You were so close with that team. You hated having to come here and were still close with them, so you must have known something," she snaps.

"I wasn't close with him, and if I knew anything I would've done something."

"Would you have? You'd stand up to your little buddies? Because for a while you were borderline harassing me, so I think you may have joined in."

I rear back like she slapped me. "You really think that? So, what, you think I forced you to be with me?"

Conflict flashes across her face and I don't know if she means what she's saying, but she's doing what she said she wasn't going to. Which is run. But this time she wants to make sure I don't come back.

"We're going back to pretending you didn't want me then, Baby Collee?"

"I...I did, but you were really pushy, and I just don't know if maybe–"

I cut her off, not able to hear more of this, "Say it, then. You think I was involved too. Tell me what a shitty person you think I am even though you know damn well that's not the truth. I may be an asshole at times, sure, but you fucking know me. You know for a fucking fact I would have never done anything with you that you didn't want. And I would never ever fucking hurt you. Or any woman and you should fucking know that."

Instead of saying anything else she just shrugs.

Just fucking shrugs.

I drop my hands, and take a step back from her, despite the hurt I see flash across her face. It must mirror mine because I can't believe this is happening. Especially after everything was so perfect just this morning.

"You know me, Brynn, you really know me and I want you to think nice and hard if you think I could do something like that."

She wraps her arms around her stomach, eyes dropping down to the floor. "You should probably go; I have a lot to deal with."

I have to fight the urge to plead for her not to do this. For her to stop fighting her feelings and see what's right in front of her. I want to bare my fucking soul for her. Lay it all out for her to know that I love her, that I would rather rip my heart out of my chest than hurt her. That I don't want to walk out of this fucking door.

But she's shut down right in front of my eyes. Her fears taking over and overriding anything I could do or say right now. So, I don't beg for her like I want to because she needs time. And the last thing I want to do right now is push.

"You think you'll still come to the game later?" I can't help but ask, even though I'm sure I know the answer.

"Probably not."

I nod once, opening the front door, but I linger for a second, my back turned to her, and I can't help but say one more thing.

"I've given you everything, Brynn, please don't throw it away because you're scared. Everything is easier to get through if it's done together and you don't have to do everything alone anymore."

When the door closes behind me, I feel like I just shut the door on so much more, but when she doesn't open it again, I know her decision has been made for now. I'll respect whatever that decision is because she already accused me of being pushy before. I refuse for that to be true now, I love her too much to try and force her to be with me.

I love her enough to have to let her go if I have to.

———

THIS GAME FUCKING SUCKS. Tensions are high between our teams, and I feel like everyone is looking at me like I'm the one the article is about. I fucking get it, but it wasn't me and I didn't know about it.

It feels like everything that was changing has gone back to square one and it's coming out in this game. We're also headed out on the road for two weeks after this game and are going against L.A. in a couple days.

The last thing I want right now is to leave town. Facing my old team is a close second.

"Wheeler, get out there," Coach barks at me, pulling me from my thoughts.

I hate how distracted I am this game, but I can't think about anything other than Brynn and what happened earlier. Hockey is always my number one except now. Now, I couldn't give a shit about this game or anything going on.

I take my position on the ice for the next puck drop. I'm positioned next to another defenseman from the other team, and he chirps, "You hear about your buddy Richardson?"

"Not my fucking buddy," I grumble, not wanting to give into his antagonizing. For once I just want to get through the game and have it end.

"I knew all you fucking Spartans were dirty players but seems like you're that way off the ice too."

I turn my head slightly, but am still watching for the puck drop that keeps getting delayed when a player goes for it too soon. "Good thing I'm not a Spartan, then. Because I'm a Dragon."

We shove at each other as the play starts. I get possession of the puck and race it down to their zone. Collee gets a perfect opening and takes it, sending the puck flying into the net.

He skates around with a minor celly, before skating up to the bench to fist bump the whole team, the rest of us on the ice follow. We end up switching lines and I sit back on the bench. I look over at my captain and think about saying something, but I don't.

He notices me looking but doesn't say anything either.

It's not the time or place to say any of the things I want to.

I'm distracted for the rest of the game that I can hardly acknowledge that we even won. I deny a post-game interview because all I want to do is go home. I check my phone before getting into the shower, just hoping that maybe Brynn texted me something. But it's radio silence. I know I'm really fucked when part of me hopes and thinks she's going to be standing in the hall once I leave the locker room.

She's not.

I check for her car in the parking lot, but it's not there.

When I'm almost home, I even think about her being there waiting for me.

She's not.

I think about texting her, especially as I climb into bed. Even for a second I think about calling her just to hear her voice. But I know she won't answer, and I don't need her to reject me again today.

So, instead, I go to bed alone. I used to prefer this, but ever since the first night I had her in my bed I have wanted to keep her here. And now I may never have her here with me again.

———

IN THE MORNING, I drag my ass to the team plane, plop down in my seat with my headphones in and close my eyes. No one tries to talk to me. And I don't try to talk to any of them. I used to want to be left alone and I finally have gotten what I wanted.

All. Fucking. Alone.

No friends, no family. Just me, once again. Only this time I hate it.

I don't even care where we're playing, my plan is to wake up, practice, eat, play, sleep. Repeat forever.

My eyes close and by the time I open them we've already landed wherever we are, I join the team on the bus to the hotel. We have practice in two hours. I make the mistake of looking at my phone once I'm in my room and see another text from my mom, which is only making my mood worse.

> Mom: How are you?

I don't know what it is about the single message today. Maybe it's the fact that I can't just call Brynn to hear her voice and distract me. Maybe it's because my entire world shattered just after I felt like it was beginning to get better. But for the first time in several months, I press the call button.

"Hello?" she answers with a raspy voice. I remember when I

was younger, she would sing to us, and she had such a beautiful voice. Now, just like everything else, that's gone.

I don't say anything. I'm not sure why I even called, and as I open my mouth to say that my mom sighs on the other side.

"Seriously Colton, why call?"

My grip tightens on the phone. "Because I wanted to see if maybe you cared to talk to me for once, but I guess that hasn't changed."

"I just asked you how you were, and you're the one that doesn't respond," she snaps defensively.

"Because I know you don't really care. You never fucking have," I explode. "I'm just an obligation, the son you have left that you didn't want. I know you'd rather have Josh than me and I'm fucking sorry that's not the case."

She's quiet and I wonder if she hung up. I've never said these things to her, after Josh died we all coexisted, not as a family just as humans sharing a house. Until I left.

"That's not true," she finally responds.

"It's not? Because I don't remember a single time since he died that you hugged me. That you told me you loved me. Dad either. You gave me whatever I wanted to shut me up and dropped me at hockey every chance you got. That's not parenting, Mom." I might be too harsh, but I feel like all the feelings I've locked and thrown away the key to are coming out right at this moment.

"Of course we have, Colton, that's ridi–"

"No. You haven't. Either of you. A single time."

We are both silent. I'm not going to be the one to break it, either.

"I'm sorry," she finally whispers, so quiet I almost think I'm imagining it.

Still, I say nothing, waiting for her.

"Losing Josh," her voice cracks saying his name. "Broke us. It broke all of us, I know it broke you too and we just...we didn't know how to be anymore."

"But I was still here. Of course it broke me too, he was my best fucking friend, but I needed my fucking parents." I'm about to break again, the tears starting to form, but I don't want to let them fall.

"I know, Colton, I know. I'm sorry. There's nothing I can say that will fix anything at this point, I know that."

I blink away the fog from the tears. "No, there's not."

Silence again.

"Maybe next time you're here we could...maybe come to your game?"

"I don't think I'll come back after this season," I snap quickly. She sighs again and I feel bad for resorting to what I always have. "But maybe I could come visit when I have the time."

"That would be nice."

Immediately I think of Brynn and how I would want to bring her, she would make it better. My parents would love her, but I shake away the thoughts because I don't think I'll get the chance to ever know.

"Okay," I nod. "I'll let you know."

"I love you, Colton. I should have showed it more, and there's nothing I can do to make up for that."

"Thank you," I reply, because I can't bring myself to say it back yet. It might be fucked up, but I just can't right now.

We hang up, and I drop onto the bed, emotionally exhausted. Part of me is relieved to have said what has needed to be said for a long time. The other part feels even worse about all of it.

The tears I tried to hold back finally fall.

I t's like we've been fed to a pack of bloody hungry sharks with the way I've had to address, dodge, and handle everything coming at Spencer since she posted her response on social media. One would think that everyone could have accepted her statement and left her out of the drama further, but her name gets publicity. Which is why they keep using it.

I'm exhausted mentally and emotionally every day from all the emails, phone calls, and social media notifications. It's almost been enough to distract me from how Colton looked when he left my apartment the other day. I saw something I didn't think I would ever see from him. At that moment, he wasn't the annoying asshole who was trying to get into my pants.

At that moment, he looked like his heart had just been shattered and I was the reason for it. I want to believe I did the right thing, but every day that passes I think I may have made a mistake shutting him out.

He's changed.

And I think I believe him that he didn't know about Kenneth and this whole bullshit.

But also, it might be better that whatever was going on ended there, before my brother found out. It's for the best.

It's that single thought that stops me from reaching out to him.

Chandler invited Audrey, Spencer, and me over to watch the Dragons against the Spartans because it's going to be a bloodbath. Kenneth hasn't been playing since the news dropped while the team decides what they're going to do, but that doesn't change how tense things will be without him.

I didn't want to go. No one knows what happened with us. I've avoided telling Spencer what happened and luckily have the excuse of the guys being gone anyway. When I tried to cancel, Chandler begged me to come and since she used Evie to guilt me, I couldn't say no.

So here I am, on the large couch, watching the announcers talk about some of the players as they skate around the ice before the game. I'm trying not to pay attention, but when his name is said I can't help my reaction, looking up and watching him, looking down at the ice as he skates.

"Colton Wheeler, a surprising trade last year, hasn't shown the improvement he should for a player of his caliber. He's solid, but his lack of teamwork has been his downfall recently."

I hardly register what they're talking about. All I can see is his face, how muted he looks. The air around him that's usually filled with his cocky energy seems gone as he continues to look down, and flicks a puck away, but hardly lifts his head.

The main thing I think as I look at him is that I miss him. *Fuck, I miss him.*

"You okay?" Spencer asks, sitting next to me.

I paste a fake smile on my face. "Yeah, of course."

She looks over to the screen just as it switches back to the announcers, but she catches on quickly. "Did something happen?"

I shake my head, already feeling like I could cry. "No, it's okay, Spence."

"Spill," Audrey prods, sitting on the other side of me.

"Nothing to spill." I shrug.

"Don't bullshit a bullshitter. What happened?"

I go to deny it, but then decide against it. I can't keep doing this, I'll push away everyone eventually, which is why I tell them everything. Starting from the beginning. We miss the start of the game, but no one seems to care as they hang on to every word. Spencer already knows most of it, but even she's enthralled as I rehash my entire...relationship? *Is that even what it was?*

"And then he left," I finish. The TV is quiet with the game commentary in the background as my friends just stare at me.

"Hold on, you just let him leave?" Spencer asks gently.

I nod. "Yeah. I'm an idiot, aren't I?"

Their chorus of "nos" ring out, but I don't believe them.

"Look." Audrey gets my attention. "I get it. I didn't want anything serious with Charlie. I was fucking terrified of anything that looked, talked, smelled, acted like a relationship. But that man loves me more than anything in the entire fucking world and I could have easily fucked it up if I didn't move past my own fears to give him a chance."

"How though?" I question.

"Leap of faith, babe," she says as she shrugs.

"What if I get hurt though? What about Brent?" I groan.

Chandler waves me off. "Don't worry about him, focus on you and what you want."

"I just want..." I pause, thinking of everything I want. My family, love, to not feel so fucking lonely all the time. But I look around at the women here and I know that they have become my family too. I may feel alone at times, but at the end of the day I'm not. I miss Bryson, Bailey, and even Brandon, but I do have a family. I have someone that helped fill in a piece of my heart, but he took it with him when he left my apartment the other day.

I don't get to finish my sentence because we're all pulled to the screen as a fight breaks out on the ice.

Colton and a player on the Spartans I don't recognize have solid holds on each other's jerseys while they exchange significant blows. The Spartan's player has his helmet knocked off and Colton is raining punches down on him in a fury. I'm horrified at the sight, while also worried about him.

When the two of them fall onto the ice, Colton doesn't let up and it takes two refs to pull them apart and as Colton is escorted to the penalty box he's still yelling at the other guy, even as the glass door shuts in his face.

The camera changes to the other player who's leaving the ice back to the locker room. Then, we see Colton looking down at his knuckles, stretching his hands out before grabbing a towel to wipe them, then his face where I see a split lip, but that's it.

All eyes swing to me, and I shrink onto the couch with a quiet, "What?"

Audrey's the first to speak up. "That was fucking hot."

Chandler and Spencer chuckle and I just groan.

"Seriously, though, what do you want?" Spencer asks, wrapping an arm around my shoulder as I lean my head against her.

"I want that stupid hockey player," I grumble gesturing toward the screen.

"But you don't trust him?" she pries.

Sighing I say, "I thought I didn't, but I've seen another side of him I don't think he's let anyone see before and...dammit."

"You want to get him back?" Chandler smiles widely.

"Yeah. What do I do, though?"

Audrey's smile is almost sinister when she says, "I have a plan."

I'm equally intrigued and scared of her plan, but I know before I can do anything she's suggesting, I'm going to have to settle one more thing in my life. Because I'm sick of keeping secrets and being one.

If we're doing this, I don't need any more drama standing in the way of it.

Chapter Forty-Four

WHEELER

24

We got back to Denver last night and I used to love to come home to my quiet empty house, but as soon as I walked in, the silence was too loud and I was missing something. No, someone.

I still haven't heard from Brynn and I'm thinking I never will. Part of why I got in that fight against the asshole from the Spartans was in hopes that she was watching and would reach out afterwards.

That, and the fact that he was chirping so much I wanted to see if he could back up his shit talk. Turns out he couldn't.

After sitting in my house for all of an hour, the quiet becomes too much. I grab the keys to my bike and take off on a drive around the city just to fucking feel something.

It's when I saw the lights from a tattoo shop that I make a split second decision. I don't give a shit if anyone thinks I'll regret it. I don't give a flying fuck if Brynn never talks to me again, she's carved her place in my heart so might as well ink a piece of her on my skin.

"You sure about this one, man?" the artist asks after placing the stencil.

"Fuck yeah I am."

———

THE NEXT MORNING, I get to practice, completely exhausted because after I finally got home I still couldn't sleep. I tossed and turned until the sun came up. Now here I am, changing into my gear, carefully pulling on my pads over my new ink. It's covered with a thin piece of Saniderm, but I've gotten enough tattoos and played hockey the next day that shit rubbing against them can be a bitch.

Out on the ice I throw myself into the drills, using this as a distraction before I have to go home to my empty house once again.

I grow increasingly agitated at every minor thing I'm yelled at by Coach. I'm fucking tired and miserable enough, I get that I'm not my best right now. But my last straw is when Collee snaps at me to pull my shit together.

Fuck it. I have nothing else left to lose.

"Say shit to me again, Collee, I didn't fucking hear you," I snap, already ready to toss my gloves across the goddamn ice.

"Practice like you actually want to be here," he barks.

And that's fucking it.

"I don't want to be here; I want to be in bed with your sister. I can still hear her screaming my name."

He's grabbing my practice jersey within a second, with his fist flying into my face. I hardly feel the pain because it feels good to feel something in this moment. And it feels even better to finally see the "perfect" Captain lose his shit.

"You motherfucker," he seethes with another punch to my jaw.

"No, just your sister." I can't help myself and it earns me another hit, my lip splitting open once again, but I want the pain. I want to keep pissing him off.

I'm gripping his jersey to keep him from tackling me onto the ice, but my own attempts at blows don't land as hard as his with the way he blocks them.

"You fucking hurt her; I'm going to kill you." He punches me again and that time I think blood sprays onto the ice.

There's chaos going on around us with the rest of our team and coaches as they try to get us to stop, but Collee isn't letting up, and I don't want him to.

"Don't worry, she loves everything I do to her," I smile a bloody smile at him right as another punch rattles my brain.

A loud whistle echoes all around us, but we don't stop. I try to land another hit on him, I feel my fist connect with his jaw, but not as hard as I intended. We're finally pulled apart by our teammates. I don't even fight them, but with Dumont and

McQuaid holding Collee back I can see him struggle to try and come at me again.

"I fucking knew you couldn't help yourself. You're a piece of shit and have been since you stepped foot in this city. You wanted to piss everyone off and only make enemies. Is that why Brynn has been so fucking depressed? Because you took advantage of her and then left her? Congratulations, how does it fucking feel to be the shittiest person possible?" He doesn't let up and his words feel worse than his punches.

Thinking about Brynn being depressed and in pain is a different type of hit. This one feels more like a stab right in the gut. So does his accusation that I'm the reason for it.

"Fuck you, Collee, she ended it with me. I would never fucking hurt her, but I know you want to make me out to be the enemy so go ahead. Fight me some more. Do whatever the fuck you want because without her I don't give a shit anymore." I shake off Mann and Jones holding me back.

"Wheeler, Collee, get the fuck into the locker room!" Coach screams and I'm already skating that direction anyway.

As I pass him, I can't help but try to put the final nail in my own coffin. "Might as well call the GM to get rid of me now."

Despite the physical pain in my face and the blood in my mouth I spit out, all I can think about is Brynn feeling half as shitty as I have since I left. And I don't care about what might be about to happen with my career, my team, anything. I just want to somehow know that she's okay.

But I worry that seeing me will only make it worse and the best thing for me is to leave.

Chapter Forty-Five

BRYNN

Chandler let me know when the guys were supposed to leave practice today so I can come over and talk to Brent. I'm obviously not about to tell him everything, but I am planning on telling him that I don't want him to be mad about my relationship with Colton. If he will even want me back.

My hands twist together in front of me as I approach the front door. My knock is weak, and I debate turning around and leaving because as confident as I've been about this plan, every second makes me more nervous.

When the door swings open, I expect to see Chandler, but it's Brent and he has the start of a black eye forming. "What happened to you?"

His jaw ticks before he answers. "Courtesy of your boyfriend."

My—Oh shit. *He knows.*

"How—"

"Why the fuck did you not tell me?" he snaps, stepping outside and shutting the door behind him. I've seen Brent in a lot of ways. Rarely it's anger and when it has been, it's never been directed at me. Not until right now.

I can't help but go on the defense, though I have so many questions, starting with why did Colton punch my brother.

"Probably because I knew you'd be mad. Which is clearly the case." I put my hands on my hips.

"I thought you were smarter than this, Brynn, seriously. I've had good teammates that asked about dating you, but you choose him?"

"I've never wanted to date any of your stupid teammates. Not like you would've been okay with it no matter what."

"I did everything for you so you could have a better life than the one we were born into, and you get caught up with a guy like that? I mean seriously, Brynn, what the fuck?" Every word he says has me tempted to punch him too, and I've never felt this way toward him. I don't like being scolded like I'm a child.

"My relationship has nothing to do with how we were forced to grow up, Brent, that's stupid. *You're* being fucking stupid."

"Oh, so it is a relationship?" he scoffs.

"It—I—why does it matter? It doesn't seem to make a difference to you no matter what. You just want to stand here and talk to me like I'm a fucking kid." I may be yelling like one at this point, but I don't care.

"It matters because I wanted better for you. I still want better for you. I gave you everything. All of you," he yells back, I know referring to our siblings.

I've reached my breaking point when he mentions them. Letting out a humorless laugh I reply, "You always tried to take care of all of us, but we didn't need you! We survived and we all got out, but the damage was done, Brent. Look at all of us. Brandon is dead, Bryson barely talks to us, and Bailey has disowned us."

I should stop, I know I'm driving the knife in deeper, but I can't help it. I'm too pissed off, so I continue. "You wanted to protect everyone, but how did that work out? You can't control everything and everyone. I'm an adult and I'm with Colton. I don't care that you don't like it, if you want, I'll just join our other living siblings and not talk to you anymore. Is that what you want?"

His mouth snaps shut so hard I hear his teeth clink right before he answers, his voice softer than it has been, his deep timbre sounding more like the controlled Brent I know, "No, of course not." The pain behind his words is evident and my heart cracks.

"I'm sorry," I say quietly, looking down at my feet. "That was too far."

I'm pulled into his large frame, and he hugs me tightly. I hug him back and can't deny how nice it feels. That's probably why I can't stop the tears from falling. He just tightens his hold on me as I cry.

"Don't apologize to me for that. You're right. I didn't need to take care of you all, but I wanted to. I wanted to get us all out of there. I wanted everything to be better and I ended up pushing everyone away. I'm sorry, Brynn."

Burying my face against him, I will the tears to stop, but it feels good to let them out.

I hear a throat clearing and look up to see Vince standing just inside the house. "If you guys are done yelling you can come in, Evie's sleeping, but it's fucking cold out there."

I sniffle with a small laugh. We walk inside and I hardly even noticed how cold I was until the warmth from the house starts to heat my body back up.

We sit on the large sectional, I lean my back against the armrest, hugging my knees to my chest while Brent stretches out and my eyes catch on his injured eye again.

"So, what happened?" I ask, hesitantly, not sure I'm ready to hear it after I defended Colton even though we aren't even actually together.

"He was being a dick like usual and I finally snapped," he answers, curtly.

"But...he told you." It's not a question.

"He said enough. I mean seriously, Brynn. Why?"

I tense. "Why are you with Chandler? Why are you okay sharing her?"

"Because I love her," he answers easily. "And so do they."

I nod, like that's my point without me having to say the words.

"You love him?" He sounds genuinely shocked.

I shrug, not wanting to admit it to my brother before even telling the man in question. "He's never hurt me, you know? We didn't get along for a while, but he's never treated me badly."

Not outside the bedroom.

"So, what happened?"

I pick at some of Ellie's fur stuck to my pants as I answer, "I got scared. I'm sure you heard the news about Spencer's ex and I kind of accused Colton of some shitty things. He respected the line I drew, but I think it was the wrong one."

Brent hums, and I can tell he's still not happy, but trying to keep his composure like he usually does. "You want to be with him?"

I nod.

He sighs, leaning his elbows on his knees, and running his hands down his face. "I was pretty suspicious on Thanksgiving, you know? I just didn't want to believe it."

"I get it. And I get why you were mad. I guess you do care about me a little bit," I tease, trying to lighten the mood a bit.

He chuckles. "Just a tiny bit."

"I'm sorry for what I said, that was messed up."

"It's okay. I get it. This isn't what I wanted for our family either. I miss them too. Even Brandon."

Brent rarely talks about our brother, and I feel the tears welling up again. "I really wanted to help him; I still feel like I could have."

He immediately shakes his head. "No, Brynn, you couldn't have. I don't want you carrying that guilt around. I did what I could for him, but he had a disease because that's what addiction is. I hate that it took his life, but at the end of the day he had to make the decision to change, we couldn't force it. I tried, with him and our parents."

"You did?" I sniff.

"Many times. Guess I did a good job protecting you from that," he tries to joke, but I don't laugh. "I gave him and our parents every opportunity to get help. Set it up, paid for it. Anything and everything. I thought that if they had access, they would just do it, but I was wrong. None of them wanted to, so even the couple times I managed to get them to go it wouldn't stick."

"I didn't know that," I say softly.

"You didn't need to. You needed to focus on growing up."

My shiny eyes meet his. "So did you."

"You all were more important. And I wouldn't change a thing, I love my life. I do wish Bryson and Bailey were around more, but this is their choice and one day I hope it changes."

I jump off the couch and hug my brother again. We may have

a fucked up past, and things may not be perfect, but I'm glad I still have him. No one's life is perfect, but we've made the best out of our situation.

We break apart and I see the way he grimaces as he asks, "So, are you going to talk to Wheeler?"

"I have a plan, if he even wants me back," I reply nervously.

"If he doesn't, I'll kick his ass again," he smirks.

I roll my eyes. "Looks to me like you got a black eye, not a good look, hotshot."

"You should see the other guy," he jokes.

"If you messed up his face, I'm going to be pretty mad at you, it's one of his best qualities. Well, that and his–"

"Stop talking."

"I was going to say his hockey skills, you're gross. I would never talk to you about his–"

"Brynn," he snaps, and I cackle.

"Are we okay?" I ask.

"Always," he answers easily. "But seriously, if he ever hurts you, I'm going to kill him."

"Yeah, yeah, I get it. I can handle myself and if he did then you wouldn't even get the chance, he would already be six feet deep."

"Thatta girl, shorty."

"Now that this is all settled, where is your girlfriend and child, I'm sick of your face and want to look at something cute." I look around for where they could be hiding since it seems like everyone ran away while we had our moment.

I try to distract myself for the day but can't help thinking about my plan tomorrow when I'm finally going to see Colton again and how I hope I won't regret it.

B y some fucking miracle I'm not on suspension or anything. I have a feeling Collee sucked someone's dick to get us off the hook, but we both have to attend this team mediation shit. The last thing I want to do is sit in a room with him and "work out our issues." My issue is I'm in love with his sister, she wants nothing to do with me and he hates me.

End of story.

It's like how it was when I first got traded when I showed up for the game. Keeping my headphones in, pump up music blasting as I change into my gear. Even when I'm forced to take them out, I avoid looking at Collee, not for any reason other than if I do I think I might beg him to talk to Brynn about taking me back.

And I'm not about to beg that fucker for anything. My lip re-split during our fight, I got another cut on my eyebrow along with a fat black eye. I'm sure people are going to wonder what happened to me once they see me out on the ice, but none of us are talking about it.

On the way out onto the ice I'm tempted to ask Mann or Colver if Brynn is here because I'm sure they would know and there's not a chance in hell I'm going to ask Collee, Dumont, or McQuaid.

I decide against it by the time my skates hit the ice. If I know she's here I don't know if I'll be able to stop myself from leaving the game to run up and see her. And if she's not it'll fuck with my head too much.

After warmups, we head back into the locker room and my eyes catch on Collee for a second where I catch the shiner I gave him. I didn't think any of my punches actually landed, but I guess one did.

I expect him to go off on me again, but he doesn't. He doesn't exactly smile either, but he also doesn't look like he wants to tear my limbs off anymore.

Progress, I guess.

The game goes surprisingly well for how much shit has been happening behind the scenes. We are even able to pull out a solid win four-to-one. It almost helps lift my mood. Almost.

Back in the locker room the guys are excited and I'm shocked when Dumont pats my shoulder. "You coming out to celebrate with us?"

"Nah, I'm beat," I answer easily. I'd rather not get caught up in any other drama if some puck bunny decides to test the waters with me and it gets back to Brynn before I get the chance to talk to her again.

"Good choice, you should probably go home," Colver adds. I looked over at him, confused why he would say that. He sends a wink in my direction, but I have no idea what for.

"Uh, yeah, I need some fucking sleep." I shake off the weird interaction and focus on getting out of here.

Just like I have every home game, I check to see if Brynn is waiting in the hallway with her friends. Just like every other game she's not there.

By the time I get home I wonder if I should have gone to her apartment, knocked on her door until she answered. Refused to leave until she would talk to me. But I can't. She said I was pushy before. I can't do that to her again. She has to want me too.

Entering my dark house, I notice the light to the hallway leading to my room is on and I'm confused because I always turn all the lights off. Unless I actually forgot, which is unusual but possible.

I walk that direction, and my eyes catch on the painting hung up in the living room, there's something hanging from the frame with an envelope on it. As I get closer, I see it's a jersey. Taking it down, I see the familiar Dragons logo, and on the back, it has "Collee 52." My heart rate immediately kicks up at the sight. And I remember the last time I saw this jersey was when she was wearing it while I fucked her in the locker room.

Brynn was here.

I opened the envelope to see her handwritten note.

COME FIND ME.

I feel like I can't breathe. She's here. And she's clearly not hiding very well if the light leading to my room is any indication.

But I don't care. I just want to see her. Which is why I rush that way, still gripping the note and jersey as I bust open the door and am met with the greatest sight I've ever laid eyes on. Brynn is kneeling in the middle of the rug, her long blonde hair falling around her shoulders partially covering the Dragon logo on the jersey she has on that's way too big for her frame. Her hands rest on her thighs and she's looking up at me through her eyelashes.

"Hi," she greets softly because I haven't been able to say anything.

Instead of trying, I drop the things in my hands and rush over to her, lifting her into my arms immediately. Holding her tightly against me. I take everything in. Her floral scent, the way she fits so perfectly in my arms, the little sigh she lets out as soon as we make contact.

She pulls back slightly, and I see the sheen of tears in her eyes, cupping her face, I use my thumb to wipe the first one that falls immediately.

"I'm so sorry, I should've listened to you. I believe you; I was just scared. I shouldn't have let you leave, Colton I'm so sor–"

"Hey," I cut her off. "You don't need to apologize. We were both scared, and I get it. You don't have to be sorry, I wasn't going to push you anymore, but fuck, I missed you so much you have no idea."

"I missed you too," she says as another tear falls.

"I want to make one thing clear to you that I should've said already. I should've told you the first time I realized it. But I fucking love you, Brynn Collee. You are and always will be everything to me. I am so fucking in love with you," I confess.

"I love you too," she whispers, and I can't wait any longer, brushing my mouth onto hers. Kissing her like she's the air I need to breathe because at this moment she is.

She opens immediately letting my tongue dip into her mouth as we sink into each other. I pull back before I really want to, and she whimpers at the loss.

"Thought I told you; I gave you that key so you could be kneeling naked in my room." I make it a point to look her up and down at her very not naked body.

"If I was naked, you would've been too distracted to talk to me," she scoffs. "Plus, I thought you'd like this too."

Backing out of my arms, I reluctantly let her put the space between us. When she turns around and I see "Wheeler 24" across her back I can't help but tug her back into me, taking her mouth in another desperate kiss. Knowing she's in my jersey for the first time, here in my house, and is my girl, has me needing her right this second.

But in my way.

My hand collars her throat, angling her head so I can kiss her deeper. She mewls into my mouth as her hands grip my button down tightly. I slide my fingers to the back of her head, tangling them into her soft hair and yanking hard so our mouths part. Hers dropped open on a gasp as she looked up at me. Lips red and puffy from mine and I want to bite them. And I will.

"On your knees again," I growl.

She listens immediately, dropping back down onto the floor in front of me. Sliding my fingers through the hair on the top of her head, she leans into my touch before I drop it. Unbuttoning my shirt as I make my way to the end of my bed. Pushing open my shirt, and unbuckling my belt, I sit on the edge of my mattress.

"Crawl to me, Princess," I command.

Moving onto her hands and knees, she does what I say, crawling across the room until she's kneeling between my spread legs.

"Such a good girl for me, aren't you?" I ask.

She nods. "Only for you."

"Fuck yeah," I practically groan. "Did you miss my cock, baby?"

She lets out a little squeak. "Yes."

"My girl is desperate to be fucked like the little cumslut she is?"

I see the way her thighs squeeze together. "Please?"

"Please what?"

"Please, Sir?"

Oh fuck. She's never said that to me before and I could get

used to it. I fucking need her.

"Stand up and get naked," I command.

Wasting no time, she scrambles to her feet and takes off my jersey and then her pants. She wasn't wearing anything underneath and I groan at the sight of her. I've missed every single piece of her, and knowing this sexy as shit woman in front of me is mine has my already hard dick ready to punch a hole through my pants.

Crooking my finger to her I say, "Get your ass over here."

She walks forward, teasingly, and I'm about to get up and yank her into me, but I wait. Until she's standing between my legs, then I pull her down so she's straddling my lap. Immediately, grinding against my erection and letting out a throaty moan.

"Fuck, baby, you're already so soaked, you're going to make a mess on my pants."

"Then you should take them off." She reaches between us, unbuttoning my pants, but I stop her with a grip on her wrists.

"Take my shirt off first," I instruct.

Brynn slides her hands up, trailing her fingers along the ridges of muscle on my abdomen, up higher to my chest. My grip on her hips tightens when I feel her brush over the tattoo on my pec on her way to push the fabric off my shoulders.

Her eyes follow her hands, and after my shirt is off, she brings them back to my chest, sliding over the ink. "What's this?" she asks.

"What does it look like, Princess?"

She traces the outline of the crown inked into my skin right next to the words "Live for me" over my heart.

"It's a crown. You just got this?"

Nodding, I grip the back of her neck, so she looks at my face. "It's for you, it didn't matter if you never spoke to me again, you have my heart and I'll always love you. I promised my brother I would live for him, and I thought I was, but I wasn't really living. Not before you. Now, I'm finally fulfilling my promise and it's thanks to you, Brynn."

She throws herself against me, kissing me fiercely, all tongue and teeth. There's nothing smooth or practiced in this kiss. It's all our need for each other. The desperation, desire, want, love. It's us.

"Need you. Please," she pleads against my mouth, and I need her too.

We both work my pants and boxers off roughly. They don't even make it past my knees before she grips my cock, angling herself over me and dropping down, taking me fully. I wrap my arms around her tightly with a moan as I'm surrounded by her tight heat, practically blacking out at the sensation.

She grips me so tightly, adjusting to my size, but I wasn't kidding about how wet she is, I love knowing how much she wants me.

"You better start riding me, Princess. Show me how much

you missed the way I fill you," I say with a sharp smack to her ass.

Lifting up slightly, she adjusts her knees on either side of me before dropping down, swiveling her hips.

"Fuck, so fucking good. So fucking mine. Say it." I bring my arms up behind her to hold on to her shoulders, pulling her down onto me as she circles her hips and I meet her thrust for thrust.

"I'm yours, Colton. *Ah* fuck. Always yours."

"That's it, baby. My needy slut, aren't you?"

"Yes, oh my God, please please more," she pleads.

"You need more? Take what you need. I'm all yours. I'll always be yours."

It's like my words are just as powerful as the way our bodies are moving together because she moans loudly, continuing to ride me, but she wants more and I'm going to give my girl what she needs.

Lifting her off my lap I stand us up, bending her over the side of the bed with a hand on the middle of her back and push her face down into the mattress as I press inside her again. She groans at the new angle.

"Harder," she cries, and I almost bust at the single word.

I move my hand up to the back of her head, grabbing a fist of her hair, pulling her head up as I pound into her roughly. Our skin slaps together loudly and I already feel myself getting there too quickly, but she needs to get there first.

Pulling out quickly, I drop down behind her to bury my tongue in her soaked pussy. She cries, falling forward onto the bed as I devour her. Licking up all the wetness she's created only for me has me feral. I fucking love her taste, the way she coats my tongue as I eat her like my favorite meal.

"Colton, oh my *fuck*," she screams right before burying her head into the comforter, her legs shake, and my mouth is flooded with the sweetest fucking taste as she comes.

I hold her up as I lap up every drop she gives me before standing. Grabbing her hips, I throw her onto the bed roughly, kicking off my pants completely before crawling up her body, kneeling over her chest.

"Get me nice and wet to fuck your needy cunt."

She grabs my throbbing cock without argument, sucking me deep into her mouth. Tasting herself on my shaft and I groan at the feeling. She gags when I reach the back of her throat. Pulling back, she dives in again, letting me slide further back this time.

"Such a good fucking girl for me, Princess."

She hums around me, and I already feel close so I pull out, and slide down so I'm lined up with her pussy. Eyes locked, I wrap my hand around her throat lightly as I push inside her once again, our eyes don't leave each other. I've never felt closer to another person than I do at this moment.

This perfect, amazing, loving woman looking at me like I'm

everything to her is all I fucking need in life. I love her and I don't even have to hold back telling her. So, I don't.

"I love you, baby," I tell her.

"I love you too, Colton." She wraps her arms around my neck, and her legs around my waist. "But right now I want you to fuck me like you don't."

"Goddammit, Princess." I slam my mouth onto hers and set a punishing pace with my hips as I fuck her into the mattress.

We're loud, sloppy, and fucking perfect as we both give each other exactly what we need. I'm close again and there's no way I'll be able to stop it this time. I bring my thumb to her clit, rubbing the little circles she needs.

It doesn't take long before her pussy is squeezing my cock tighter than a fucking vice as her orgasm rips through her body. I follow right behind, filling her with my cum as I groan against her neck.

We're sweaty, sticky, breathless, and yet neither of us try to move for several minutes. We stay like this for so long I feel myself start to harden inside her once again, but she needs to be taken care of.

Rolling my body off hers, I go to the bathroom, get a warm washcloth, and return to find her exactly how I left her. When I press the fabric to her center she hisses.

"Are you sore?" I ask dumbly.

"Mm, in the best way." She smiles at me, and I don't know how I ever existed without this fucking woman, I swear it's cheesy as shit, but she completes me in a way I didn't think was fucking possible.

Crawling into bed with her, I wrap her in my arms. We should talk more, I know that and I'm sure she does too, but that can happen later because we both fall asleep easily. And it's the best fucking night of sleep I've gotten since my dumbass walked out of her front door.

M y body is sore, but there's a smile on my face before I'm even fully awake. I know it's all thanks to the owner of the heavy tattooed arm that's draped across me so I couldn't move even if I wanted to.

Good thing I don't want to. I wiggle slightly so I'm pressed completely against Colton and feel his already hard cock against my ass. He doesn't react, so I rub against him again, this time he lets out a throaty groan.

His arm tightens slightly as his face nuzzles in the back of my neck.

I push back again and this time his teeth sink into the skin where my neck meets my shoulder. "Baby Collee," he says like a threat, and I shiver at his deep, gravelly voice.

"Mhmm," I hum, grinding against him harder.

"Does my little cockwhore need her ass fucked this morning?" he growls with another nip to the side of my neck, and I arch against him making a needy noise in agreement.

He rolls me on to my back, pinning my arms above my head while hovering above me. "Tell me one thing first."

"Anything," I breathe.

"Tell me you still love me and that you're still mine."

I can't help the smile that spreads across my face; I never thought I would love someone so possessive. Someone who pushes me like Colton does. But it's hard to deny how he also compliments me in ways I didn't even know I needed.

It's the perfect balance, which is why my answer comes as easy as breathing.

"I'll always love you, and I'll always be yours." My eyes catch on the tattoo on his chest, and I can't believe he did that, even before he knew he would get me back. I love him even more for it.

He leans forward, his lips ghosting over mine and says, "Such a good girl for me, now spread your legs and give me what's mine."

———

AFTER BEING LOST in each other for so long I don't even know what time it is. We're showering to clean up and as Colton is washing my hair when I have a panicked thought, turning around so quickly my wet hair slaps him.

"Don't you have practice today?" I gasp.

He chuckles. "Yes, but it's not for another hour, you woke us up really early rubbing your tight little ass against my dick."

"Oh." My cheeks flush as I turn back around to finish cleaning up.

His hands snake around my middle, holding me against him. "Promise you'll still be here when I get back?"

I lean to the side as he trails his lips along the column of my throat. "I have to go check on Ellie, but I'll be here."

He shakes his head. "I miss her too, I'll come over instead."

I turn with a raised eyebrow. "You miss my cat?" I ask skeptically.

"Yeah, I'm a fan of all your pussies."

I roll my eyes. "You're annoying."

He chuckles. "Yeah, but you love me anyway."

"Eh," I joke. He splashes water in my face making me laugh right before he takes my mouth in a deep kiss that has my toes curling. And we fall into each other once again just like we always do.

———

COLTON LEAVES for practice and I go home to see Ellie. After checking her food, water, and litter box, I find her curled up on

the top of her cat tree. I scratch behind her ears, and she immediately starts purring, rubbing her head against me.

"Colton is coming over later. I guess we kind of like him, so
be nice," I tell her, even though she's always been nice to him
like a little traitor.

When he steps through my front door a couple hours later,
she proves that by walking right up to him and rubbing against
his leg.

"She missed me too, didn't she?" he teases, and I smack his
chest lightly. He grabs my hand, keeping it trapped there as he
leans down to press his lips to mine. It's over too soon, but I
have a couple questions I never got around to ask during our
reunion.

"Guess so," I say as I shrug.

The three of us settle on the couch, Ellie takes Colton's lap
and I scowl at her which makes Colton laugh at me.

"You didn't tell me what happened with my brother." I start
with the main thing. Brent wouldn't give me details and I want
Colton to explain it anyway.

"What did he tell you?" he asks.

I explain how I was a bit caught off guard by the fact that he
already knew when I asked about the black eye he gave him. He
smirks at the mention of it.

"I figured I had nothing left to lose. I didn't have you, and I
went a little off the rails when he pissed me off. I'm sorry for

what I said, but I think him and I getting into it was a long time coming. It's good for him to lose it every once in a while."

I sputter out a laugh because the last point is probably true. "Are you done being a dick to each other then now that you got it out of your systems?"

"Probably not, but he's not a bad guy, I know that. And for you I'll do anything, even if it's being nice to your brother."

"Thank you," I say softly, taking his hand in mine since my cat still won't leave his lap, even though that's the spot I want to be in right now.

He tells me about his conversation with his mom and asks if I would come with during the offseason.

"One condition," I tell him.

"Anything."

"We stay at a hotel because I know you're going to try to have sex with me there, and I would die if your parents heard us." I shiver just thinking about that.

"Done," he smiles and gently moves Ellie off his lap to pull me onto him. "Any other conditions before I officially ask you to be my girlfriend?"

I tap my chin to pretend like I'm thinking. "Unlimited orgasms."

"Done."

"Unlimited access to your glorious bathtub."

"Done."

"Unlimited love for me."

He smiles, leaning into me, brushing his lips against mine, "Done."

BRYNN

TWO YEARS LATER

It's Spencer's wedding day.

It took Jared a long enough time to propose, I swear Spence was losing her mind waiting for it to happen. When Jared told me his plan to do it during one of her shows, I helped him organize it after she sang their song, "Only Forever." It was beautiful and the crowd went insane.

I had to dodge a bunch of hate from her ex after it happened. The asshole got booted from the Spartans and no team in the league wants anything to do with him. He pops up every once in a while to try and make Spencer's life miserable, but I'm the one that gets all the messages. I'm also the one that presses "delete" on every single one of them.

No one thinks about him, and we all intend to keep it that way.

Now, a year later we're here helping her get ready. Chandler got Evie dressed in her flower girl outfit she keeps twirling around in. She's fallen a couple times after being so dizzy, but she just laughs and gets up again. Her brown hair is curled and turquoise eyes shine with her laughter.

When Audrey was changing, Spencer noticed her nipple piercings and that sparked a whole discussion because she wanted a distraction from her nerves.

"Do they hurt?" Spencer asks.

"Getting them did, but not anymore, they feel amazing now," Audrey explains. "Would you ever get them?"

Spencer shakes her head. "No, I don't think I could go through with it. I only have the one tattoo and I may do that again, but I'm not sure."

She displays her "Only Forever" tattoo on her ribs proudly.

"What about you, Brynn, want to join me in the pierced nipple club? I know Chandler won't." Audrey gives Chandler a pointed look.

"Nope, you've tried and failed many times," Chandler responds.

I shrug. "Maybe. I only have one tattoo right now, but I would consider it."

Audrey looks me up and down like she's searching for the ink through my clothes. "I never knew you had a tattoo. What is it and where?"

Slightly embarrassed, I pull down my lip to reveal it. It's a little faded at this point, but still readable and I see the moment she reads it. "Good girl, damn I knew I always liked you." Audrey winks and I chuckle.

"What about Colton, does he have any secret piercings or tattoos?" She wiggles her eyebrows at me.

"No piercings, he does have a princess crown tattoo for me." I feel the blush on my cheeks.

"That's so cute," Chandler joins in. "Brent just has the one piercing on his d–"

"EW! Oh my God, no! Don't ever talk about anything Brent has on his body or talk about him at all. In fact, I don't even know him." I gag at the new knowledge. She didn't even need to finish her sentence for me to know what she was about to say, and I feel like I'm about to pass out.

Spencer and Audrey keel over with laughter at my expense.

"I always knew your brother was a secret freak," Spencer says through her laughter.

"Sorry, I forget you're related sometimes," Chandler apologizes, and I don't even know if I can look at her right now.

"I'm leaving this room before I end up even more traumatized."

I leave the large bridal suite and run into a large body immediately, for a second I worry it's my brother and I think I'll throw up on him if I see him. Luckily, as soon as the hands grip my biceps, I know who it is and I relax.

"What are you doing?" I ask Colton.

"I came to check on you guys, Colver is freaking out and I was the one suckered in to make sure his bride didn't run away."

I chuckle, appreciating the distraction from the trauma I just experienced. "She's in there and she's not going anywhere. They've been best friends forever; you'd think he wouldn't be worried."

"Yeah, who the fuck knows. I also wanted to see you." He leans down to press a kiss to my lips, but I stop him with my hand on his mouth.

"I'm wearing lipstick."

"Good, I want to fuck it up."

Before I'm able to stop him, he kisses me roughly and I let him because I don't care if it gets messed up, I'll never get used to how it feels when Colton kisses me. Our love has only grown, and I wouldn't have ever guessed we would be where we are today.

When he pulls away, he asks, "Would you want this someday?"

"The marriage or wedding?"

"Both."

"With you, of course."

He kisses me again, but I push him back. "This doesn't count as a proposal though; I still expect a real one."

He chuckles. "I'll always give you anything you want."

When our lips meet this time, I don't want to break apart. I don't care who finds us, I don't care if we miss the wedding, as long as I'm here with him I'm so happy.

"Get a room," a voice booms and I look up to see Matt, Vince, and Brent standing at the opening of the hallway.

Brent looks disgusted and I'm glad because that makes two of us.

"On second thought, maybe we should just elope," I whisper to Colton.

"Done."

The End

Want a little more Brynn and Colton?
Download their spicy BONUS SCENE

WHAT'S NEXT?

An all new dark MMA romance, coming early 2025.
Preorder Uncaged Desires HERE
The date on Amazon is a placeholder.

Keep an eye out in my future releases where certain Collee siblings may make an appearance...or maybe their own story.

WHAT'S NEXT?

ALSO BY MADI DANIELLE

Signed Books available on my website:

www.madidaniellewrites.com

ACKNOWLEDGMENTS

Wow. I can't believe this series is over. When I wrote The Hat Trick at the beginning of 2023 I never expected it to become what it has. I never expected to make the friends I have, gotten the opportunity to do the things I have and it's all because of you that have read it so thank you so much for loving these characters as much as I have.

As always thank you to my best friends Ashley and Julia because I wouldn't be on this journey without them and their support. They provide me the most content for my books between the outrageous things they say and do and their love for me. So I love you and thank you.

Thank you to Sarah Beth, always. You've been here since my very first book and I can't believe it! Here we are, 6.5 books later and you're still my biggest supporter. I love you so much.

Thank you to my alpha readers Maggie and Jenna. You were a couple of the first to meet Colton and I'm glad he lived up to your expectations. Even if he's an asshole.

Thank you to my beta readers Ari, Jaeann, Jessica, Katelyn, Rachel, Sydney, Billie, Tiffany and Kalie. All your comments keep me going in when I'm in the thick of editing and want to gouge my eyes out.

Thank you to my editor, Kay, I can't begin to express how thankful I am we found each other and have been on this journey together ever since. You're never getting rid of me, so don't even try.

Speaking of never getting rid of me, thank you my PA,

Chelsey, I'm so glad you have you in my life and our insane voice notes. You listen to my ideas and complaints like a champ and I'm so happy to have you along for this process.

Thank you to Candice for some Inso on a couple Colton lines (you know the ones ;)) I love our unhinged conversations and get ready for the next one, you may be ready to commit me after it.

Thank you to Amanda who let me use her cat Ellie as inspiration for...well, Ellie!

Final thank you to every single person who has read any of my books I seriously can't even begin to explain how much it means to me. Because of you I get to live my dream creating stories for you all. Thank you, thank you! Let's do it some more!

ABOUT THE AUTHOR

Madi is 20 something trying to figure out what "adulting" is. Madi has been writing stories since she was a teenager she continues to express all her emotions in her writing. She's also an avid reader, especially of dark romance. Madi lives in the PNW where she attended college after moving from the unforgiving heat of Arizona. Madi spends her free time with her husband, daughter and family of pets (3 dogs and 2 cats).

If you want to be kept up to date on news regarding my next release, follow me on Instagram, TikTok and my Facebook reader group!"

Made in the USA
Middletown, DE
28 November 2024